SERMONS AND SODA-WATER

The three linked stories related in *Sermons and Soda-water* show the brilliance of John O'Hara's gifts as a writer of the novella of a hundred pages or so—gifts which in recent years have tended to be overshadowed by his stature as a writer of novels on the largest plan.

The Girl on the Baggage Truck, *Imagine Kissing Pete*, and *We're Friends Again* admirably fulfil their author's intention which is 'to record the way people talked and felt' during the troubled interim from the end of one world war to the end of another 'and to do it with complete honesty and variety'. Variety is indeed the spice of the life he imaginatively and succinctly records—in New York, Pennsylvania, and Hollywood; in speakeasies, country clubs, grand hotels, and war factories; and in the homes of many sorts and conditions of men and women.

JOHN O'HARA

SERMONS
AND
SODA-WATER

LONDON : THE CRESSET PRESS : 1961

First published in Great Britain in 1961 by
The Cresset Press, 11 Fitzroy Square, London W.1

Printed in Great Britain by Richard Clay and Company, Ltd.,
Bungay, Suffolk

Contents

THE GIRL ON THE BAGGAGE TRUCK

WHEN I was first starting out in New York I wrote quite a few obituaries of men who were presumably in good health, but who were no longer young. It was the custom on the paper where I worked that a reporter who had no other assignment was given this task, which most reporters found a chore but that I rather enjoyed. The assistant day city editor would tell you to prepare an obit on some reasonably prominent citizen, you would go to the office library and get out the folder of the citizen's clippings, and for the remainder of the afternoon you would read the clippings and appropriate reference books, and reconstruct a life from the available facts, keeping it down to forty lines or whatever length the subject's prominence had earned. It was good experience. One time I had to look up Jack Smedley, one of the richest oil men in the United States, and I discovered that his folder was so slim that you could have mailed it for the price of a two-cent stamp; while a Bronx politician of almost the same name had six bulging folders that cluttered up my desk. Later, when the two men died, the rich man was a Page One story all over the world, and the Bronx politician got thirty lines halfway down the column on the obituary page. You got what in more recent times was called a sense of values.

It was through an advance obituary assignment that I first learned that Thomas Rodney Hunterden was born in my home town. I had never known that, and my ignorance was certainly shared by most of my fellow townsmen. The baseball players, concert singers, vaudeville performers, Grade B Wall Street figures, clergymen, army officers, gangsters, and other minor celebrities who were natives or one-time residents of the town were always claimed with varying degrees of civic pride. The people in my home town not only remembered its former residents; they also clung to the memory of the famous visitors to the place—Theodore Roosevelt, John Philip Sousa, Colonel William F. Cody, Ruth St. Denis and Ted Shawn, Ignacy Paderewski, Harry Houdini, DeWolf Hopper, E. H. Sothern and Julia Marlowe, the Borax 20-Mule Team, a stuffed whale on exhibition in a railway coach, the dirigible *Shenandoah*, two reigning Imperial Potentates of the Ancient Arabic Order of the Nobles of the Mystic Shrine, James J. Corbett, Arthur Guy Empey, Leopold Stokowski and the Philadelphia Orchestra, Paul Whiteman and His Orchestra, Billy Sunday, Dr. Frank Buchman, Dr. Russell H. Conwell, and William Jennings Bryan, to name a few who had passed through or over the town. The people of my town were as quick with reminiscences of a suffragan bishop who lived in New England as they were with stories about a whoremaster who operated in Atlantic City, and it just was not in character for them to forget Thomas Rodney Hunterden.

The next time I was home on vacation I had a beer with an old-time newspaper man who knew everything about everybody. "Claude, did you ever hear of Thomas R. Hunterden?" I asked.

"Thomas Rodney Hunterden, d, *e*, n? Sure. Why?"

4

"Did you ever know him?"

"How would I know *him*?"

"Because he was born in Gibbsville, and he's about your age."

Claude shook his head. "He wasn't born in Gibbsville. I'd know it if he was," said Claude quietly.

"I could take some money away from you on that," I said.

"I'll bet you a new hat."

"No, no bet. I *know*."

It was afternoon, and the public library was open till nine in the evening, so we had a few more beers and then went to look up Thomas R. Hunterden in *Who's Who in America*. My friend Claude Emerson, who was half Pilgrim stock and half Pennsylvania Dutch, was so miserable at being caught in an error that we went back to the speakeasy and drank more beer, but he was not so talkative. Several weeks after I returned to New York a note came from Claude.

Dear Jim:

If Thomas R. Hunterden claims to have been born in Gibbsville, the man is a liar. I spent an entire day at the Court House in among the birth and tax records. No one named Hunterden was ever born in Lantenengo County since records have been kept, nor has anyone paid taxes under that name. You have aroused my curiosity. Wish I could track this down. If you get the opportunity to interview Hunterden, would be much obliged to hear what you learn.

Yours sincerely,
Claude Emerson

The opportunity to interview Thomas R. Hunterden was a long time coming. I was fired from the paper and it was several months before I got a job as a press agent for a movie company. My interest in Hunterden was non-existent until one morning when I was at Grand Central Terminal, meeting the Twentieth Century Limited. Charlotte Sears, who was one of my employer's not-quite-top stars, was coming in on the Century, and I was there to handle the reporters and photographers. There were three photographers and a reporter from the *Morning Telegraph*, and we were a little group down on the platform, conspicuous only because the photographers had their cameras out and camera cases hanging from their shoulders. The fellow from the New York Central press department came to me with the information that the car in which Charlotte had a drawing-room would be at a point farther up the platform, and our group accordingly moved on.

I noticed casually that a tall gentleman in a Chesterfield and carrying a silver-mounted walking stick was standing at approximately the point towards which we were headed. He paid no attention to our group until he saw the cameras, then there was no mistaking his reaction for anything but panic. He saw the cameras, he put a yellow-gloved hand to his face, and he quickly walked—almost ran—past us and up the ramp and out of sight. I vaguely recognized him as a man whose photographs I had seen but whom I had not seen in person. In a minute or two the Century pulled in and I had other things to think about than a man who did not want his picture taken. I had my job to do.

I re-introduced myself to Charlotte Sears, whom I had

met on previous occasions, and we posed her sitting on a baggage truck with her legs crossed and an inch or two of silk-stockinged thigh showing. The little man from the *Telegraph* asked her the usual questions about the purpose of her visit, the future of talking pictures, the rumoured romance with an actor who everyone in the industry knew was a drug addict and a homosexual, and the chance of her doing a stage play. The photographers and reporter finished their jobs and Chottie Sears and I were alone. "I have a limousine to take you to the hotel," I said.

"I think I'm being met," she said.

"I'm afraid not," I said, guessing. "I think the photographers frightened him away."

"Mr. Hunterden? Oh, Lord, of course," she said. "But he *was* here?" I immediately identified Hunterden as the man with the cane.

"Yes, he was here," I said. "But as soon as he saw those cameras . . ."

"Of course. I should have warned him. All right, Jim, will you take me to the hotel? Have you had your breakfast?"

"I had a cup of coffee," I said.

"That's all I've had. Have breakfast with me."

On our way to the hotel I told her about the interviews we had scheduled for her and the public appearances she was expected to make. "I hope you haven't booked me for any evening engagements," she said. "If you have, that's your hard luck."

"A charity ball," I said. "At the Astor."

She shook her head. "Nothing in the evening. Tell Joe Finston I have other plans."

"*You* tell him."

"All right, I'll tell him. And believe me, when Finston knows who the plans are with, he won't raise any objections. Well, *you* know. You saw him at the station. To think how close he came to getting his picture in the papers. That was a narrow escape. I should have warned him. Do you know him, I mean personally?"

"No, I've never met him."

"He hates reporters and those people. He has a positive aversion to them. Are you married, Jim?"

"No."

"I know you weren't the last time I was here, but things happen fast in this life. Why I asked is, while I'm in town will you do the honours? Take me out and so forth?"

"That's no hardship, and it's what I'm paid for anyway."

"The only trouble is, you'll have to sort of stand by. I won't know when I'll need you."

"I could guess that," I said.

She took a bath while breakfast was on the way to her suite and I was disposing of the telephone calls from high school interviewers, jewellery salesmen, and furriers. "No call from that certain party?" she said.

"Not unless he was pretending to be from New Utrecht High," I said. "Or maybe he was the man just in from Amsterdam. I don't know his voice."

"You don't have to know his voice," she said. "The manner gives him away. He's used to giving orders."

"So I'd infer, although I have nothing to do with the stock market. Eat your breakfast. It's a cold and wintry day."

8

"I wish he'd call, damn it."

"He will. Have some coffee."

"What do you know about his wife?"

"Mrs. Thomas Rodney Hunterden, a name on the society pages. A doer of good works, I gather. That's all. I could look her up if you want me to."

"No, I just thought you might have some information offhand."

"I don't get around in those circles," I said.

"You and me both," said Chottie. "The way I was brought up, anybody that finished high school is in society."

"Oh, come on," I said.

"Really," she said. "I can do simple arithmetic and I read a lot, but that's the extent of my culture. And travel. It's a good thing I liked to travel or I'd have been bored to death by the time I was twelve. But I liked it. Split weeks in Shamokin and Gibbsville, Pa."

"Be careful. That's where I come from."

"Shamokin?" she said. "The Majestic Theatre."

"No, Gibbsville."

"The Globe. I played the Globe in vaudeville, twice, and I did a split week in Gibbsville with a road company of *The Last of Mrs. Cheyney*. You didn't happen to catch me in that, did you?"

"I'd left there by then," I said. I do not know why I refrained from mentioning Gibbsville as the birthplace of her Mr. Hunterden. I think it was because she was upset about the photographers at Grand Central and nervous about the telephone call that had not yet come.

"I was young for the part," she said. "But I was glad to get the job. I had to get out of New York. I don't

9

mean I had to because I was forced to or anything like that, but there was a young polo player in love with me. A strong infatuation, call it. He was a nice kid, but a kid. His parents made life very difficult for me."

"Threatened you?"

"Anything but. They belonged to the school that thinks a young man ought to sow his wild oats, and I was his wild oats. Tame wild oats. I didn't have a bad reputation, and they sort of approved of me as Junior's girl friend, just as long as I didn't show any signs of wanting to marry him. Oh, I visited them and I went for a cruise on their yacht. But then I began to ask myself, what was I? What was I getting out of it? I was a combination of nursemaid and mistress. It was a dandy arrangement—for them and for Junior. Then I began to get sore. I hate being a chump. Other girls I knew would have taken him for plenty. They figured I was just too nice to be that kind of a girl. So I got out of New York."

"But why? There's something missing here."

"Because I was beginning to get a little stuck on the kid and there was no future in it. I wasn't in love with him, but he had charm and I wasn't going out with anyone else, so I began to get stuck on him. But two weeks on the road and he was nothing to me, nothing." She had a sip of coffee. "When I'm on the road I'm a great sightseer. I go for walks. Other people on the bill, or in the company, they travel all over the country, thousands of miles, and all they ever see is the inside of one theatre after another. All they ever read is *Billboard* and *Zit's*. Maybe the *Racing Form* and the *Christian Science Monitor*. But they never read the local papers, or books or magazines. Some of them don't even bother to read their notices, because half the time the hick critics are on the take from the local theatre manager. Those that aren't, they pan everything. We got one notice on *Mrs. Cheyney* that didn't even know Freddie Lonsdale was an Englishman. What a business!" The telephone rang. It was Joe Finston, welcoming the star to New York and inquiring whether she was being well taken care of.

She hung up. "Joe Finston. That heel. Last year he'd have been here in person, but the grosses are down on my last two pictures, so he uses the telephone. This call was to soften me up. He'll be nice to me because he wants to talk me out of my contract, but fat chance he has. I have three more years to go, raises every year automatically. The only way I'll let him out of the contract is if he pays me one hundred per cent of what the contract calls for."

"You know what he'll do, don't you?"

"Sure. Put me in one stinker after another till I holler for help. But it won't work with me. I'll be on the set and made up at six o'clock every morning. I'll go on location to Patagonia. I know all the tricks. Stills that make me look fifty years old. But I worked a lot harder for sixty dollars a week than I do now for six thousand. Finston doesn't know that. Finston isn't show business. He's a picture-business nephew. He doesn't realize that it would be cheaper to settle the contract for a hundred per cent on the dollar now than put me in four or five stinkers."

"Would you settle now?"

"Did he tell you to ask me that?"

"No."

"Then I'll tell you, yes. I'd settle now, this minute. Do you know how much I have coming to me on the contract? Only $1,488,000. That's forty weeks left of this year, and three more years with raises. If you figure interest, that's over a million and a half. I won't get it. He won't settle. But he'd be much smarter if he did, because if you put a star in a stinker you have a bigger stinker than if you had no star."

"You said it. Would you quit the movies if you got all that money at once?"

"Nobody ever quits the movies, Jim. They go into enforced retirement. The talkies killed off those that couldn't read lines or had voices that wouldn't record. But they didn't quit. A queen doesn't—what's the word?"

"Abdicate?"

"Abdicate. And that's the way you're treated while you're a star. Like a queen. Bring in those grosses, and you're treated like royalty. Begin to slip a little, and choose the nearest exit. But that isn't abdicating. That's escaping from the angry mob. I'll do what others have done. I'll take the money and come back here and wait for a good play. The difference is, if you have a flop on Broadway, it doesn't count against you the next time out. And if I happen to get a hit on Broadway, the next time I go to Hollywood I'll start at ten thousand! And maybe Joe Finston will be the one who pays it. Wouldn't that be nice?"

"It sure would." I got up and looked at the scrambled eggs that were being kept warm over an alcohol burner. "You sure you won't have some solid food?"

"All right," she said.

I started to dish out the eggs and the telephone rang. "You want me to go in the other room?" I asked.

"I'll go."

We both guessed it was Hunterden, and we were right. She went to the bedroom and was gone about fifteen minutes. When she came back she was calm and self-possessed. Whatever had been said on the telephone, her composure was now that of a star. I dished out the eggs again and she ate a big breakfast, speaking very little. "I was hungry," she said. "I want to go to the theatre every night I'm in town. Will you arrange for the tickets? I may not *get* there every night, but when I can't, you take some friend of yours. Here." She handed me a $100 bill.

"What's this for? I'll get the tickets from a scalper and have them put on your hotel bill."

"Your expenses."

"I put in an expense account at the office."

"I'm trying to give you a little present, you idiot," she said.

"Oh. Well, thanks. I can use it. Thanks very much."

"I should thank you. You got me through a difficult two hours. Imagine what I'd have been like, missing him at the station and then sitting here fidgeting."

"You go for this guy in a great big way, don't you?"

"I guess I do. Why else would I give a darn? Why else would I keep all my evenings free?"

All this was thirty years ago, as remote-seeming to many people today as the Gay Nineties had seemed to me. New York now is as different from New York then as New York then was from London. The one pervasive factor in all our lives was Prohibition, which made law-breakers of us all and gave a subtly conspiratorial, arcane touch to the simple act of dining out. Even that was phony, for there were only a few speakeasies which you could not talk your way into, where you had to be known. Indeed, it is harder to get a table at the best restaurants today than it was to gain admittance to the illegal cafés of those days. The other pervading factor, whose influence has been exaggerated in retrospect, was the national greed, the easy dollar in the stock market. But Prohibition, with the speakeasy, and the stock market, with the lucky dollar, facilitated romances like that between Charlotte Sears and Thomas R. Hunterden. Men like Hunterden have always had mistresses like Chottie Sears, but the speakeasy made it all so much simpler and the stock market paid the bills.

In the beginning I mentioned an oil millionaire whose newspaper clippings failed to fill a single folder. That was not true of Thomas R. Hunterden. His record filled three or four folders, and when I visited the library of the newspaper from which I had been fired, and checked what I had read, I now noticed that not a single clipping was dated prior to 1917. According to the other information available, Hunterden was in his early forties when the United States entered the war. His age had kept him out of the army draft, but there was no mention of any war activity whatever, either in his clippings or in the standard reference books of the period. In his brief *Who's Who* sketch he stated that he was born in Gibbsville, Pa., on April 2, 1876, and educated in "public schools" but did not say where; and there was no mention of his parents, a most unusual oversight if it was an oversight. The next item stated that he married Alice Longstreet in 1919. If there were any children they were not mentioned. After that followed a list of corporations of which he was board chairman: American Industrial Corporation, British-American Transportation, Throhu Petroleum, Omega Development, and Omega Holding. He then listed his clubs: the New York Yacht, the Bankers, and several golf and yacht clubs in Florida and South America. The only address he gave was his office on Lower Broadway. The Social Register provided one additional bit of information: Alice Longstreet was not her maiden name. She had been married to a man named Longstreet and her maiden name was Alice Boyd.

I then looked up all the Longstreet clippings and I found what I wanted. In 1918 Forrest Longstreet committed suicide by jumping from a window in his office in the financial district. Surviving were his wife, the former Alice Boyd, and two daughters. Longstreet had been quite a fellow. In the clippings he was often described as the sportsman-financier, prominent clubman, big-game hunter, aeronaut, foxhunter, and so on. He had played football at Harvard and had once set a record for driving his racing car from Rome to Paris. The newspaper photographs of him showed a handsome man with thick black hair and eyebrows, a black moustache, and white even teeth. The pictures confirmed my guess that he had been a wild man. It was not a particularly shrewd guess; the clippings gave the clues. Sporting accidents, expeditions into Africa, a suit for breach of promise, a swimming race from the Battery to

Bedloe's Island. I was too young and too deep in the Pennsylvania mountains to have heard of Longstreet, but now he interested me as much as Hunterden, and I knew that in finding out about the one I would be learning about the other.

I had a speakeasy friend named Charley Ellis, who was my age and who was my principal connection with New York society, as I was his with the Broadway-theatre-newspaper world. Charley had a job that he did not take very seriously, and he was easily persuaded to have me to lunch at his club.

"Why the sudden interest in old Forrest Longstreet?" he asked, when I began to question him. "Not that he was so very old. I guess he'd be about fifty-five or six if he'd lived. He was a friend of my old man's."

"Did you know him yourself?"

"Oh, sure. He used to take me for rides in his car. He had a car called a Blitzen-Benz. We'd go like hell out the Vanderbilt Parkway and on the way back he'd give me cigarettes. Now that I think of it, I guess he was my godfather. Yes, he was."

"Why did he do the dry dive?"

"What's this for? You're not going to put it in the paper, are you?"

"What paper? I don't work for a paper any more."

"No, but you might again. This has to be under the hat."

"It will be."

"Well, Forrie Longstreet was mixed up in some very suspicious stock promotion, and when he killed himself his family gave out the story that he did it for the insurance. The insurance was supposed to pay back his friends that went in on the stock deal. Actually, they were paid back by other members of his family. He blew all his own money, but the Longstreets still had plenty and they came through. My old man collected something, I know."

"What about his wife?"

"What about her?"

"Well, how did he leave her fixed?"

"Oh. Well, it didn't really matter, I guess. She married a fellow called Hunterden, supposed to be in the chips."

"Which one don't you like? Hunterden, or Long-street's widow? You're holding out on me."

"I know I am, Jim. I don't know what you want this information for, and I liked Forrie Longstreet. Let him rest in peace."

"I think Hunterden is a phony. I know he is, in some things, and I want to find out how much of a phony. I have no intention of writing an exposé, or giving it to the papers, but I've had my curiosity aroused. He's having an affair with Charlotte Sears, and I like her. It's none of my business. She's a big girl now and not a great friend of mine, but she's on the up-and-up. I did a little digging on Hunterden and I happened to come across Longstreet's name."

"Charlotte Sears is much too good for him, but as you say, if she's having an affair with him, what business of ours is it to interfere?"

"Not interfere, but be ready when the roof caves in. She trusts me, and she's a good egg. Would you like to meet her? I'm taking her to the theatre tonight. Meet us at Tony's, twelve o'clock."

"I've met her. She was going around with Junior Williamson a couple of years ago. Not that she'd remember me, but I'd like to see her again."

We said no more about Forrest Longstreet or Thomas Hunterden. Late that night Charlotte Sears and I went to Tony's, a speakeasy that was a meeting place for theatrical and literary people, and Charley Ellis joined us. He was too polite to remind her that they had met in the past, but she remembered him and he was pleased. "What's Junior up to these days?" she asked.

"Oh, he's talking about going into politics."

"Is that his idea, or his wife's?"

"His, I guess. He doesn't know what to do with himself."

"I guess when you have as much money as he has, it gets to be a problem. You don't feel like making any more money, and if you're in love with your wife, you don't go on the make. At least not yet. But he will. There isn't much there, you know. This may sound like sour grapes, but Junior's a mama's boy."

"That's no secret," said Charley Ellis.

"Maybe not, but it's the secret of his charm."

"How could it be?"

"A man wouldn't understand that, Mr. Ellis. As soon as a girl discovers that Junior's a mama's boy, every girl thinks she's going to be the real mama."

"A strange way to look at it."

"You're talking to somebody that learned it through experience. Oh, well, he was a nice kid and I guess he always will be. The women will vote for him. Once. What's he going to run for? Governor?"

"He hasn't said, but I doubt if he'd run for governor."

She laughed. "I could defeat him."

"You'd run against him?"

"Hell, no. I'd support him. The minute I opened my mouth the Democrats would thank me for saving them the trouble. Can you imagine the horror at Republican headquarters if I came out for Junior?"

"You should have been a politician," said Charley.

"Should have been? I am, every day of my life. Ask Jim. In our business Al Smith wouldn't last a minute. By the way, Jim, Joe Finston is taking me to lunch tomorrow, apropos of nothing at all."

Two acting couples invited themselves to our table and in a little while we all went to the Central Park Casino. Before saying goodnight Charley Ellis asked me to meet him for lunch the next day, and I said I would be glad to.

"That was fun last night," said Charley Ellis, at lunch.

"Yes, we didn't get home till after seven. We went to Harlem."

"I have to go through the motions of holding down my job," he said. "She's a good egg, Charlotte Sears. Confusing, though. I kept thinking she was still carrying the torch for Junior Williamson."

"Maybe she is."

"She's wasting her time. I didn't want to say anything, but Junior has his next wife all picked out already. Sears is right. There isn't much there. I like Sears."

"Yes, I can tell you do. Why don't you grab her away from Hunterden?"

"Somebody ought to. Hunterden is bad business."

"Take her away from him. She liked you. She said so."

19

He smiled. "She said so to me while I was dancing with her. As a matter of fact, Jim, and very much *entre nous*, I'm seeing her tonight."

"Good work," I said. "Fast work, too."

"Well, I thought it was worth a try. Maybe she just wants to talk about Junior, but we'll get on other subjects."

"I'm sure you will. I wonder what she plans to tell Hunterden," I said. "You know, I never got the feeling that she was in love with Hunterden as much as she was afraid of him."

"He's bad business. And you want to hear about Forrie Longstreet. He didn't kill himself over money."

"You more or less implied there was another reason."

"It was his wife. Forrie was a wild man. Cars and airplanes and all that. But he was crazy about Aunt Alice. We weren't related, but when I was a kid I called her Aunt Alice. Absolutely devoted to her, Forrie was. And apparently she was in love with him till this Hunterden guy came along. Hunterden went to Forrie with a business proposition that looked like easy money, just for the use of Forrie's name, and that's how Hunterden met Alice. Forrie lost his dough, his good name, and his wife, all to the same guy. My old man told me Alice didn't even wait six months before she married Hunterden. But I guess she's paying for it."

"How so?"

"Everybody dropped her like a hotcake. My mother wouldn't have her in the house, even before she married Hunterden. My mother of course was one of those that knew what was going on between Alice and Hunterden, and I gather she had a talk with her, but Alice wouldn't listen. You think you come from a small town, but what you may not realize is that there's a very small town right here in New York, composed of people like my mother and father. They never see anyone outside their own group and have no desire to, and believe me, the gate was closed on Alice Longstreet. The portcullis is lowered and the bridge over the moat has been raised, permanently."

"I see her name in the paper all the time."

"Yes, and you should hear my mother on the subject. 'Alice still doing public penance, I see.' That's what Mother says about Alice and her charities."

"How do the boys downtown feel about Hunterden?"

"Depends on what boys you're talking about. My old man and his friends give him the cut direct, and any time they hear he's in anything, they stay out of it."

"How did he get in all those clubs?"

"There's a funny thing about clubs. If the right people put you up, a lot of members hesitate to blackball you. The members figure that a man's sponsors must have their own good reasons for putting him up, and the members are inclined to respect those reasons, even in a case like Hunterden's. And there are some clubs he'll never get in."

"This one, for instance?"

"Oh, hell, this isn't what it used to be. I mean it isn't as hard to get in. There was a time when all the members knew each other. Now as I look around I don't even know all the guys my own age. This is where Forrie Longstreet used to hang out. I'll take you upstairs and show you some pictures of him."

"I've seen some. He was a dashing figure."

"In everything he did. He belonged in another age, when all gentlemen carried swords."

"I don't know, Charley. In Walpole's time fellows like Longstreet got into debt and had to do business with guys like Hunterden."

"So they did, but the Hunterdens never met the Longstreets' wives."

"I wonder."

"Well, maybe they did," said Charley Ellis. "You *like* to think things were better long ago."

"Better for whom?" I said. "Two hundred years ago I wouldn't be sitting here with you."

"If you say that, you know more about your family two hundred years ago than I do about mine. I'm not an ancestry snob, Jim. Maybe you are, but I'm not. My objection to Hunterden isn't based on who his grandfather was. Neither was my father's or mother's. It's what Hunterden himself was. And is. I consider Charlotte Sears more of a lady for dropping Junior Williamson than I do Alice Longstreet for marrying Hunterden. When I was in prep school I remember seeing pictures of Charlotte Sears, before she had a reputation as a movie actress. Around the same time Alice, Aunt Alice Longstreet, was a beautiful lady who was a friend of my mother's. But now Charlotte Sears is the beautiful lady, and Alice Hunterden is a social climber, trying to climb back. And having hard going."

"Very instructive conversation," I said. "And that isn't sarcasm."

"A little sarcasm. You know, Jim, people from your side of town, they choose to think that all the snobbery is concentrated in people like my mother and father. But all my father and mother want to do is see their friends and mind their own business. That's the way they like to live, and since they can afford it, that's the way they do live. And incidentally, money has very little to do with it. I know damn well my old man has friends that don't make as much money as you do. But they *are* his *friends*. Whereas, on Broadway, and the Hollywood people, a big star doesn't want to be seen with anyone that isn't just as big a star or a little bigger. And among those people there's nothing worse than a has-been. With my father and mother there is no such thing as a has-been." He smiled to himself.

"What?" I said.

"I said to the old man this morning that I'd been out with Charlotte Sears last night. 'Tell me about her,' he said. 'What's she like?' He's never met her, but he's seen her movies and plays, and he was really interested. But he doesn't want to know her any better, and neither would my mother. That isn't snobbishness, but you might think it is, and I guess Charlotte would too. You're the snob of us two."

"Why do you say that? It may be true," I said.

"One night when you took me to that place called Dave's Blue Room."

"I remember," I said.

"We sat down at a table, a booth, and you knew everybody there. They all said hello to you and they gave me the cold stare till you introduced me. 'Charley Ellis, of the *Daily News*.' Then they relaxed."

"Why was I a snob? Maybe they were, but why was I?"

"Because you were embarrassed in your own crowd, to be seen with somebody that wasn't a member of the crowd. You had to explain who I was. If you hadn't been a snob, you'd have just introduced me as Charley Ellis, or even Charley Ellis, customer's man at Willetts & Ellis."

"You're right," I said.

"Well, Charley Ellis, customer's man, has to make a few phone calls, but if you'd like to hang around for a while I'll play you some pool."

"Thanks, but I'm going up to see La Sears. She has a fan-magazine interview at four o'clock. Any message for her?"

"Just that I'm looking forward to seeing her tonight."

Chottie's maid let me in and I had a half-hour wait before Chottie turned up. It was immediately apparent that her luncheon with Joe Finston had not gone well. "Do you know a good cheap gangster that's looking for a night's work?" she said.

"I know several. Your candidate's Finston?"

"Who else? He offered me a picture that's been turned down by everybody on the lot, and of course when I said no, he said he was going to offer it to me by registered letter, and then if I turned it down he'd put me on suspension."

"That's what you pay an agent for."

"I know, but my agent is on the Coast and this little manoeuvre is all Finston's, in New York. Oh, I'll figure out something, but this heel, this nephew, Finston, he's doing all he can to spoil my visit. He wants to get out of the contract and then show his uncles what a smart boy he is. To show you how cheap he is, he said if he

24

wanted to, he could legally notify me in New York, today, and if I refused to do the picture, I'd not only go on suspension. I'd even have to pay all my expenses while I'm here."

"Well, from what I know of him, he'd do it."

"Jim, you stay out of it. I know you're on my side, but I don't want you to lose your job on account of me."

"Finston won't fire me, not right away. He wants to get some personal publicity in the New York papers and he's convinced I'm the one that can get it for him. Chottie, I haven't been with the company very long, and you have, but I know something you may not know."

"What's that?"

"Finston has his eye on the Coast. He'd do anything to get in the production end. But his uncles don't want any part of him out there. They don't even like it when he takes trips out there. Don't forget, it's his mother that's a Rosenbaum, not his father. The Rosenbaum brothers want to keep Joe Finston here in the home office, as far away from production as he can get."

"I knew some of this, but not all. I didn't know he was trying to get into production."

"Oh, yes. When he was in college he wanted to be a writer. He told me that himself. He wants to fire all the writers on the Coast and get all new ones. Also directors. He thinks he knows about directing."

"He couldn't direct a blind man across the street."

"I'm sure of it. Well, if I were you, I'd stall him till you go back. Let him say or do anything he pleases. Then when you get back to the Coast, go see Morris

Rosenbaum and tell him you understand Finston is getting ready to take over production. If he recovers from his stroke, you tell you heard a lot of rumours to that effect while you were here. In fact, you say to Morris you got that impression because Finston wanted you to star in this turkey and tried to talk you into it all the time you were in New York."

"I think I'll marry you, Jim."

"Just the way I am? I ought to go out and buy a few things. And you have a date tonight with a friend of mine."

"Well, he asked me. And you didn't."

"I didn't, because it's my job to take you out, and I do it on company money. I don't mean anything to you, Chottie, so don't pretend I do."

"Truthfully, you never did before, but this trip—I don't know. I never knew you before. I'll break the date with Ellis?"

"Oh, no. You keep the date with Ellis."

"Will you meet us later?"

"No."

"Well then, don't be jealous of Ellis. Jealous of Ellis! Well listen to the girl."

I decided to catch her off balance. "Where is Hunterden?"

"Hunterden? Why?"

"Okay, it's none of my business."

"No, it isn't," she said haughtily, so haughtily that I guessed something had gone wrong.

"Sorry I mentioned it," I said. "Now about this dame that's coming to interview you. She's new, but watch her. She's meek and mild, and asks innocuous questions, but she's out to make a score and we've had a little trouble with her. She doesn't write the usual fanmagazine slop."

"Everybody's out to make a score, in one way or another. I wish I had six children and lived in Chillicothe. Any Chillicothe, just so it wasn't New York or Hollywood."

"You've seen all those towns, but you never lived in them, and you never could."

"Don't be hard on me, Jim. I don't know where I'm at. If you want to know the truth, I'm scared."

"Of what?"

"Hunterden. Ellis. Finston. Junior Williamson. Oh, *he* phoned. He saw in the paper I was in town, and he quote just called up to chat unquote. So don't you add to my troubles, please. On the train East I had everything all worked out so neatly. Hunterden would meet me and we'd see each other and maybe get a few things settled. But he ran away from the photographers. And then I met your friend Ellis and I liked him, but he's on the make. Not that I blame him, but here I go with Junior again, only this time his name is Ellis. And I'm scared of Finston. He has a mean little face and I don't think it's going to be easy to fight him." She stopped. "I'm ashamed of myself, Jim. I tried flirting with him, but he wasn't having any. Ashamed and scared. An ugly little man like that ought to be easy to handle, but he just looked at me like I was another man. No, not like another man. He wouldn't have the guts to look at another man with such contempt. Do you know what he said? I can hardly repeat it."

"Don't if you don't want to."

"There we were in the middle of Sardi's and I was trying to use my feminine wiles, hating it but acting. And he said, 'Any time you want to put your clothes back on, let's talk contract.'"

"Did you have any answer to that?"

"Yes, I said I hoped he got a good look because the only way he ever would would be in his imagination. That's when I wished I could mention Hunterden's name, but how can I? I haven't seen Hunterden since I've been in New York. If you were a woman you'd know what I'm going through with Finston and Hunterden. Slapped in my famous teeth by a little horror I wouldn't even step on, and given the absent treatment by a big shot. And what's in between? An ex-college boy on the make, your friend Ellis. Don't be hard on me, Jim. I'm scared."

"I'll get you out of this interview."

"Can you? I couldn't face a tough dame this afternoon."

"You go downstairs and wait in the limousine. I'll wait till she gets here and tell her you're launching a battleship, or something. I'll get rid of her. I suggest you go for a drive through the Park and come back in about an hour."

"I don't want to be alone," she said. "Please, Jim. You get rid of her and then come down and go for a drive with me."

"Well then, park the car up Fifth Avenue and I'll join you as soon as I can."

I was not in love with Chottie and I never could be. She was a public person and I had already observed that a public person could only be in love with another public person; in Chottie's case another star, a famous young heir, a mysterious but nonetheless public figure like Hunterden. And yet as I made my way to the limousine, and as we drove through the Park and over to Riverside Drive, I wanted to protect her, to keep her from injury, to shield her from roughness. In the Park she reached over and took my hand.

"What are you thinking about, Jim?"

"You."

"I thought so," she said. She did not go on, and neither did I. If I told her that I wanted to protect her, I would be taking away her strongest protection, which was her belief in her own toughness. I saw her clearly as something gay and fragile that could be hurt and even destroyed, but she was as proud of her independent spirit as she was of her beauty and talent. I let her think whatever she was thinking, and for the remainder of the ride she encouraged me to talk about myself and jobs I had had. Back at the hotel entrance she said, before getting out of the car: "Do you want to keep the car?"

"You mean, don't come up," I said.

"That's what I mean. Don't come up. This would be a very bad time to start anything, if we ever are."

"And if we don't now, we probably never will," I said.

"Probably," she said. "I'll give you a wonderful kiss and you'll always know we could have."

"If you give me a wonderful kiss, we will," I said.

"Yes, I guess so. Then no kiss, but when you get old and think back on your girls, I give you permission to include me. We just as good as. Thank you, Jim."

She left me, and I found that the factual part of my

mind was busy wondering how old she was. Until that moment she had been among those actresses whose beauty and fame, while they last, make them impervious to questions as to their real names and real ages. But we had come very close to making love, and she herself had been the one to mention age. It was on her mind, and now it was on mine. Until then I would have accepted any age under thirty as a true one for her. With some sense of treacherous guilt I told the driver to take me to my newspaper alma mater, and I passed the next two hours in the files.

Allowing for margins of error, I found that she was no less than thirty-five, and quite possibly thirty-eight. Shows and plays she had been in, the kinds of roles she had played, established her age within those three years. My first thought when I considered her age was that at the time that I was begging my father to buy me an air rifle, Charlotte Sears had her name in lights in Herald Square.

In the morning I was at my desk, doing my routine chores that consisted of making up small items for the movie news columns, and I was summoned to Joe Finston's office. I went upstairs and waited to be admitted.

"Hello, Jim," he said. "Sit down. Two things. First, I'd like you to look this over and see if there's a story in it. It's about me when I was managing a theatre out in Rockaway. It has some amusing stuff in it about how I started in the industry. Don't read it now. I just sort of batted it out because I thought it'd be kind of amusing. The other matter is this Sears dame. We're getting ready to give her the old heave-ho. The key cities are howling bloody murder over her last two pictures and I got nothing but telegrams from all over the country. 'Don't give us any more Sears pictures,' is what they unanimously agree. I don't know what those production guys can be thinking of. I think some of them get softening of the brain from that California sunshine. I can tell you, from my experience as an exhibitor, this dame is costing us. You should see what her last two or three did, the grosses."

"Well, two costume pictures in a row," I said.

"Costume pictures are all right if they make money, but they don't with her in them. What I want you to do, I don't want this dame to have a line, not a line, as long as she's in New York. Cancel all interviews and don't give out any releases on her. I don't care if she climbs the Statue of Liberty, marries the Prince of Wales, she gets no publicity through this office. If you want to plant it that she's on the way out, the gossip writers are all friends of yours."

"Whatever you say, Joe. But I can't ask the gossip writers for any more favours just now. They're laying off the Hunterden story."

"What Hunterden story? Thomas R. Hunterden?"

"Yes, and Sears."

"Our Sears? Charlotte Sears and Hunterden? I don't know about that story. You have to enlighten me."

"Well, now you've got *me* confused. I thought she was all set here because she's Hunterden's girl friend."

"The first I knew about it," said Finston. "Where did you hear it from?"

"I didn't *hear* it. He was there to meet her at the station, the day she came in. And he called her up while

I was with her at the hotel. He's married, but I don't know why the gossip writers don't hint at it."

"You saw him at the station?"

"Did I? You should have seen him scatter when he saw those photographers."

"You positively couldn't be mistaken?"

"Not a chance. Thomas R. Hunterden was born in my home town. Gibbsville, Pa. Look him up."

"Does she admit it, Sears? I mean about being his girl friend?"

"Oh, sure. She has nothing to lose."

Finston removed his glasses and chewed on the tortoiseshell. "Then it's true, eh?"

"What?"

"Well, you hear things and half the time you don't pay any attention, the rumours and gossip you hear." He was trying to lie his way out of his ignorance of the Hunterden–Sears affair, and doing it so badly that I was almost embarrassed for him. He looked at his watch, and I knew he was reckoning the time on the Pacific Coast. "Tell you what you do, Jim, you read that material I gave you and let me know what you think of it. I'll let you know later about the Sears publicity. I still want to think it over a while longer."

"Whatever you say, Joe." I went out, and I stood a moment to light a cigarette near his secretary's desk. Finston's voice came through the intercom.

"Get me Mr. Morrie in Hollywood," he said. "Home, if he isn't at the studio."

I could have been quietly noble about what I had done for Chottie Sears, but she needed some good news and I had it for her. It amused her, too, that I had accidentally but quite truthfully been able to make use of the two men who were giving her the most trouble, to play them against each other without telling a lie. "You know who would have enjoyed this was my grandfather, Pat Somerville," she said. "Did you ever hear of Pat Somerville? An old-time song-and-dance man. And playwright. He wrote dozens of plays and acted in many of them. A good Mick, like yourself, and it was always a feast or a famine for him and my grandmother. Unfortunately it was all famine by the time I came along, and I never got the benefit of any of the feast. But my mother had a lot of wonderful stories about him. One day they'd be putting on the ritz with servants and horses, and the next day men would come and start moving the furniture out of the house." She paused and studied a diamond ring she was wearing. "My mother used to tell me those stories, but she had more spunk than I have. My father—they had an act together—lit out and left her stranded in Pittsburgh without a nickel and she never heard from him again. He took all their money and her diamond ring. In those days show people used to put their money in diamonds when they were working, and of course hock them when there was a long layoff. They boarded me in a house in Brooklyn in those days, so I could go to school. She got back to New York and partnered up with another man and went out again doing the same act. All she said to me was that my father was taken sick with consumption and in a sanitorium. Being a show-business kid, I'd often heard of that. TB was very common among show people, and I guess I cried a little

33

but my father had never been much to me. Or me to him. My mother'd make him come to see me in Brooklyn when they'd lay off during the summer, but he never tried to pretend that I didn't bore him. And the three of us never lived together after I was about eight years old. I was taking violin lessons and it used to drive him crazy when I'd practice, so they always lived in a hotel and I went on boarding in Brooklyn.

"Finally, when I finished eighth grade my mother and her partner got Willard K. Frobisher to write them a new act that I could be in. Songs, dances and witty sayings, and me on my fiddle doing a toe dance. Damn near ruined my legs, that toe-work. Thank God I gave *that* up in time."

"What was the name of the act? Did your mother marry her new partner?"

"The original name of the act was Dowd and Somerville. My real name is Catherine Dowd. Then the new act was Snow and Somerville *introducing* Charlotte Sears. Sears was the name of a face powder my mother used, and Charlotte—just a fancier name than Catherine, and there were thirty-five thousand Kitties, so I became Charlotte Sears. Society people ask me if I have relations in Boston, and out in the sticks they ask me how's Mr. Roebuck. But I was named after a face powder and a famous empress. Who went nuts, didn't she?"

"Yes, I think so."

"Well, I can sympathize with her, the last couple of days. But I feel better now, temporarily," she said. "Anyway, Jim, the story of my life isn't very interesting, but I left out what I really started to tell you. I don't want to be poor. *I* don't want to be stranded in Pittsburgh. I haven't got as much spunk as my mother. Not that I *am* poor. When I began earning my own living at fifteen, I saved something out of every week's pay. I never missed a week. Never. No matter where I was, I'd go to the post office and send back a money order, even if it was only two or three dollars. There was a bank here that show people used to use for that. So I'm not poor. But it isn't only the money. It's something else. All the years I've been in show business, every new job paid me more money than the last one. I've never taken a cut, and I've never taken a job that didn't pay me more than I'd been getting. That's why I'll fight Finston. It isn't only Finston I'm fighting. It's—oh, hell, you know what it is. Do I have to say it?"

"No."

"Do you know the picture I turned down? Do you know the story?"

"No, I haven't seen the script."

"I play the mother of a seventeen-year-old girl. That is, I would if I took the picture. I could very easily have a daughter seventeen, but I'm not going to let fifty million people see me playing a mother to a seventeen-year-old girl that everybody knows is twenty-two. Jean Raleigh. I'm not going to play Jean Raleigh's mother, because then the public will think I must be over forty, and I'm not. I may not have ten years to go before I'm forty, but I'm not there yet. And regardless of how old I am, your friend Ellis doesn't think I'm so old. And Junior Williamson called again today. He won't take no for an answer, that one. You know, it's almost as if he were taking advantage of me."

"How so?"

"This way. He's very anxious to see me and I've told him absolutely no. But he's not going to give up. He told me so. Well, last night Ellis took me to that speakeasy on 49th Street, Jack and Charlie's. I'd never been there before, and who should be there but Mr. Thomas R. Hunterden? He was with two other men."

"Did you speak to him?"

"No. But he kept looking at me and at Ellis, and he didn't like it a bit that I was with Ellis. Ellis and I had a quick dinner and left to go to the theatre and Hunterden was still there with the two men. Well, what I'm getting at is, what if I showed up there again tonight, this time with Junior Williamson? Or tomorrow night? Or every night?"

"Why hasn't Hunterden got in touch with you?"

She did not immediately answer me. "You risked your job for me, so I'll tell you," she said. "But this is between you and me and nobody else."

"All right," I said.

"The reason he hasn't *seen* me is because he can't. He's in the middle of the biggest deal he ever made. One of the men he was with last night was an Englishman, and the other one I guess was a Turk. He wore a fez, so I guess he was a Turk. Hunterden told me yesterday that there were some men in town that he was going to have to be with until they left. In fact, he said he wasn't going to let them out of his sight. I thought he was lying, but I guess those were the men."

"Sounds like it," I said. "Then he still loves you?"

"Love? Hunterden would choke on that word. A man like Hunterden doesn't think about love, although I shouldn't complain. It's a long time since I've said it

36

and meant it. Jim, maybe you'll be famous some day and then you'll understand certain things."

"What would I be famous for?"

"Writing, maybe. You have something, or I wouldn't be attracted to you. Politics, maybe. Or you might be head of a studio."

"Well, what is it that I'll understand that I don't understand now?"

"Two people like Hunterden and me. We're very much alike. I don't know anything about him—that is, the kind of things I told you about myself. I've only known him less than a year. He came out to the Coast and I met him and I fell for him. Not love. And not just sex. I didn't even know who he was, but naturally he had to be *somebody*, to be invited to Morrie Rosenbaum's to dinner. I guessed that much about him. I didn't sit near him at dinner, but after dinner he sat with me and the first thing he asked me took me completely by surprise. He said, 'Miss Sears, if you owned the Rosenbaum Studio, what other company would you like to merge with?' I said I wouldn't merge with any, not if merging meant equal partnership. I said I'd go into competition with one particular studio and drive them out of business, and then buy them out cheap. 'How would you do that?' he said. And I told him I'd steal their biggest stars and best directors. He asked me how I'd do that and I said if he'd give me the Rosenbaum Studio and plenty of money I'd show him how. Well, he wanted to know how I'd go about getting a certain star. I won't tell you her name. Miss Smith. How would I go about getting Miss Smith, who was under contract to a certain other studio? I said in that particular case I wouldn't go after Miss Smith herself, I'd go after a certain cameraman. It isn't so much that he's one of the famous cameramen, but if Miss Smith ever made a picture without him, she'd soon find out that fifty per cent of her success in pictures is due to him. She'd see herself photographed by someone else, and she'd follow the cameraman as soon as she could.

" 'Very interesting,' he said. Then he wanted to know who I'd keep if I suddenly got control of the company, and I said in other words he wanted to know who I'd fire. 'Not quite,' he said. So I told him I'd keep Morrie Rosenbaum, because he was more interested in making pictures than in the stock market.

"Then he made his first personal remark. He said, 'You know, Miss Sears, there's enough for everybody in this business, but if you and I had known each other ten years ago, we could have had most of it.'

"And I said, 'Well, Mr. Huntington, let's take what's left.' I thought his name was Huntington.

" 'No,' he said. 'Let's take our share, and then look into other possibilities, and see what we have ten years from *now*.' That particular moment was when Ruth Rosenbaum decided everybody ought to play poker. It was all right. I won about two thousand dollars, but I didn't see Hunterden alone till four or five days later. A Sunday noon. He came to my house unannounced, without calling up in advance. He came down to the pool, where I was reading the Sunday papers, and he said, 'Am I too late for breakfast, or too early for lunch?' He stayed till Tuesday afternoon, and then he had to go back to New York. Incidentally, Wednesday or Thursday of that week I saw in the trade papers that Guy

Smallwood had just signed a new contract with the Rosenbaum Studio. He was the cameraman. You can guess who the star was."

"Oh, sure. She's with us now."

"And getting a picture I wanted to do."

"But I'm surprised that Morrie Rosenbaum didn't know about you and Hunterden."

"We never went out together in Hollywood, and the few times we went to speakeasies in New York, other people were along with us. Hunterden has a deadhead that works for him, and if anybody saw the four of us out together they wouldn't know whether I was with Hunterden or his straight man."

"You started to tell me you and Hunterden are very much alike, then you got side-tracked."

"We are. If I were a man I'd be the same way with Charlotte Sears as he is. I understand where I fit into his life and where I don't. In fact, I don't have to be a man to understand all this. If I were on the crest of the wave, I might be treating Hunterden the way he's treating me. But I'm not on the crest of the wave. I have things worrying me, and when that happens I'm not as sure of myself. No spunk. I'm best at figuring things out when the heat's not on me. Hunterden has this big business proposition bothering him, and he doesn't want to be bothered with a woman too till it's all settled." She smiled. "I wish you were just a moron. Then you could make love to me and I could forget about Hunterden. But if you were a moron I wouldn't want you to make love to me."

"I'm very close to making love to you right this minute."

39

"I know, and it's exciting. But we better not, Jim."

"If it means so little, why not? Who'd know?"

"I would. The next man that I let make love to me—you don't know what I'm like. I try to run your life, I'm jealous."

"You're not with Hunterden."

"No, because I'm afraid of him. There ought to be another word for love, for people like Hunterden and me. Attraction. Respect. Success. I'm successful, a star. He respects that in me and we're attracted to each other. I know he's a big shot, a star in his own line. So there's a strong attraction that leads to sex. Well, I won't knock sex. I've had affairs that were nothing else and I've stayed up all night waiting for that phone to ring, just like anybody else. But with Hunterden—if I'd refused him on the sexual side, he wouldn't have bothered with me any more, but sleeping with me wasn't all he wanted. I suppose you might say I'm like one of his businesses, but I'm more than that to him and yet it isn't love.

"I don't know about love, anyway, Jim. I've been in love, all the symptoms. Happiness and thrills and desperation. Once I had them change my bookings so I could be on the bill with a magician I was in love with. Oh, he was a bad man, too."

"Did he want to saw you in half?"

"You think you're joking, but he gave me a beating one Saturday night in Baltimore that I never thought I'd make the Monday matinée in Philly. I had to wear black tulle over my arms and shoulders, and I had a mouse under my eye that I had to have leeches for. I was doing a single and up to the last minute I wasn't sure I could go on. But then I saw him grinning at me and I said to myself, 'You so-and-so, you go out there and wow them, and that'll show him.' I did, too, although I was half dead."

"No spunk, eh?" I said.

"Oh, I'll fight. By no spunk I mean I don't have the endurance that my mother had. The long pull, as they say down in Wall Street."

"I think you underestimate yourself all around," I said.

"Not to hear me talk about what a success I am," she said. "Well, a week from now and I'll be getting off the train at Pasadena, with a lot of new clothes and probably a whole trunkful of new headaches. I have two more days in New York."

"How do you figure that?"

"I'm going away for the week-end. To Long Island," she said. She waited for me to say something, but I remained silent. "You won't ask me where?"

"It's none of my business," I said. I could not keep the huffiness out of my tone, and she laughed.

"I like to tease you," she said.

"In more ways than one," I said.

"Oh, now that's not fair. I didn't tease you the other way, and I could have."

"You didn't do so well with Finston," I said, knowing as I said it that it was a cruel and vicious thing to say; but I had no control over, no knowledge of the depth of, the frustration I felt.

She looked at me very calmly. "After that remark you can't stay here any longer," she, the movie queen, said.

I got my hat and coat out of the foyer closet and went down the hall and pushed the button for the elevator. I put on my coat and watched the indicator as the elevator climbed and then began its descent. It was two or three stories above me when I heard her voice. "Jim? Come on back."

I went back and she was holding the door open for me. She closed it behind me and stood leaning against it. We looked at each other and then as naturally as we breathed we embraced, and I kissed her. She reached back her hand and turned the deadlatch. "It's what you want, isn't it?" she said.

"Very much," I said.

"Then I do too," she said.

I had seen, as a hundred million others had seen, the outlines of her body many times, but the extraordinary beauty of it as I saw her in the next few minutes was beyond my past imaginings. There was no bad disposition or sorrow in her love-making; she was pleased and she was happy to be pleasing. I think she was glad to be friends again, to heal the hurt I had inflicted on her and to do so by an ultimate generous act of her own, without waiting for me to express my regret, without pausing to forgive.

I was young, not inexperienced, but young, and my experience counted for little in this new lesson. I was learning for the first time that a woman could be gracious in a calculated act of love, that she could deny the pleasure to many who wanted it, who even wanted to trade love for it, but that she could make a present of pleasure and of the honour of her trust without asking for promises or tokens. Both of us knew that this would

42

not happen again, and that her earlier warning to the next man who might make love to her did not now apply. I had enjoyed what she gave, she had enjoyed the giving. She lit a cigarette for me and asked me if I wanted to sleep, and as she sat on the edge of the bed she seemed reluctant to get dressed again.

"Don't you want to go to sleep?" I said.

"Oh, no. But you can. I'll let you sleep for a half an hour." She took my cigarette and inhaled once, then put it out in the ash tray. "I'll remember this when you're famous," she said.

"I'll have you to the White House," I said.

She shook her head. "No, this is just between us, you and me. You did a lot for me out of niceness, and I couldn't let you think I was a teaser."

"I didn't think that."

"You might have. You did. You thought I was teasing you about the week-end, and I guess I was. Yes, I was. I didn't think I was, but I was. Don't be stubborn, Jim. Ask me where I'm going."

"Where are you?"

"The Williamsons'."

"The father and mother's?"

"No, Junior's house. His wife invited me."

"I didn't know you knew her."

"I don't. At least I've never met her. Have you met her?"

"Hell, no. Or him either. I don't know those people. I only know Ellis through a speakeasy that's open in the morning."

"From something Ellis told me, Junior's wife is quite desperate. And she's pretty clever, too. Junior has his next wife picked out, according to Ellis, and the present one I *think* would like me to break that up. She knows I had an affair with Junior, and I guess she thinks the next Mrs. Williamson won't like it a bit if I show up again. You're not listening. Go to sleep."

"I heard every word you said," I said, and then I dozed off.

It was dark and the traffic sounds of early evening in New York—the beep horns, the protesting second speeds of the buses, and the cab starters' whistles—brought me back to consciousness. Charlotte Sears in negligee and panties, was sitting at her dressing-table. "You rejoining the party?" she said.

"Where's your maid?"

"She'll be here in a little while. I couldn't hide anything from her, so I don't try. I had your suit pressed."

"Have I got a date with you tonight?"

"Well, I have theatre tickets and I have no other date."

"Fine."

"You can do me a great favour, if you will. Have you got a car?"

"No."

"Well, will you hire one and drive me out to the Williamsons' tomorrow afternoon?"

"Sure."

"She offered to send a car for me, but I want to do it my way. If I feel like getting the hell out of there, will you come out and rescue me?"

"Of course."

"Hunterden phoned while you were asleep."

"I thought I heard you talking."

"You didn't hear a thing. You were really out. Anyway, he wants to see me Sunday night, in town, so even if I don't call you before then, will you come out and get me Sunday afternoon?"

"Sure."

"Finston has lost," she said.

"Good work. Did you find that out from Hunterden?"

"I sure did. Morrie called Hunterden from the Coast and said he had good news for him. The Studio was giving me the lead in *Rhapsody on Broadway*, a musical that I'm dying to do. Morrie giggled and said he just thought Hunterden would like to know. Hunterden was taken completely by surprise, but he wasn't annoyed. In fact he was pleased. But the man that really swung the whole thing—little old you."

"Great," I said. "Tomorrow I'll watch Mr. Finston crawl."

"I'm going to do something worse. I'm not going to answer the phone when he rings. I'll let him hang for a week. But doesn't that please you, how it worked out?"

"It certainly does."

"And yesterday I was down at the bottom of the bottomless pit. Do you like champagne?"

"Not much."

"But let's have some tonight, even if we don't drink it all."

"Company money," I said.

"What kind of a car would you like? I mean to own?"

"Don't buy me a car, Chottie. It'd be a waste of money."

"All right, then, not a car, but I'm going to give you something. You wouldn't wear a diamond ring, would you?"

"No."

"How about a trip to Europe?"

"Well, it would be fun to go as a passenger. I've been to Europe, but I worked my way."

"The *Ile de France*? Would you like that?"

"Who wouldn't?"

"You decide when you want to go, and the boat, and I'll pay your fare both ways and all your hotel and travel expenses for a month. Can you get a leave of absence?"

"I don't know, but it won't make the slightest difference. I'll just go."

"Just tell me when, and the trip is yours."

"Thank you."

We had dinner at Jack and Charlie's. It was a small room, low-ceilinged, and no table would seat more than six comfortably, but it was the best speakeasy in New York; the food was excellent, and there were many rumours to explain the high quality of the liquor, the recurring one being that certain highly placed financiers had got Andrew Mellon to allow the Bermuda rum-runners to slip through the Coast Guard patrols. Everything was expensive, and I seldom went there when I was not spending company money.

"Over in the corner, the table that's hidden by the bar," said Charlotte Sears.

"Who?" I said.

"Hunterden and the Turk and the Englishman. Now he sees me." She bowed. "Might as well speak to him if Morrie knows about us. He's coming over."

Thomas Rodney Hunterden, expensively tailored in a black suit and wearing a black silk necktie with a smoked pearl stickpin, shook hands with Chottie. "How do you do, Miss Sears," he said.

"Hello, Mr. Hunterden. I saw you here last night but you didn't recognize me. Will you join us? This is Mr. Malloy, of our publicity department."

"Could I sit with you for a minute?" He included me in the question, but he did not wait for my answer.

"I've seen you before, haven't I, Mr. Malloy?"

"Well, I get around," I said.

"What part of the country do you come from?" he said.

"I come from a place called Gibbsville, Pennsylvania."

"Oh, yes. In the coal regions."

"Oh, you've heard of it?"

"I was born there, but I left when I was very young."

"You two were born in the same town?" said Chottie.

"But I persuaded my parents to take me away when I was two years old," he said. It was not very funny, but it was a remark that put me in my place. "I saw your picture in the paper, Miss Sears. Will you be in town long?"

"Leaving for the Coast Monday."

"Well, I hope we run across each other again. Nice to see you. I have a very good friend in your organization, Mr. Malloy. Remember me to him if you see him."

"Who's that, and I will?"

"Morrie Rosenbaum. Have to get back to my friends." He rejoined the Turk and the Englishman.

"Dying to know who you were," said Chottie.

"And to make sure I didn't get any ideas. He has a very good friend in my organization."

She patted my knee. "Don't let him annoy you. After all, two hours ago."

"What do you think kept me from telling him to go to hell?"

"Me."

"True," I said.

"You can be as independent as you please, but I can't."

"But you are."

"No, I'm not. I cheated with you, Jim, but he's my big moment. He always will be. We didn't find a word to use instead of love, but whatever it is, that describes it. And it's the same with him. He had to know who you were."

"Why not call it love, Chottie? Nobody's going to fine you for misusing the word."

"You get over love. I won't get over this."

"Then you're worse than in love."

"Oh, I know that. That's what I've been trying to tell you."

"I'm a very unimportant guy," I said. "He didn't have to threaten me by telling me what good pals he is with M. R."

"He shouldn't have done that, but he couldn't help it. And don't forget, Jim. His instinctive jealousy was right. Where were you and I two hours ago? The man is no fool."

"I never thought of it that way."

"The same instinct that made him pick me out at Ruth and Morrie's dinner party. He said to me one

48

time, the secret of his success was to find out everything he could about, well, about a business. Get all the facts, and then play his hunches, even when the facts seemed to lead in another direction. Just now he followed a hunch. Maybe I was sitting too close to you, or enjoying myself too much. But he had a hunch, and he was right. Although he'll never know he was right."

"Yes, but maybe he'd be jealous of anybody."

"He wasn't jealous of Ellis. There goes that rhyme again. He saw me with Ellis, but he didn't come to the table. He had no hunch about Ellis, and he did about you. Give him credit." She paused. "Also, I don't like to say this, but watch your step. I'm going to lie to him when he asks me about you, but he may not believe me, although he'll pretend he does. And he might make up some other excuse to have you fired."

"Oh, he wouldn't do that to another Gibbsville boy," I said.

Abruptly Hunterden rose and came over to our table again. "Have you and Mr. Malloy been to the Florence Club, the Chez Florence? I'm taking my friends there later if you'd care to join us. About two o'clock? It doesn't start till late, or is that no news to Mr. Malloy?"

"I've been there quite a few times," I said.

"Miss Sears?"

"All right, fine," she said.

"I see you're just finishing dinner, so I infer you're going to the theatre. Two o'clock, then? Splendid." He went back to his table.

"Well, that was pretty smart," I said.

"Why?"

"Don't you get it? We go to the theatre and we get out after eleven, probably go some place for a drink, meet him at two, and stay under his watchful eye till four or five. The whole evening taken care of, in case I get any ideas. That was damned smart. And at five o'clock tomorrow morning, or whenever, he'll deposit me right at my door, in his beautiful big Rolls-Royce."

"How do you know he has a Rolls?"

"There's one parked outside, so I guess it's his."

"It is. I recognized the chauffeur."

I had failed to anticipate the degree of Hunterden's strategy. At the Florence Club he and his companions were with three show girls from Mr. Ziegfeld's production. The Turk did not drink, but the Englishman and I drank a lot, while Hunterden nursed a highball until about half-past four. Hunterden then made his excuses and departed with Chottie, and the Turk, the Englishman, and I were left with the show girls and Hunterden's Rolls. The girl who got me was sore as hell, as she might well have been, to have had such an unprofitable evening, but at least I got four hours' sleep before going to the office.

I telephoned Chottie. "Do you still want me to drive you out to Long Island?"

"Why? You're not running out on me, are you?"

I laughed. "You're a fine one to be talking about running out. Is everything okay?"

"Blissful," she said, and she meant it. "Will you call for me around five-thirty?"

"Yes. What am I supposed to be, I mean am I your brother or cousin? In case I have to act a part at Mrs. Williamson's."

"You be a devoted admirer that likes to do things for me. That's real type-casting."

"It's a part I like to play, Chottie," I said. I liked this woman in a way and to a degree that probably only another man would understand, although it was a woman—she herself—who had come closest to putting it into words when she declared that you get over love, but you don't get over "this".

I drew some expense money and went up to Columbus Circle and picked out a second-hand Duesenberg S-J, which was on sale for $18,000. It was a phaeton with a tonneau windshield. "I want to hire it for the week-end," I said.

"Not a chance," the salesman said.

"Don't be so hasty," I said. "I want to hire it, and I don't want to pay you a nickel." I introduced myself and told the man that I was squiring Miss Charlotte Sears around Long Island society, and if he didn't want the publicity, I'd just as soon give it to another car. He said he'd have to talk to the manager.

"Get me a picture I can blow up and put in my window, and the car is yours," the manager said. "With Miss Sears at the wheel, of course."

"Of course," I said.

I then got my coonskin coat out of hock and Charlotte Sears and devoted friend drove out to the Williamsons' in style. The Williamson butler was not impressed, but Mrs. Williamson was. "What a beautiful car," she said. "Did you drive from California?"

"It isn't my car," said Chottie.

"It's yours, Mr. Malloy?"

"For the time being," I said.

"I've never driven one," said Mrs. Williamson, wistfully. "Are you in a terrible hurry? Couldn't the three of us . . .?"

The butler removed Chottie's luggage and we went for a ride out the North Country Road. Polly Williamson took the wheel, and she was a good driver. On the stretch past the Hutton place she hit ninety m.p.h., and after we turned around she took the same stretch at slightly more than a hundred. Her delight was simple and disarming. "I've never done that before in my life. What a wonderful car. Thank you, Mr. Malloy." She herself was simple and disarming, unlike the person I had expected her to be. She was not pretty by the standards of the three girls I had seen the night before; but she had a good figure and legs, and if her hands had not been strong we would have landed in a ditch. The Duesenberg was not a woman's car, and I guessed that Polly Williamson was accustomed to handling big Irish hunters.

She was wearing a checked suit and was hatless, and her blonde hair was in disarray from the spin. When we got out of the car at her house she patted the door and smiled. "Can you come in and have a drink?" she said.

"Thanks, but I have to be on my way," I said.

"I hope I didn't make you late. If you're going to be in the neighbourhood why don't you come in Sunday afternoon? Don't call or anything, just come if you can."

I almost hated to leave, and Polly Williamson, by her unexpected friendliness, had made me feel I was welcome to stay. She was in her middle twenties, the age of most of the girls I was taking out at that period of my life. She had two small children, and I knew that she was having trouble with her husband. But where I had been led to expect a neurotic, jealous woman, I could see only a young wife who was making an effort to save her marriage by resorting to the kind of intrigue that I was sure was new to her. I do not wish to imply that I saw her as a simple, suburban housewife; the butler wore silver-buttoned livery; the Junior Williamsons' house was only the second largest on the estate, perhaps a quarter-mile distant from the main house whose chimneys and roofs we could see above the trees on a hilltop; and while we were saying goodbye a toothless little man in breeches and buttoned canvas puttees rode past us on a lathery gelding, leading another horse with the stirrup irons tucked up, on his way to the stables. The little man tipped his cap to Polly Williamson. "Just back, Peter?" she said.

"Yes ma'am, just these five or ten minutes," he said, without halting.

"My husband and a friend of his," said Polly Williamson. "They must have stopped in at the big house, but you sure you can't wait to meet them?"

"Afraid not, but thanks very much, and Chottie, see you Sunday if not before?"

Chottie Sears was grinning at me and my not well-hidden admiration of her hostess. "I hope you can make it Sunday," she said.

"I'll try," I said, and put the Duesenberg in gear. I had plans for the week-end; I was not going to waste the Duesenberg; but I drove away reluctantly. I suppose that at that period I was about as fancy-free as it is possible for a man to be, which in my case, however, meant also that I was ready to fall in love with almost any attractive girl. There was an element of pity in my admiration of Polly Williamson, and that element nullified what would otherwise have been the awesome effect of her possessions.

I took the Port Washington ferry and spent Friday and Saturday nights with friends in Connecticut. At noon on Sunday, while we were having breakfast, I was called to the telephone. It was, of course, Chottie Sears. "Duty calls," she said.

"How's it going?" I said.

"Not so good. Can you get here around five? They're having some people in and I have to stay for that, but I want to be ready to go any time. I'll be packed and everything, so we can leave here before eight. You don't have to play any part. Polly Williamson knows who you are. We've gotten to be friends. Her whole plan collapsed last night after dinner. Junior got plastered and he and his lady friend disappeared about eleven and never came back. We'll see how things are at lunch, but as of now this marriage is a fiasco, and for her sake I'm sorry. She wanted to make it go, but he's a silly, spoiled brat. Wait till you see what took him away from Polly."

The other guests had not arrived when I got to the Williamsons' house, and without prior information I could not have guessed that all was not serene. Junior Williamson, dressed for town in a blue suit, black shoes, and stiff collar, pretended to me that I had cost him money he could not afford. "My wife wants a Duesenberg just like yours," he said.

"She can have mine, because it isn't mine. I rented it," I said.

"Isn't it a new car?"

"No, it's second-hand. They want eighteen thousand for it."

"That's quite a come-down from the original price, isn't it? Don't they sell for over twenty thousand?"

"Around twenty-two, I think," I said.

"That's a lot of money. I'm in favour of renting cars. I always do when I go abroad."

"Yes, but if people like you don't buy those cars, they'll stop making them," I said.

"No, not really. There'll always be guys like Thomas R. Hunterden to buy them. You know, Thomas R. Hunterden, the holding-company guy?"

"He's coming here this afternoon," said Polly Williamson.

"That's what made me think of him," said Williamson. "Somebody told me he kept a Rolls in New York, one in London, and one in Paris. And they're not rented."

"Well, I suppose a fellow like that can make sixty thousand dollars in one day," I said.

"Easily, but think of the upkeep. My father and I together, I think there are about eighteen cars on this place, with the two small trucks. A ton-and-a-half Dodge truck and a Ford. That may seem like a lot, but we have a full-time mechanic, an absolute genius with cars, and we get a good discount on gasoline and oil, quantity buying. It probably doesn't cost us as much to keep a Pierce-Arrow going as it does some fellow that has one Chevrolet. And I'll bet you—no. I was going to exaggerate. I was about to say we could run our whole garage on what a fellow like Hunterden spends for three cars in three cities. I was thinking about three chauffeurs, garage bills, and so forth. I suppose the actual outlay is less for Hunterden, but our cars are always in use. That's where the big difference is. Every car on this place is in actual use. My mother, my father. My wife. Taking one of the children to school. Servants to church. Marketing. Actually, if we had room in the garage, my father was thinking of buying a horse van *as an economy*. He gets awfully tired of paying a fellow in Roslyn every month for vanning. Five dollars a head, just from here to Meadow Brook."

The fascinating thing about Williamson's monologue was his taking for granted that I shared his problem: I was in his house, I had his highball in my hand, and I therefore was a sympathetic listener. I had once experienced the same blind, uncomplimentary acceptance when I was sent to interview a Princeton professor who had won a prize for some scholarly research in Sanskrit. Both Williamson and the professor assumed, without the courtesy of inquiring into my interests and my ignorance, that their language was also mine. Williamson had paid no attention to my remark that I was renting a second-hand car, other than to assume that my reason for renting a second-hand car would be the same as his for hiring cars in Europe. If his wife had not been present I would have made a burlesque of his father's persecution by the Roslyn horse-vanner, but I did not want to add to her troubles. I also did not want to kid this humourless man into giving me a punch in the nose. He glowed with health and strength; in the downward turn of the corners of his eyes there were warnings of a bad temper, and he had the meaty hands of a former oarsman. Four—six—eight years of rowing gives them a good fist that they keep all their lives.

Williamson was ready to change the subject, and did. "It's been awfully nice having Chottie here again," he said. "Chottie, you mustn't ignore us the way you've been doing."

"Hollywood isn't exactly around the corner, Junior," said Chottie Sears.

"I know, but don't you have to come to New York a lot?" he said.

"Not often enough," said Chottie.

"Why can't they make their pictures just as well in New York? I read an article not so long ago, about making movies over in Long Island City. Ever since the talkies they have to film everything inside a studio, it said. So the California sunshine isn't an advantage any more."

"Real estate," said Chottie. "The picture companies have a lot of money tied up in real estate."

"California bores me," said Williamson. "That everlasting sunshine."

"Go there during the rainy season," said Chottie.

"The what? I didn't know it ever rained there. But I suppose it must sometime."

I was beginning to understand Williamson and his attraction for women. In ten minutes he had proved to me that he was one of the stupidest men I had ever met, but the society girl and the movie queen watched every move he made and attended every trivial word. He would take a sip of his drink, and they would watch the elevation of the glass, the lowering of it, and then their gaze would go back on his face. His wife had hardly spoken a word since my arrival, and I noticed for the first time a phenomenon of her attentiveness: when Williamson was speaking, she would look at his mouth, and her lips would move in a barely discernible, unconscious forming of his words. Polly Williamson was a rich girl in her own right, from a family as rich as the Williamsons, and was therefore not dazzled as Chottie Sears might be by the Williamson fortune. In an otherwise masculine face Williamson had a feminine, cupid's-bow mouth, and I now recalled Chottie's remark about his being a mama's boy. He was indeed a mama's boy, with the mouth of a pubert and the appetites of a man; the brainless cruelty of a child, and the strength to arouse in a woman an urgent need to give him pleasure. With the addition of my own observations I agreed with Chottie's epithet. Williamson also had a rather musical voice, not at all unpleasant, and he spoke in the accent of his class. He would pronounce third and bird as though they rhymed with an r-less beard. Polly Williamson's pronunciations were identical with his and her voice was nicely modulated, so that in the present company the Williamsons' accent and voices were harmonious, while Chottie Sears, deep-voiced and with a smoothed-over Brooklyn enunciation, and I, with a harsh voice and an Eastern Pennsylvania twang, were two soloists against a duet. Our voices, our accents, and we ourselves were out of place in this house, in this room. I cannot say whether I became conscious of our vocal sounds first and of Polly Williamson's silent lip-moving second or that the order

of observation was reversed. But my more vivid re-
collection is of Polly Williamson's lips. Chottie Sears,
experienced in turning on and simulating facial expres-
sions, gave no indication of her thoughts while Williamson boldly dismissed the telephone calls he had been
making since Chottie's arrival in New York. He
correctly assumed that she would play his game in spite
of his having shown a preference for another woman the
night before.

Williamson was a study of an arrogant aristocrat at
work. He represented strength and vitality, three or
four generations of careful breeding (with some rather
distinguished citizens in his blood lines), and great
wealth. He had begun to serve on many boards of
trustees that governed the policies of philanthropies and
cultural activity of the city and the nation, which had
been preceded by his earlier participation in polo and
fox-hunting committees and his support of Yale ath-
letics. I had no doubt that he sincerely believed that a
seat in the House, to be followed by a seat in the Senate,
a Cabinet office and an ambassadorship in London or
Paris, all would and should be his. As these things raced
through my mind I looked over at Polly Williamson
and wanted to tell her that her marriage was safe
temporarily: Williamson would not ask for a divorce
until his maiden political campaign was over. But I
also would have had to tell her that in the event of his
defeat (which I regarded as certain), the marriage was
finished.

At that point we were joined by a tall, handsome
woman of about twenty-eight. I looked at Chottie
Sears, who gave me a quick pair of nods, and glanced

from the newcomer to Williamson. This, she was telling me, would be the next Mrs. Williamson. Her name, as she was introduced, was Mrs. Underwood; her first name, as she was greeted by the Williamsons, was Eunice.

Eunice Underwood was actually not very tall and not very handsome, but she had chic in abundance. She wore a small black hat with a rhinestone pin on the left side, and as she entered the room she slipped off her mink coat and handed it to a maid, revealing a black satin dress, of which the fringed skirt was cut on the bias. The dress had long, close-fitting sleeves that came down over her wrists. She wore sheer black stockings and black suede shoes that had rhinestone buckles that matched the ornament on her hat. From a platinum chain around her neck hung a large diamond. Two words came to mind: the word dramatic, and the word mistress. I suppose the first word made her costume a success, even though I would not tell her so; and I suppose the second word was in my mind before I saw her, although I might have had the same verbal association without advance preparation. She was black, white, and sleek. Her hard, high little breasts pointed forward against the shiny satin. I had seen breasts like them on an expensive whore: all nipple and little flesh.

She went up to our hostess and said "Hello, Polly," but did not kiss her or shake hands.

"Hello, Eunice," said Polly Williamson.

"Hel*lo*, there," said Junior Williamson, exuberantly.

She reached out and smoothed down his necktie. "Hello," she said. "Hello, Miss Sears." She then was silent while I was being introduced, but she looked at me and my ready-made suit during the utterance of our names, and I was out of her life before she said "Howja do." She immediately turned away from me and handed Williamson an ivory cigarette holder into which he fitted a cigarette from his own case. I suspected that she had made him change to her brand, since there was no discussion over that. She put the holder in her mouth and Williamson lit the cigarette.

"Have you got crowds more people coming, Polly?" she said.

"Between thirty and forty."

"Oh, well, that's not so bad. I'll be able to find a place to sit with only that many."

"Wouldn't some nice gentleman give you a seat?" said Chottie Sears. Polly Williamson suppressed a smile.

"They're not as polite here as I'm sure they must be in Hollywood," said Eunice Underwood. "That reminds me, not that I've seen many films, but I don't think I've ever seen anyone sitting down in one. They're all so busy shooting at each other or throwing pie in each other's faces."

"A lot of them do sit down, though," said Chottie Sears. "There's a trick to it. We call them prat-falls."

"Do you know where your prat is, Eunice?" said Williamson, laughing.

"I can imagine. Where did *you* learn where it is? From Miss Sears?"

Williamson laughed again.

"Steady, girl," said Chottie Sears.

"You two," said Williamson, laughing. "I swear."

A group of six men and women now entered. Three of the men and one of the women were slightly tight, and Eunice Underwood slowly moved away to a chair in a far corner of the room. "Hey, Eunice," said one of the men.

"Stay where you are, Billy. Don't come over and bother me. You spray people when you're plastered."

"We could do with a little spraying around here," said the woman who was tight, and whom I took to be Billy's wife. A maid brought in a trayful of drinks which apparently has been ordered by the new guests on arrival. The butler stood in the doorway and watched the drinks being served, and then disappeared. Almost immediately another group of six arrived and among them was Charley Ellis.

"Have you been here all week-end?" he said.

"No, I just got here a little while ago," I said.

"I hear there was a bit of a *crise* last night. I thought you might be able to tell me about it."

"Can't tell you a thing," I said. "I was on the other side of Long Island Sound."

"I'll be back after I've said hello," he said. He left me and kissed Polly Williamson and shook hands with Chottie Sears.

Eunice Underwood called to him: "Charles, come here and sit with me a minute."

"I'll sit with you," said one of the other men.

"I didn't ask you, I asked Mr. Charles Ellis."

"I'm giving you your last chance," said the man.

"Is that a threat or a promise?" said Eunice Underwood. "Polly, if I were you I'd tell McDonald to dilute the drinks."

"Oh, I don't think so, Eunice," said Polly Williamson.

"Well, in that case I'm going to have to get tight in self-defence. Junior, get me a martini in a champagne glass, please."

"How'd it be if I got you champagne in a martini glass?" said Williamson, laughing.

"Oh, don't be the life of the party," said Eunice.

Charley Ellis rejoined me. "Where is *Mister* Underwood?" I asked. "Or isn't there any?"

"Eunice's husband? He's feeding the fishes. He got drowned in Bermuda a couple of years ago."

"Oh, that's why she's all in black?"

"No, I don't think that has anything to do with it. She didn't waste many tears on him. Not that he would have on her."

"Has she got a lot of dough?"

"Well, she has enough. But let's just say that if she hooks Junior she'll change her scale of living, not downward."

"Where is she from? She wasn't one of this crowd originally, was she?"

"No, she's from Brooklyn. Her father was a minister."

"Oh, she wants to be a nun," I said.

"I hadn't heard *that*," said Charley. "But I'm told she's tried everything else, and believe me, if she doesn't get Junior she's going to have to change her scene of operations."

"Not very popular?"

"Well, not with the women. Decidedly not with the women. Most of these people have known each other all their lives. Some of them were engaged to be married and married somebody else, but it's a closed

63

corporation, and Eunice, the complete outsider, married Buddy Underwood and played it straight for a while. But she was in too much of a hurry. You can't hurry these people. They've been together too long."

"What was she in a hurry to do?"

"Oh, I suppose get rid of Buddy and make a better marriage. If she'd stuck by Buddy, who wasn't much good, she'd have gotten ahead faster. But instead she went after the men. She's a good rider, and she used that, and she's quite a good tennis player."

"She doesn't look the athletic type."

"She is, though. Don't let that slinky get-up fool you. She rides sidesaddle, and in a top hat and skirt she's even more impressive than she is today. Plenty of guts, too. And knows she's hated. Junior is sort of her last chance, and she knows that. If she doesn't land him, she knows she'll have to clear out. She gets invited everywhere because nobody wants to snub the next Mrs. Junior Williamson, but this is the ninth inning, two out, nobody on base, and she's at bat. A scratch single isn't going to do it for her. She has to knock one out of the ball park."

"Why is she after you?"

"After me? She isn't after me. Polly's my cousin, and Eunice would like to line up a few of Polly's relations on her side. She isn't after anybody but Junior, and everybody in this room knows it. That's why I asked you about last night. If she had an open spat with Polly, that would cook her goose for fair, because Junior doesn't want to be hurried. Don't forget, old Mr. Williamson and Mrs. Williamson are still very much alive. Junior takes Eunice to their house every chance he gets, but the old boy and Mrs. Williamson like Polly and they're crazy about those grandchildren."

"Why would Thomas R. Hunterden be invited here this afternoon?"

"I didn't know he was. That'll be a new face, and you don't see many of them in this house. He'd never be asked to the big house, so I guess Junior invited him."

"Why not Polly?"

"Well, anything's possible. Let's see if Alice comes with him. If she does, then it just means that Alice and one of her hospitals has been working on Junior and one of his hospitals. I don't know. You see anybody you'd like to make a play for?"

"Yes. Your cousin."

He shook his head. "No. Anything's possible, but I wouldn't like to see you make a play for Polly now. If a son of a bitch like Hunterden wants to, that's different. But not a friend of mine. If on the other hand she ever gets a divorce from Junior, I'll be as helpful as I can."

"Thanks," I said. "I could go for her."

"I think she's about the best we have to offer, and I'd like to see her shake loose from Junior, but she isn't ready to give up. See anybody else?"

"The blonde in the blue tweed suit."

"Mary Day? Can be had. The coast is absolutely clear, there. Billy's forever on the make for Eunice and it makes Mary sore as a wet hen. Hey, Mary."

The girl called Mary Day sauntered over.

"Here's a friend of mine that thinks you're pretty darn attractive."

"Why shouldn't he? I think he is, too. And a stranger in our midst. Where are you from?"

"He's a Pennsylvania boy," said Charley Ellis.

"Oh, God. Another Biddle?"

"No, I'm one of the anthracite Malloys."

"Oh, Scranton. I was in a wedding there once and I never saw people drink so much—except here, of course. But somehow it shocked me to see out-of-town people do it. Maybe you were at the wedding. It was——"

"I'm not from Scranton. I'm from Gibbsville."

"Oh, Gibbsville. Well, I know a girl that lives *there*. Caroline Walker, married to somebody called English. I spent one god-awful year at Bryn Mawr and she was one of the few bright spots. How is she?"

"Well, I saw her the last time I was home. She was looking well."

"She invited me to her wedding and I invited her to mine. End of correspondence, but I liked her. She was very nice to me. You give her my love when you see her. Mary Patterson. Can you remember that?"

"Mary Patterson. Sure. I'll remember."

"Are you visiting Charley? I didn't see you at lunch, did I?"

"I'm squiring Charlotte Sears."

"Oh, I want to hear all about her. Is it true that she's going to break up this thing between Junior and Eunice? I *may* have had one too many cocktails, don't you think? I shouldn't drink on Sunday. He who drinks on the Sabbath will live to fight some more. What did you say your name was?"

"James Malloy."

"It won't stick. I've forgotten it already," she said.

66

She was sitting on a sofa between Charley Ellis and me, holding her cocktail glass in both hands. "What did you say it was again? Spell it."

"M, a, l, l, o, y."

"Mallory."

"No, there's no r in it."

"Like oysters."

"Yes. I'm out of season."

"I don't think you are. I think you're very much *in* season, and if you want to know the truth, so am I. You wouldn't like to take me out of here, would you, Mr. Mallory?"

"Where would you like to go?"

"I don't know. I'm open to suggestion."

"I'd love to take you anywhere, if we can be back here by eight o'clock."

"Oh, I don't think we would be. I really don't think we would. In other words, you're spoken for?"

"Not exactly spoken for, but I'm here to drive Miss Sears back to New York."

"Too bad. Or maybe not. Now this old gossip won't have any sleuth. Except that he did hear me proposition you."

"Am I the old gossip?" said Charley Ellis.

"What is sleuth?"

"I thought you were a friend of Caroline's. Sleuth is gossip. An old Bryn Mawr word for gossip. Talk-gossip. But Charley Ellis is a talker-gossip. If you want to know anything about anybody here, ask Charley. Isn't that right, Charley?"

"Just about," said Charley Ellis, not at all offended.

"*But*—if you want to know everything about

67

Charley, you have to ask *me*. That's right, too, isn't it, Charley?"

"Just about."

"Ask him something about me," said Mary Day.

"Anything at all?" I said.

"Anything."

"All right," I said. "Has she had her appendix out?"

She laughed. "Go ahead answer him. I want to see what you say. You're in a spot. You don't know whether to be chivalrous or truthful. Go on, Charley, answer his question."

"You answered it for me," said Charley. "I didn't have to say a word—and I still haven't. So stop calling me a gossip, Mary. You get a few too many drinks in you and talk too much, and then you accuse other people of gossiping."

Mary Day turned to me. "Ask me whether *he's* had *his* appendix out? The answer is yes. And have you had yours out, Mr. Mallory?"

"You're not going to find out as easily as that."

"Well said, Jim," said Charley.

"Has Charlotte Sears had hers out?" said Mary Day. "*Why, look at him! He's blushing!* I took him completely by surprise."

"I wouldn't know," I said.

"Oh, come on, it's too late. You got as red as a beet. Why, Mr. Mallory. And you're the one that started this whole thing about appendixes. That's rich."

"You jump to conclusions, Mrs. Day," I said.

She was staring at Chottie Sears, who was sitting between two men, laughing with them and enjoying their admiration. "Some women just have it, that's all," said Mary Day. "I wonder if she ever got tight over some damn man." She got to her feet and slowly, rather shyly, joined Chottie and her admirers.

"She's a swell girl till she drinks, and then—bang! No inhibitions. Says anything that comes into her head, no matter who gets hurt in the process." He was trying, I knew, to avoid the topic of Chottie Sears and me, but he believed Mary Day had made a discovery and he was resentful of it. He had his masculine pride, and I was his successful, deceitful rival.

"Well, as she herself said, she oughtn't to drink on Sunday," I said.

"Or between Sundays. She does most of her damage on Sunday, because there are more people around. But Sunday isn't the only time she drinks too much. She's another of those girls around here that set their caps for Junior, and who got him? Her best friend, Polly. I know what fixed that, too. Mary gave up everybody else for Junior, wouldn't even let people cut in at dances. No dates with anyone else, and behaving like an engaged girl, although Junior was going his merry way. And as against that possessiveness, there in the background, so to speak, was Polly Smithfield, the logical one, waiting to be asked. And she got asked and Mary didn't. That was some wedding. Mary the maid of honour instead of the bride, eyes red going up the aisle. Tight as a tick at the reception, and eloped with Billy Day the next week. She was back here and settled down before Polly and Junior got back from their wedding trip."

"Day isn't so much, is he?"

"He never used to be, but Junior has helped him

along and he's doing very well. He has a seat on the Stock Exchange that I understand Junior put up the money for, and downtown Billy's known as Junior's man. Considering what he would have been without Junior's help, that's nice going.

"You know, when you have forty or fifty million behind you, that money does double service. Triple. Quadruple. For instance, McDonald isn't just a butler. He's Junior Williamson's butler, with forty million behind him. Junior Williamson's tailor isn't just a tailor. He has a forty-million-dollar customer. And downtown, Billy Day is Junior's man and that much closer to the money, even if he never gets his hands on it. I could probably get Junior's business. Polly's my cousin. But I think Polly wants Billy to have it, and in any case I wouldn't want to be known as Junior's man. Or anybody else's. When my father dies . . ." He cut himself off.

"What?"

He shook his head. "Don't know you well enough, Jim," he said, with finality. "If I talk about it, I won't do it."

"You wouldn't tell me if I guessed, would you?"

"No, but I'd be interested to hear your guess."

"You want to write," I said.

"Well, it's an interesting guess," said Charley Ellis.

"You're probably not kidding your father one bit."

"Probably not. But time is on his side. The longer he lives, the better the chances that I'll give up any crazy ideas I have."

"Why don't you just up and go?"

"The time to do that was when I graduated from

70

college, and never to have gone downtown at all. That was *my* mistake and where the old man was clever. Hell, look at the guys in this room. At least half of them wish they were doing something else. I could tell you about most of them. Eddie Patterson wishes he could be a guide in Canada. Mike Bell should have been a vet. He studied it at Cornell, but now he's a big trader in oil stocks."

"I always wanted to be something else, too," I said.

"You did? What?"

"A millionaire."

Charley smiled. "Do you mean a million a year, or a million all told?"

"I wasn't greedy. At least, not till you said a million a year."

"There are both kinds of millionaire in this room. See if you can tell them apart."

"I guess I couldn't."

"No, I don't think you could, just by looking. Mike Bell probably has a million-dollar income, and Billy Day probably has around a million capital."

"But why does a guy like Bell give up what he wants to do when he has all that money?"

"It's the system, my boy. Or what I call the system, and you know the old saying. 'Don't buck the system or you're liable to gum the works.' Mike went to St. Mark's and then his father allowed him to go to Cornell and study animal husbandry. Then when he graduated, Mr. Bell told Mike he needed him downtown, just about the way my old man did me. You start going downtown, you get a lowly job as a runner or something, and you want to earn a promotion to prove that

71

you could do it if you wanted to. So you earn that promotion and they give you some responsibility, which you have to fulfil. Pride. Meanwhile you're having a very pleasant time. You have lunch with your friends, go to parties, come out here week-ends, get married, start having children. You're in the system. You're part of it. And what you wanted to be, or do, that becomes your hobby. In Mike's case, he's an amateur vet. You see, Jim, the best of these guys would have been good at something else. The others, let's not worry about them. They're the Billy Days."

"And what about the Junior Williamsons?"

"How many are there? Not more than half a dozen. Let's not worry about them, either. They're the royalty, and the others are the nobility, the peerage."

"Where are the commoners?"

"Well, there aren't any, not in this group. Not really *in* this group. Eunice is one, and the only way she'll be anything else is by becoming Junior's wife."

"What if I married Polly Williamson?" I said.

"Well, you wouldn't marry her unless you were in love with her and she was in love with you, and we'd know that. You'd get credit for marrying her in spite of her dough and not because of it. But you could never look at another woman, not even flirt a little. You couldn't start spending her money on yourself. You'd have to get something to do that her money wouldn't help you with. *And* if Polly had an affair with another guy, you'd take the rap. It would all come back to your marrying her for her money. And I wouldn't be surprised if that's why Polly wants to save her marriage.

She's a very intelligent girl, and she knows there aren't many Junior Williamsons around."

"This is all based on the assumption that I'd give a damn what people said about me."

"Of course it is."

"Well, I don't."

"Well you damn soon would, my friend," he said. "Where are you and Polly going to live? Here? Then you'd be surrounded by Polly's friends. Gibbsville, Pennsylvania? I'll bet your friends would be tougher on you than Long Island. You may think you wouldn't give a damn about Polly's friends or your friends, but people is what people have to live with. And if you're surrounded by hostile people, your friends or Polly's or strangers, your marriage wouldn't last. Oh, just coming in. A perfect example of the commoner."

"I resent that," I said.

"No you don't," said Charley Ellis.

The newcomer was Thomas Rodney Hunterden, dressed for the Scottish moors in August in a tweed jacket and matching plus-threes, tab garters, and fringed-tongue brogues. "Lord Plushbottom," I said. There were others in the room similarly dressed, but the stiffness had not gone out of Hunterden's suit and shoes, nor out of him.

"New York Yacht Club tie," said Charley.

Hunterden made straight for Polly Williamson.

"No Alice," said Charley.

Most of the men showed that they had met Hunterden or recognized his name, but the only woman who greeted him with any informality was Chottie Sears. To my astonishment Junior Williamson took Hunterden's arm and steered him among the men and women, taking care of the introduction. "Mr. Ellis, and Mr. Malloy," said Williamson.

"Mr. Ellis," said Hunterden. "Mr. Malloy, I've had the pleasure. Did you get home safely the other night, Malloy?"

"Yes, did you?"

His quick anger was beautifully controlled. "Quite safely."

"Hunterden, what will you drink?" said Williamson. "Sherry, please."

Williamson nodded to McDonald. "Damned sensible, I must say. I ought to stick to sherry. I hate the damn stuff," said Williamson.

"Do you? I don't. I like a glass of sherry at this time of day," said Hunterden.

"I don't even like it in soup. I come of a long line of whisky drinkers, myself," said Williamson. He again took Hunterden's arm, and said: "Well, have you thought that over?" He piloted Hunterden away from everyone else and the two men sat off by themselves, engaged in private conversation. If I was curious, I was no more so than the other men in the room, who were curious and baffled.

"Be interesting to watch the stock ticker tomorrow morning," said Charley Ellis. "I predict a steady rise in Omega Development. That's one of Hunterden's companies. It'll go up a couple of points between opening bell and twelve-thirty. It'll remain steady while these boys are exchanging information at lunch, and then it'll begin to drop off a little because nobody's going to be able to find out a damn thing and the timid ones will take a quick profit. Would you like to make a few dollars, Jim? I'll put in an order for you first thing in the morning, and sell out at twelve noon."

"Do you know how much money I have in the bank?"

"None, the way you say it."

"None."

"Well, I'd lend you some but not to play the market on a tip I gave you."

"Thanks very much, Charley," I said. "I've never been in the stock market, so I didn't lose anything when the crash came."

"Well, that put you on even terms with a lot of guys that had been in it," he said. "At least we found out that Hunterden isn't here on Polly's invitation, and frankly I'm relieved."

"So am I," I said. "They're still gabbing away, Williamson and Hunterden."

"I'm going to see what I can find out from Polly," he said. "Very little, I'm sure, but I'll have a try at it."

The party had grown in size, but there was no individual or group that I felt would welcome my presence, so I waited alone while Charley Ellis spoke to his cousin. She laughed at something he said and shook her head, shrugged her shoulders. Then she stopped smiling and looked over at me and was confused to see me looking at her. Charley Ellis rejoined me.

"Couldn't get a thing out of her," he said.

"I know. So you changed the subject and told her I liked her."

"Yes," he said.

"But she didn't want to sit with us."

"That's exactly right. Can you read lips?"

"No. I almost wish you hadn't said anything about me."

"Would you like to hear what she said? It was nice," he said.

"Sure, of course I would."

"She said she met you at exactly the wrong time. From that I infer that any other time would have been the right time."

"Excuse me," I said. On an impulse I got up and went to Polly Williamson, who was talking with a man and woman. "May I see you a minute, please?"

We stood alone. "Charley told me what you said."

She nodded quickly.

"I have to tell you this. It may be the wrong time, Mrs. Williamson, and it may not last, and I know I'll never see you again. But I love you, and whenever I think of you I'll love you."

She turned away. "I know, I know. Thank you for saying it. It was dear of you."

I left her then and went back to Charley. "You see," he said. "I couldn't have done that."

"You don't know what I did."

"Yes, I do, Jim. You told her you love her."

"Yes, God damn it, I did."

"Did she thank you? If she didn't, I do, for her."

"Yes, she thanked me. Mrs. Williamson." I laughed. "I don't know her well enough to call her Polly, but I had to tell her I love her. How did you know what I was saying?"

"What else would take possession of a man so completely? What else would you have to say to her that was so urgent? And—what else could make her look the way she did when she was first married to Junior? Oh, that was a damn nice thing to do, to make her feel love again. The existence of it, the urgency of it, and the niceness. How long since any two people in this room had a moment like that? Or ever will? You know who I wish *I* could say that to, don't you? You must know."

"No, I don't," I said.

"To *her*! To Polly! I've never loved anybody but my first cousin, and I never will. But it isn't because we're first cousins that I haven't told her so."

"Why haven't you?"

"Well, yes, it is because we're first cousins. Closer than friends. Different from brother and sister. But she'd be shocked and frightened if she ever knew what it really is. It happens, and it works out, but when I was eighteen and she was fourteen I was ashamed because she was so young. And then when we got older she fell in love with Junior. So I've never told her. But now you see why I understand how you feel. You can't have her either." He smiled. "It seems to me we have a lot in common. I haven't slept with Chottie Sears, and you haven't slept with Mary Day, and I'd like to sleep with Chottie and you'd like to sleep with Mary. And neither of us will ever get anywhere with Polly. I've got drunk with friends of mine on less excuse than that. Shall we just quietly start putting it away, beginning with two double Scotches?"

"I'll have a double Scotch with you, but I have an eighteen-thousand-dollar car and a two-million-dollar movie queen to deliver safely. If you're going to be in New York tonight, I'll meet you anywhere you say."

"I think this would be a good night to get drunk. Don't you? How about if I go in with you and Chottie?"

"That would be fine. We drop her at the hotel, put the car in the garage, and start out at Dan's." I stood up. "I'll go over and speak to our friend."

Chottie made room for me beside her on the sofa. "Are you about ready to go?" she said.

"Entirely up to you," I said. "You don't mind if Charley Ellis rides in with us, do you?"

"Not a bit. Love to have him. How soon will you be ready to go?"

"I'm ready whenever you are. I've had all I want of this party, and if I stay much longer I'll only get too plastered to drive."

"You're not plastered now, are you? That's a big drink you have, Jim. And I noticed you jumping up and down and whispering things to Polly. Tell me if you're tight, because I'm scared to death to drive with anybody's had too much."

"No, I'm not tight. But in another hour I might be."

"You don't seem tight, but . . ."

"But what?"

"Well—just suddenly springing to your feet and taking Polly off to one side. You were like a wild man. What made you do that? Whatever you said, it had a big effect on her. First I thought she was going to cry, and then instead of that she turned all smiles. And you hardly know her."

"I told her her slip was showing."

"But it isn't. No, you didn't tell her any such thing. You sure you're not tight?"

"I'm not tight, and I won't take any more till I deliver you at the hotel." I placed my glass on the table in front of us, and she crooked her finger at Hunterden. He said something to Williamson and then came over to Chottie.

"Did you signal me?" said Hunterden.

She made sure that no one was listening, and said: "Can I drive in with you?"

It was obviously an interference with his schedule. "I understood this fellow was to take you in."

"She thinks this fellow is stewed," I said. "Where do you get that this-fellow stuff, Hunterden?"

"Jim," said Chottie. "Please?"

"Hunterden, you're a phony. You don't even tell the truth about where you were born. Where *were* you born, anyway? Not Gibbsville, Pa. I know that much. And don't this-fellow me. Nobody ever heard of you in Gibbsville and your name isn't even in the Court House records."

"There's no doubt about it. He is stewed," said Hunterden. "You drive in with me and I'll take care of this nobody tomorrow. One phone call, Malloy."

"Save your crooked nickel. I won't show up at the God damn office." I now knew I was tight; I had not known it before.

"Was your father a doctor?" said Hunterden.

"Yes, my father was a doctor."

"I thought so. I didn't like *him*, either."

"But I'll bet you never told him. If you had, you wouldn't be here."

He turned to Chottie. "This fellow is trying to create a scene, and I don't want a scene here, now."

"Well let's not have one. Take me out of here and stop arguing," she said. "Jim, I don't think I'll ever forgive you for this. You're just impossible. I don't know what ever came over you all of a sudden."

"I'm not used to good booze," I said.

"Come on," said Hunterden. He put his hand under her elbow and they went to speak to Polly Williamson. She turned and said something to McDonald, and I guess he got her luggage from upstairs. Charley Ellis came and sat with me.

"What was that all about?" he said.

"I told him off, and it was damn unsatisfactory. I didn't tell him half the things I wanted to."

"Are you plastered?"

"I didn't think so, but I guess I am."

"Can you drive?"

"Oh, I think I can drive. I'm not that kind of tight. I just want to tell people off, and I'd like to give that Hunterden a crack in the jaw."

"He's twice your age and you have fifteen pounds on him. Don't do that. Don't spoil Polly's miserable party."

"I won't."

"There's something brewing between Junior and Hunterden, and you could spoil it and Junior would blame Polly."

"Oh, I realize that."

"We'll give them a chance to leave, and then you and I can go. I'll drive."

"All right."

He studied my face. "What came over you?"

"What ever possessed me? I'm like Mrs. Day. I shouldn't drink on Sunday, I guess."

Thirty years later I remember most of that spring as well as I do some things that happened a month ago. In this morning's paper they treated Charlotte Sears rather well. She did not make Page One, but they gave her two-column top heads in the *Trib* and the *Times*, called her an "early Academy Award winner" who had come out of retirement in 1958 to win a nomination for best supporting actress as the mother superior in the Joseph S. Finston production, *Benediction at Dawn*. She was described as the last member of a theatrical family that had been prominent in vaudeville during the Nineteenth Century, who had become an outstanding success in the so-called drawing-room comedies of the Twenties and Thirties. Her career, it said, was abruptly terminated in 1930, when an automobile in which she was riding was struck by a train at a grade crossing in Roslyn, Long Island, and she received facial injuries that disfigured her and forced her into a long retirement. In the same accident, Thomas R. Hunterden, in whose car Miss Sears was riding, was fatally injured. Hunterden, a stock promoter (it said), was facing indictment on six counts of fraudulent conversion and other charges. His tangled financial affairs resulted in court action over a period of three years, and his manipulations were instrumental in bringing about the creation of the Securities Exchange Act of 1934. Hunterden, a native of Gibbsville, Pa., was a somewhat mysterious, publicity-shy figure who had made a fortune through speculations during the First World War. Later he sought to gain control of motion picture companies and at the time of his death he had failed in a last-minute attempt to enlist the financial support of a syndicate headed by Ethridge B. Williamson, Jr. During the investigation of Hunterden's financial affairs Miss Sears was questioned by the district attorney in an effort to locate securities worth more than $2,000,000 which could not be accounted for, but no charges were made against her . . .

I remembered that. I went to the hospital every afternoon and read the morning and afternoon papers to her. I would sit by the window so that I could see the print; she would not allow the electric light to be turned on. There were dressings on her nose and chin, and her arm was in a cast.

She had other visitors besides me. Polly Williamson came in at least twice a week. Morrie Rosenbaum made a special trip from the Coast to tell her not to worry. She could have had more visitors, but we three were the only ones she wanted to see. When Morrie Rosenbaum heard that she was going to be questioned about the missing bonds, he telephoned me from Hollywood. "Mally," he said (at $125 a week I did not rate a correct pronunciation), "Miss Sears don't have none of them hot bonds. I stake my life on it. So I got her a lawyer. Not my lawyer. I got her Percy Goodfellow. You know who *he* is? Lawyer to the biggest firms in Wall Street. Bishops he has for clients. The very picture of integrity and a God damn shrewd man. I told him I want him there every minute they're asking her questions."

"Yes sir," I said.

"Oh, why am I telling you? Because you go to hospital and tell her she don't see no district attorney without Goodfellow being there every single minute. You understand? She can't talk to me over the phone, you understand, so you give her my instructions. You tell that little lady we don't want her worrying about a thing. Mally?"

"Yes sir?"

"Tell her love from Ruthie and Morrie. Ruthie is Mrs. Rosenbaum, my wife." He then hung up.

I was never there when Polly Williamson came to see her, but I always knew when she had been there, and not only by the flowers that she continued to bring on every visit. She would stay only ten minutes—a total of twenty minutes a week—but Chottie would always have something to say about her. "It took me a couple of weeks before I got over something," said Chottie.

"What was that?"

"Wishing she wouldn't come. I didn't want her coming here because she felt guilty, because if I hadn't gone to her place this never would of happened. I didn't want you coming for that reason, either. But with you—well, maybe you had another reason."

"I did blame myself," I said. "It was the first thing I thought of when I read about it. If I hadn't got drunk——"

"I know. But you had a man-and-woman reason for coming. I'm in your memory-book. And you're in mine, too, Jim."

"I hope so."

"But Polly doesn't blame herself. I don't think she

ever did. She comes here because the night before it happened, when Junior went off with that Underwood dame, Polly knew I was mad as hell at Junior being so insulting. So crude. He was crude. But now when Polly comes to see me, she only stays ten minutes, but she always makes me feel that if she were here instead of me, she'd want me to visit her. Do you see what I mean? She'd *want* me to come. And I've never had another girl that was that kind of a friend. Even if I look like Lon Chaney when I get out of here, it won't all be a total loss."

Another time she said: "Polly was here earlier this afternoon. She came today instead of tomorrow because Etty, the boy, has to go and have his tonsils out tomorrow, poor kid. A wonderful mother, that Polly. But am I glad I don't have children. If I'd of married any of those hambo boy friends of mine—present company excepted—I'd of wanted children. But if I had a son or a daughter waiting for me to get out of here, I just couldn't face them. The first time they'd see me with my face all banged up. I read something one time about Helen of Troy, if she had a nose that was different by a fraction of an inch, it would have changed the history of the world. Well, mine's going to be different, but it sure as hell isn't going to change the history of the world."

My reading to her was usually confined to the theatrical and movie news and reviews, book reviews, the gossip columns, the principal news stories, and occasionally the sail-and-arrive items on the society pages. "Ah, Eunice Underwood sailed yesterday in the *Ile de France*, to be gone a year," I said.

"No matter how I look when I get out of here, I'll have a better figure than she ever had," she said. "I had a lovely figure."

"And still have."

"I wonder what I'll do about that? Oh, I guess I'll find somebody."

She was depressed.

"They're all the same from the top row in the balcony," she said. "They're all the same with a bag over their heads. I saw a comedy bit in a two-reeler one time. The comic, I forget who it was, he sees this girl in a one-piece bathing suit, great figure, and he follows her up the beach and tries to pick her up. Then when she turns around she has a face like Bull Montana. The comic did a Bobby Vernon grando and ran. I don't think it's as funny now as I did when I saw it. Now don't give me false encouragement."

"How do you know I was going to give you any?"

"Because I can see you, even if you can't see me. And you were going to say something encouraging. Don't. They're gonna do what they can, the doctors. I'll have a different nose, and they've got this wire in my jaw. I'll be able to put make-up over the scar in my cheek. I was thinking of changing my name and starting out playing character bits, but everybody'd know it was me. That'd be too good a story for you boys in publicity."

"It would get around, even if we laid off."

"Yes, and the last thing I want is stuff about brave little Charlotte Sears. If I have to be brave I don't want to be brave in public."

"You have spunk, just like your mother."

"That's one satisfaction. I'm beginning to get over

85

my inferiority complex about her. But I'm only—well, I'm under forty, and I hope and pray I find a good man. God protect me from gigolos. God keep me from paying a man to sleep with me."

She in her wisdom had thought it all out, the danger she faced that had been my secret worry for her. We both knew actresses who kept gigolos, and we knew that the gigolos laughed at them and that some of the actresses even made cruel jokes at themselves.

"You have plenty of money," I said. "Look around and get something to do."

"Don't think I haven't thought about that. I could be an agent. I know this business cold, and I have the contacts. A lot of things I *could* do, like being a script girl. Wardrobe. But I was a star, and I don't need the money. I've been trying to think what I could do out of show business entirely. I wish I'd gone to high school, then I could go to college and study to be a doctor. I guess I'll get over that as soon as I get out of here, but it was one idea I had. Open a shop, but I'd soon get tired of that. Interior decorator. Doesn't interest me."

"Charity work," I suggested.

"No. I'm too accustomed to making my own living. I have to do something I'll be paid for, even if it isn't much at first. By the way, Jim. You're still going to take that trip to Europe."

"No."

"Yes. I didn't mention it before because I needed you here. But in another three or four weeks I'll be going back to the Coast."

"I don't want to go to Europe. As soon as you leave I'm quitting Rosenbaums'. I start a new job the first of

August. Second-string dramatic critic. It's a job I want. Pretty good pay, and time to start writing a novel."

"Morrie's paying my bills here, you know, so it isn't a question of money."

"Be honest, Chottie."

"Well, I'll tell you. Morrie is paying all my bills and I'm letting him do that. He really wants to, and I want him to. It makes him feel good, he and Ruthie. But of course I'm through at the Studio. I'm going to sell my house and have that money for capital. The money I've invested will keep me the rest of my life, not in luxury, but comfortably. I'll get a little house out in the Brentwood section for me and my maid, and I'll live quietly out there. Morrie told me I'd never have to worry about money, and he's one that keeps his word. Well, if he gives me as much every year as I have been getting every week, finances won't worry me. Morrie says he'll figure out a way to keep me on the payroll. Story department, most likely. He knows I'm a great reader, and if I give them one story idea a year, like suggesting a magazine serial they ought to buy, I'll be earning my pay."

"You certainly will."

"There's one thing I've always been interested in and it's why I always used to go for walks. Remember me telling you I used to go for those long walks when I was on the road? You know, in most towns I played, if you walk steadily for fifteen-twenty minutes, you're out of the business section and you start getting in the residential."

"It's only about a hundred-yard dash where I come from."

"Yes, it varies with the size of the town. But when you get out of the built-up section, you come to the thing that interested me the most. Hold on to your seat."

"I'm holding on."

"Flowers. I love flowers. I used to ask the stagehands who had the best gardens in every town I went to. The wise-guys used to ask me if I meant beer gardens. Sometimes I'd take the trolley to look at a garden, if it was too far out to walk. If there was a real famous one, big, I'd even take a taxi. I have over a hundred books on flowers and gardening. You know, Polly Williamson I discovered knows a lot about flowers, but I have to admit, I know more. You know, most flowers have at least two names. Different names in different countries, like larkspur for delphinium, bachelor's button for cornflower. That's in addition to the Latin names. I never got as far as Latin, so I don't know many Latin names, but I guess I've learned about fifty, the more common flowers. Our California flowers——" She halted. "That's enough of that. When I start talking about our California flowers. Do you know who loved flowers?"

"Who?"

"Loved flowers, and had a great knowledge of them. Tom Hunterden. A discovery we both made by accident. One day he was at my house and he got up and walked over slowly towards one of my rose bushes. 'What's the matter?' I said. 'Do you see a snake?' Up where my house is we get rattlers. 'No,' he said. 'This is a hybrid tea rose, and I've been thinking of putting them in at home.' We didn't spend *all* our time talking about picture business, Jim. Even if you didn't like him, he was a fascinating man."

"Why were you afraid of him? You told me once you were."

"I wasn't afraid of him. But he inspired fear in me. It wasn't only the fear of losing him. It was just fear, Jim. A lot of times just thinking about him would make me afraid of something, I didn't know what. He believed in hunches himself, and hunches are nothing but intuition. I had the same thing after I got to know him. Not hunches. But intuitive fear."

"A premonition?"

"Yes, I guess it was, considering what happened. When I came to New York this last time, when he didn't meet me at the station, I was upset but I was relieved. I thought maybe he and I were through and I'd get over this fear I had. I was glad to make love with you, because that showed me that I wasn't hypnotized by Hunterden. But I guess maybe I was hypnotized by him, if you remember later that night. By the way, did you sleep with that show girl?"

"No."

"She was a real gold-digger. She was a Ziegfeld edition of Eunice Underwood. That's one thing nobody could ever say about me. Will you write to me, answer my letters if I write to you?"

By agreement I did not see her off when she left the hospital, and I did not know the condition of her face. She took the less fashionable trains, and had reservations under fictitious names. Ruth Rosenbaum met her in Los Angeles and helped her to find the house in Brentwood that she bought as Catherine Dowd. With make-up to cover the scar, she did not look too awful unless you remembered the original, but in the new house she had no photographs of herself before the accident, and she was gradually trying to get used to the new face and the old name. All this I learned in her occasional, chatty letters, which came less frequently as time went on. Brentwood was not fancy enough for the movie stars who were buying and building in Beverly Hills, although Greta Garbo lived not far from Chottie's house. "She vants to be alone and so do I," wrote Chottie, "but I really am. I went shopping in Santa Monica and nobody recognized me. I have not got up nerve enough to shop in Beverly but I will."

Then one day, about a year after the accident, she wrote that she had bought a greenhouse, which she was calling Dowd & Company, and her letters became few and far between. We exchanged Christmas cards, but I stopped hearing from her until 1934, when my novel was published and she sent me some California reviews. She had bought a copy of the book but had not had a chance to read it but would read it before I got to California, which she knew would be as soon as she had read that I had signed with Paramount.

I drove out to have dinner at her house and I realized on the way that I had never seen her face after the accident. I found her house with some difficulty. The place was surrounded by an eight-foot hedge that gave her complete privacy, and since I knew I was to be the only guest for dinner, I parked my car in the short driveway and rang the front doorbell.

She opened it herself, swung it wide and stood smiling.

"Would you have recognized me?" she said.

"Not immediately, not unless you spoke." I kissed her and she hugged me.

"You don't have to be careful what you say. I'm all right. It's so good to see you again. You're older, and more attractive that way. You've been married and divorced, and you've written a fine book, and what kind of a deal did you make at Paramount?"

"One of those seven-year option things. I signed the first contract they offered me because I wanted to get out of New York. How is Dowd & Company?"

"Doing very well. It was tough in the beginning, but I survived the first year, and the second year I just about broke even on the business, and now there's a lot of real-estate activity in this section and that means business for us."

"Us? You have a partner?"

"You'll meet him." She nodded without looking at me. "I found somebody."

"That's the best news, Chottie."

She nodded again. "Yes. I did the other, though. What I was afraid I'd do, out of loneliness and desperation. He wasn't a gigolo with patent-leather hair. He was a young writer, very unsuccessful *and*, I found out, not very talented. I had a hard time getting rid of him."

"How did you?"

"I gave him money to go to Mexico."

"That doesn't always work."

"Not if you have no one else, but now I have someone else."

"Tell me about him."

"Oh, I will. He's married, of course. Separated from

his wife. He's fifty, has two grown children that live with her, down in Whittier. That's on the other side of Los Angeles. He's a landscape architect and that's how I met him."

"And what of the future?"

"His wife won't give him a divorce till the daughter gets married, but that will be in June, when she finishes college. Then we have over a year to wait, but what's a year? The wife is as anxious to get out of it as he is, but not before the girl is married off. He has a room over in Santa Monica. Most of his work is around here. Brentwood Heights. Beverly. Bel-Air. He isn't really my partner yet, but I don't know what I'd do without him. I couldn't."

We had a good dinner, starting, as Californians do, with a salad, and we talked without pause until ninethirty, when the doorbell rang. "That's Lou. On the dot. By the way, he knows about you and our one matinée, so don't mind if he sizes you up."

Louis Grafmiller was a stocky, sunburned man with close-cropped iron-grey hair. "Hello, Catherine," he said, and kissed her on the lips. He shook hands with me and it was a firm handshake.

"Glad to know you, Mr. Malloy," he said. "This girl is always singing your praises."

"Well, she's just finished singing some of yours," I said.

"Have a drink, Lou?"

"Oh, a glass of wine, maybe. Some of that Chianti? You just get in from the East?"

"Monday."

"Your first visit to California, Catherine said."

"Yes, I'd never been west of the Mississippi before."

"It's a big country, and a good country. People don't realize how big or how good. They ought to get around more and see what they have before they turn it over to the Communists. I know I didn't vote to take it away from Wall Street just to hand it over to those other bastards."

I had a quick revelation of what he would do to Chottie's gigolo writer if he ever showed up again. She was well protected now.

"I understand your book is a big success. Do you know Ernest Hemingway?"

"No."

"I like his kind of writing. Catherine gave me your book but I haven't started it yet."

"Are you going to write another, Jim?" said Chottie.

"Yes, when I go back. I don't think I'll stay out here past the first option."

"Don't you like California?" he smiled.

"Not yet. I don't dislike it yet, either. But I'll never be a Californian."

"That's what I said twenty-five years ago, but I'm still here. There are only two states that have everything. California and Pennsylvania."

"I'm from Pennsylvania."

"I know. So am I. Pittsburgh. You're from the other end of the state. I have cousins in Reading."

Now slowly I was conscious of Chottie's changed face as she listened to our conversation; it was very right that her face should be different when she herself was so different as well. Her face, her name, and the domesticity were all new to me. I was still very fond of what

93

I could remember, but when I left her house she shook hands with me, did not kiss me, and we were both reconciled to the finality of the farewell. Grafmiller walked with me to my car and gave me directions for getting back to Hollywood, and I could not help thinking that he had likewise directed Chottie, but not in the way I was headed. We did not bother to shake hands. Neither of us regarded the introduction as a true meeting, and we paid this silent respect to our harmless mutual animosity.

I never heard from her after that night, although I often went to Hollywood to work on movie scripts. Once on an impulse I looked up Grafmiller in the telephone book and his address was the same as the house where I had met him, hers. Then I heard somewhere that he had died, but the information came long after his death and I did not write to Chottie. She was swallowed up in the anonymity of former movie stars living in Los Angeles—the easiest way for a former movie star to become obscure—until Joe Finston put her in *Benediction at Dawn*. In today's obituaries there is mention of Louis Grafmiller, but not a word about their greenhouse, and for some reason or other that pleased me. On the same page there was an obituary of a man who had once won the 500 mile race at Indianapolis but who died while playing shuffleboard at St. Petersburg, Florida.

I close this reminiscence with one more fact. Thomas Rodney Hunterden was born Thomas Robert Huntzinger in Gibbsville, Pa. I have no idea why he disliked my father, and I am long past caring.

IMAGINE KISSING PETE

To those who knew the bride and groom, the marriage of Bobbie Hammersmith and Pete McCrea was the surprise of the year. As late as April of '29 Bobbie was still engaged to a fellow who lived in Greenwich, Connecticut, and she had told friends that the wedding would take place in September. But the engagement was broken and in a matter of weeks the invitations went out for her June wedding to Pete. One of the most frequently uttered comments was that Bobbie was not giving herself much opportunity to change her mind again. The comment was doubly cruel, since it carried the implication that if she gave herself time to think, Pete McCrea would not be her ideal choice. It was not only that she was marrying Pete on the rebound; she seemed to be going out of her way to find someone who was so unlike her other beaux that the contrast was unavoidable. And it was.

I was working in New York and Pete wrote to ask me to be an usher. Pete and I had grown up together, played together as children, and gone to dancing school and to the same parties. But we had never been close friends and when Pete and I went away to our separate prep schools and, later, Pete to Princeton and I to work, we drifted into that relationship of young men who had known each other all their lives without creating anything that was enduring or warm. As a matter of fact,

I had never in my life received a written communication from Pete McCrea, and his handwriting on the envelope was new to me, as mine in my reply was to him. He mentioned who the best man and the other ushers would be—all Gibbsville boys—and this somewhat pathetic commentary on his four years in prep school and four years in college made an appeal to home town and boyhood loyalty that I could not reject. I had some extra days coming to me at the office, and so I told Pete I would be honoured to be one of his ushers. My next step was to talk to a Gibbsville girl who lived in New York, a friend of Bobbie Hammersmith's. I took her to dinner at an Italian speakeasy where my credit was good, and she gave me what information she had. She was to be a bridesmaid.

"Bobbie isn't saying a word," said Kitty Clark. "That is, nothing about the inner turmoil. Nothing *intime*. Whatever happened happened the last time she was in New York, four or five weeks ago. All she'd tell me was that Johnny White was impossible. Impossible. Well, he'd been very possible all last summer and fall."

"What kind of a guy was he?" I asked.

"Oh—*attractive*," she said. "Sort of wild, I guess, but not a roué. Maybe he is a roué, but I'd say more just wild. I honestly don't know a thing about it, but it wouldn't surprise me if Bobbie was ready to settle down, and he wasn't. She was probably more in love with him than he was with her."

"I doubt that. She wouldn't turn around and marry Pete if she were still in love with this White guy."

"Oh, *wouldn't* she? Oh, are you ever wrong there. If she wanted to thumb her nose at Johnny, I can't think of a better way. Poor Pete. You know *Pete*. Ichabod McCrea. Remember when Mrs. McCrea made us stop calling him Ichabod? Lord and Taylor! She went to see my mother and I guess all the other mothers and said it just had to stop. Bad enough calling her little Angus by such a common nickname as Pete. But calling a boy Ichabod. I don't suppose Pete ever knew his mother went around like that."

"Yes he did. It embarrassed him. It always embarrassed him when Mrs. McCrea did those things."

"Yes, she was uncanny. I can remember when I was going to have a party, practically before I'd made out the list Mrs. McCrea would call Mother to be sure Pete wasn't left out. Not that I ever would have left him out. We all always had the same kids to our parties. But Mrs. McCrea wasn't leaving anything to chance. I'm dying to hear what she has to say about this marriage. I'll bet she doesn't like it, but I'll bet she's in fear and trembling in case Bobbie changes her mind again. Ichabod McCrea and Bobbie Hammersmith. Beauty and the beast. And actually he's not even a beast. It would be better if he were. She's the third of our old bunch to get married, but much as I hate to say it, I'll bet she'll be the first to get a divorce. Imagine *kissing* Pete, let alone any of the rest of it."

The wedding was on a Saturday afternoon; four o'clock in Trinity Church, and the reception at the country club. It had been two years since I last saw Bobbie Hammersmith and she was now twenty-two, but she could have passed for much more than that. She was the only girl in her crowd who had not bobbed her hair, which was jet-black and which she always wore with plaited buns over the ears. Except in the summer her skin was like Chinese white and it was always easy to pick her out first in group photographs; her eyes large dark dots, quite far apart, and her lips small but prominent in the whiteness of her face beneath the two small dots of her nose. In summer, with a tan, she reminded many non-operagoers of Carmen. She was a striking beauty, although it took two years' absence from her for me to realize it. In the theatre they have an expression, "walked through the part", which means that an actress played a role without giving it much of herself. Bobbie walked through the part of bride-to-be. A great deal of social activity was concentrated in the three days—Thursday, Friday, and Saturday—up to and including the wedding reception; but Bobbie walked through the part. Today, thirty years later, it would be assumed that she had been taking tranquilizers, but this was 1929.

Barbara Hammersmith had never been anything but a pretty child; if she had ever been homely it must have been when she was a small baby, when I was not bothering to look at her. We—Pete McCrea and the other boys—were two, three, four years older than Bobbie, but when she was fifteen or sixteen she began to pass among us, from boy to boy, trying one and then another, causing several fist fights, and half promising but never delivering anything more than the "soul kisses" that were all we really expected. By the time she was eighteen she had been in and out of love with all of us with the solitary exception of Pete McCrea. When she broke off with a boy, she would also make up with the girl he had temporarily deserted for Bobbie, and all the girls came to understand that every boy in the crowd had to go through a love affair with her. Consequently Bobbie was popular; the boys remembered her kisses, the girls forgave her because the boys had been returned virtually intact. We used the word hectic a lot in those days; Kitty Clark explained the short duration of Bobbie's love affairs by observing that being in love with Bobbie was too hectic for most boys. It was also true that it was not hectic enough. The boys agreed that Bobbie was a hot little number, but none of us could claim that she was not a virgin. At eighteen Bobbie entered a personal middle age, and for the big social occasions her beaux came from out-of-town. She was also busy at the college proms and football games, as far west as Ann Arbor, as far north as Brunswick, Maine. I was working on the Gibbsville paper during some of those years, the only boy in our crowd who was not away at college, and I remember Ann Arbor because Bobbie went there wearing a Delta Tau Delta pin and came back wearing the somewhat larger Psi U. "Now don't you say anything in front of Mother," she said. "She thinks they're both the same."

We played auction bridge, the social occupation in towns like ours, and Bobbie and I were assimilated into an older crowd: the younger married set and the youngest of the couples who were in their thirties. We played for prizes—flasks, cigarette lighters, vanity cases, cartons of cigarettes—and there was a party at someone's house every week. The hostess of the evening usually asked me to stop for Bobbie, and I saw her often. Her father and mother would be reading the evening paper and sewing when I arrived to pick up Bobbie. Philip Hammersmith was not a native of Gibbsville, but he had lived there long enough to have gone to the Mexican Border in 1916 with the Gibbsville company of mounted engineers, and he had gone to France with them, returning as a first lieutenant and with the Croix de Guerre with palm. He was one of the best golfers in the club, and everyone said he was making money hand-over-fist as an independent coal operator. He wore steel-rim glasses and he had almost completely grey hair, cut short. He inspired trust and confidence. He was slow-moving, taller than six feet, and always thought before speaking. His wife, a Gibbsville girl, was related, as she said, to half the town; a lively little woman who took her husband's arm even if they were walking only two doors away. I always used to feel that whatever he may have wanted out of life, yet unattained or unattainable, she had just what she wanted: a good husband, a nice home, and a pretty daughter who would not long remain unmarried. At home in the evening, and whenever I saw him on the street, Mr. Hammersmith was wearing a dark-grey worsted suit, cut loose and with a soft roll to the lapel; black knit four-in-hand necktie; white shirt; heavy grey woollen socks, and thick-soled brogues. This costume, completely unadorned— he wore a wrist watch—was what he always wore except for formal occasions, and the year-to-year sameness of his attire constituted his only known eccentricity. He was on the board of the second most conservative bank, the trustees of Gibbsville Hospital, the armoury board, the Y.M.C.A., and the Gibbsville and Lantenengo country clubs. Nevertheless I sensed that that was not all there was to Philip Hammersmith, that the care he put into the creation of the general picture of himself—hard work, quiet clothes, thoughtful manner, conventional associations—was done with a purpose that was not necessarily sinister but was extraordinarily private. It delighted me to discover, one night while waiting for Bobbie, that he knew more about what was going on than most of us suspected he would know. "Jimmy, you know Ed Charney, of course," he said.

I knew Ed Charney, the principal bootlegger in the area. "Yes, I know him pretty well," I said.

"Then do you happen to know if there's any truth to what I heard? I heard that his wife is threatening to divorce him."

"I doubt it. They're Catholics."

"Do you know her?"

"Yes. I went to Sisters' school with her."

"Oh, then maybe you can tell me something else. I've heard that she's the real brains of those two."

"She quit school after eighth grade, so I don't know about that. I don't remember her being particularly bright. She's about my age but she was two grades behind me."

"I see. And you think their religion will keep them from getting a divorce?"

"Yes, I do. I don't often see Ed at Mass, but I know

he carries rosary beads. And she's at the eleven o'clock Mass every Sunday, all dolled up."

This conversation was explained when Repeal came and with it public knowledge that Ed Charney had been quietly buying bank stock, one of several moves he had made in the direction of respectability. But the chief interest to me at the time Mr. Hammersmith and I talked was in the fact that he knew anything at all about the Charneys. It was so unlike him even to mention Ed Charney's name.

To get back to the week-end of Bobbie Hammersmith's wedding: it was throughout that week-end that I first saw Bobbie have what we called that faraway look, that another generation called Cloud 90. If you happened to catch her at the right moment, you would see her smiling up at Pete in a way that must have been reassuring to Mrs. McCrea and to Mrs. Hammersmith, but I also caught her at several wrong moments and I saw something I had never seen before: a resemblance to her father that was a subtler thing than the mere duplication of such features as mouth, nose, and set of the eyes. It was almost the same thing I have mentioned in describing Philip Hammersmith; the wish yet unattained or unattainable. However, the pre-nuptial parties and the wedding and reception went off without a hitch, or so I believed until the day after the wedding.

Kitty Clark and I were on the same train going back to New York and I made some comment about the exceptional sobriety of the ushers and how everything had gone according to plan. "Amazing, considering," said Kitty.

"Considering what?"

"That there was almost no wedding at all," she said. "You must promise word of honour, Jimmy, or I won't tell you."

"I promise. Word of honour."

"Well, after Mrs. McCrea's very-dull-I-must-say luncheon, when we all left to go to Bobbie's? A little after two o'clock?"

"Yes."

"Bobbie asked me if I'd go across the street to our house and put in a long-distance call to Johnny White. I said I couldn't do that, and what on earth was she thinking of. And Bobbie said, 'You're my oldest and best friend. The least you can do is make this one last effort, to keep me from ruining my life.' So I gave in and I dashed over to our house and called Johnny. He was out and they didn't know where he could be reached or what time he was coming home. So I left my name. *My* name, not Bobbie's. Six o'clock, at the reception, I was dancing with—I was dancing with *you*."

"When the waiter said you were wanted on the phone."

"It was Johnny. He'd been sailing and just got in. I made up some story about why I'd called him, but he didn't swallow it. '*You* didn't call me,' he said. '*Bobbie* did.' Well of course I wouldn't admit that. By that time she was married, and if her life was already ruined it would be a darned sight more ruined if I let him talk to her. Which he wanted to do. Then he tried to pump me. Where were they going on their wedding trip? I said nobody knew, which was a barefaced lie. I knew they were going to Bermuda. Known it since Thursday. But I wouldn't tell Johnny . . . I don't like him a bit after yesterday. I'd thought he was attractive, and he *is*, but he's got a mean streak that I never knew before. Feature this, if you will. When he realized I wasn't going to get Bobbie to come to the phone, or give him any information, he said, 'Well, no use wasting a long-distance call. What are you doing next week-end? How about coming out here?' 'I'm not that hard up,' I said, and banged down the receiver. I hope I shattered his eardrum."

I saw Pete and Bobbie McCrea when I went home the following Christmas. They were living in a small house on Twin Oaks Road, a recent real-estate development that had been instantly successful with the sons and daughters of the big two- and three-servant mansions. They were not going to any of the holiday dances; Bobbie was expecting a baby in April or early May.

"You're not losing any time," I said.

"I don't want to lose any time," said Bobbie. "I want to have a lot of children. Pete's an only child and so am I, and we don't think it's fair, if you can afford to have more."

"If we can afford it. The way that stock market is going, we'll be lucky to pay for this one," said Pete.

"Oh, don't start on that, Pete. That's all Father talks about," said Bobbie. "My father *was* hit pretty hard, but I wish he didn't have to keep talking about it all the time. Everybody's in the same boat."

"No they're not. *We're* on a *raft*."

"I asked you, please, Pete. Jimmy didn't come here to listen to our financial woes. Do you see much of Kitty? I've owed her a letter for ages."

"No, I haven't seen her since last summer, we went out a few times," I said.

"Kitty went to New York to try to rope in a millionaire. She isn't going to waste her time on Jim."

"That's not what she went to New York for at all. And as far as wasting her time on Jim, Jim may not want to waste his time on her." She smiled. "Have you got a girl, Jim?"

"Not really."

"Wise. Very wise," said Pete McCrea.

"I don't know how wise. It's just that I have a hell of a hard time supporting myself, without trying to support a wife, too," I said.

"Why I understood you were selling articles to magazines, and going around with all the big shots."

"I've had four jobs in two years, and the jobs didn't last very long. If things get any tougher I may have to come back here. At least I'll have a place to sleep and something to eat."

"But I see your name in magazines," said Pete. "I don't always read your articles, but they must pay you well."

"They don't. At least I can't live on the magazine pieces without a steady job. Excuse me, Bobbie. Now you're getting *my* financial woes."

"She'll listen to yours. It's mine she doesn't want to hear about."

"That's because I know about ours. I'm never allowed to forget them," said Bobbie. "Are you going to all the parties?"

"Yes, stag. I have to bum rides. I haven't got a car."

"We resigned from the club," said Pete.

"Well we didn't *have* to do that," said Bobbie. "Father was going to give it to us for a Christmas present. And you have your job."

"We'll see how much longer I have it. Is that the last of the gin?"

"Yes."

Pete rose. "I'll be back."

"Don't buy any more for me," I said.

"You flatter yourself," he said. "I wasn't only getting it for you." He put on his hat and coat. "No funny business while I'm gone. I remember you two."

He kept a silly grin on his face while saying the ugly things, but the grin was not genuine and the ugly things were.

"I don't know what's the matter with him," said Bobbie. "Oh, I do, but why talk about it?"

"He's only kidding."

"You know better than that. He says worse things, much worse, and I'm only hoping that don't get back to Father. Father has enough on his mind. I thought if I had this baby right away it would—you know—give Pete confidence. But it's had just the opposite effect. He says it isn't his child. *Isn't his child!* Oh, I married him out of spite. I'm sure Kitty must have told you that. But it *is* his child, I swear it, Jim. It couldn't be anybody else's."

"I guess it's the old inferiority complex," I said.

"The first month we were married—Pete was a virgin —and I admit it, I wasn't. I stayed with two boys before I was married. But I was certainly not pregnant when I married Pete, and the first few weeks he was loving and sweet, and grateful. But then something happened to him, and he made a pass at I-won't-say-who. It was more than a pass. It was quite a serious thing. I might as well tell you. It was Phyllis. We were all at a picnic at the Dam and several people got pretty tight, Pete among them. And there's no other word for it, he tried to rape Phyllis. Tore her bathing suit and slapped her and did other things. She got away from him and ran back to the cottage without anyone seeing her. Luckily Joe didn't see her or I'm sure he'd have killed Pete. You know, Joe's strong as an ox and terribly jealous. I found out about it from Phyllis herself. She came here the next day and told me. She said she wasn't going to say anything to Joe, but that we mustn't invite her to our house and she wasn't going to invite us to hers."

"I'm certainly glad Joe didn't hear about it. He would do something drastic," I said. "But didn't he notice that you two weren't going to his house, and they to yours? It's a pretty small group."

She looked at me steadily. "We haven't been going anywhere. My excuse is that I'm pregnant, but the truth is, we're not being asked. It didn't end with Phyllis, Jim. One night at a dinner party Mary Lander just slapped his face, in front of everybody. Everybody laughed and thought Pete must have said something, but it wasn't something he'd said. He'd taken her hand

and put it—you know. This is *Pete! Ichabod!* Did you ever know any of this about him?"

"You mean have I heard any of this? No."

"No, I didn't mean that. I meant, did he go around making passes and I never happened to hear about it?"

"No. When we'd talk dirty he'd say, 'Why don't you fellows get your minds above your belts?' "

"I wish your father were still alive. I'd go see him and try to get some advice. I wouldn't think of going to Dr. English."

"Well, you're not the one that needs a doctor. Could you get Pete to go to one? He's a patient of Dr. English's, isn't he?"

"Yes, but so is Mrs. McCrea, and Pete would never confide in Dr. English."

"Or anyone else at this stage, I guess," I said. "I'm not much help, am I?"

"Oh, I didn't expect you to have a solution. You know, Jim, I wish you would come back to Gibbsville. Other girls in our crowd have often said it was nice to have you to talk to. Of course you were a very bad boy, too, but a lot of us miss you."

"That's nice to hear, Bobbie. Thank you. I may be back, if I don't soon make a go of it in New York. I won't have any choice."

During that Christmas visit I heard other stories about Pete McCrea. In general they were told as plain gossip, but two or three times there was a hint of a lack of sympathy for Bobbie. "She knew what she was doing . . . she made her bed . . ." And while there was no lack of righteous indignation over Pete's behaviour, he had changed in six months from a semi-comic figure to an unpleasant man, but a man nevertheless. In half a year he had lost most of his old friends; they all said, "You've never seen such a change come over anybody in all your life," but when they remembered to call him Ichabod it was only to emphasize the change.

Bobbie's baby was born in April, but lived only a few weeks. "She was determined to have that baby," Kitty Clark told me. "She had to prove to Pete that it was anyway *conceived* after she married him. But it must have taken all her strength to hold on to it that long. All her strength *and* the baby's. Now would be a good time for her to divorce him. She can't go on like that."

But there was no divorce, and Bobbie was pregnant again when I saw her at Christmas, 1930. They no longer lived in the Twin Oaks Road house, and her father and mother had given up their house on Lantenengo Street. The Hammersmiths were living in an apartment on Market Street, and Bobbie and Pete were living with Mrs. McCrea. "Temporarily, till Pete decides whether to take this job in Tulsa, Oklahoma," said Bobbie.

"Who do you think you're kidding?" said Pete. "It isn't a question of me deciding. It's a cousin of mine deciding if he'll take me on. And why the hell should he?"

"Well, you've had several years' banking experience," she said.

"Yes. And if I was so good, why did the bank let me go? Jim knows all this. What else have you heard about us, Jim? Did you hear Bobbie was divorcing me?"

"It doesn't look that way from here," I said.

"You mean because she's pregnant? That's elementary biology, and God knows you're acquainted with the facts of life. But if you want to be polite, all right. Pretend you didn't hear she was getting a divorce. You might as well pretend Mr. and Mrs. Hammersmith are still living on Lantenengo Street. If they were, Bobbie'd have got her divorce."

"Everybody tells me what I *was* going to do or *am* going to do," said Bobbie. "Nobody ever consults me."

"I suppose that's a crack at my mother."

"Oh, for Christ's sake, Pete, lay off, at least while I'm here," I said.

"Why? You like to think of yourself as an old friend of the family, so you might as well get a true picture. When you get married, if you ever do, I'll come and see you, and maybe your wife will cry on my shoulder." He got up and left the house.

"Well, it's just like a year ago," said Bobbie. "When you came to call on us last Christmas?"

"Where will he go now?"

"Oh, there are several places where he can charge drinks. They all think Mrs. McCrea has plenty of money, but they're due for a rude awakening. She's living on capital, but she's not going to sell any bonds to pay his liquor bills."

"Then maybe *he's* due for a rude awakening."

"Any awakening would be better than the last three months, since the bank fired him. He sits here all day long, then after Mrs. McCrea goes to bed he goes to one of his speakeasies." She sat up straighter. "He has a lady friend. Or have you heard?"

"No."

"Yes. He graduated from making passes at all my friends. He had to. We were never invited anywhere. Yes, he has a girl friend. Do you remember Muriel Nierhaus?"

"The chiropractor's wife. Sure. Big fat Murial Minzer till she married Nierhaus, then we used to say he gave her some adjustments. Where is Nierhaus?"

"Oh, he's opened several offices. Very prosperous. He divorced her but she gets alimony. She's Pete's girl friend. Murial Minzer is *Angus McCrea's* girl friend."

"You don't seem too displeased," I said.

"Would you be, if you were in my position?"

"I guess I know what you mean. But—well, nothing."

"But why don't I get a divorce?" She shook her head. "A spite marriage is a terrible thing to do to anybody. If I hadn't deliberately selected Pete out of all the boys I knew, he'd have gone on till Mrs. McCrea picked out somebody for him, and it would almost have had to be the female counterpart of Pete. A girl like—oh—Florence. Florence Temple."

"Florence Temple, with her cello. Exactly right."

"But I did that awful thing to Pete, and the first few weeks of marriage were just too much for him. He went haywire. I'd slept with two boys before I was married, so it wasn't as much of a shock to me. But Pete almost wore me out. And such adoration, I can't tell you. Then when we came back from Bermuda he began to see all the other girls he'd known all his life, and he'd ask me about them. It was as though he'd never seen them before, in a way. In other ways, it was as though he'd just been waiting all his life to start ripping their clothes off. He was dangerous, Jim. He really was. I could almost tell who would be next by the questions he'd ask. Before we'd go to a party, he'd say 'Who's going to be there tonight?' And I'd say I thought the usual crowd. Then he'd rattle off the list of names of our friends, and leave out one name. That was supposed to fool me, but it didn't for long. The name he left out, that girl was almost sure to be in for a bad time."

"And now it's all concentrated on Murial Minzer?"

"As far as I know."

"Well, that's a break for you, *and* the other girls. Did you ever talk to him about the passes he made at the others?"

"Oh, how could we avoid it? Whoever it was, she was always 'that little whore'."

"Did he ever get anywhere with any of them?"

She nodded. "One, but I won't tell you who. There was one girl that didn't stop him, and when that happened he wanted me to sleep with her husband."

"Swap, eh?"

"Yes. But I said I wasn't interested. Pete wanted to know why not? Why wouldn't I? And I almost told him. The boy was one of the two boys I'd stayed with before I was married—oh, when I was seventeen. And he never told anybody and neither have I, or ever will."

"You mean one of our old crowd actually did get somewhere with you, Bobbie?"

"One did. But don't try to guess. It won't do you any good to guess, because I'd never, never tell."

"Well, whichever one it was, he's the best liar I ever knew. And I guess the nicest guy in our whole crowd. You know, Bobbie, the whole damn bunch are going to get credit now for being as honourable as one guy."

"You were all nice, even if you all did talk too much. If it had been you, you would have lied, too."

"No, I don't think I would have."

"You lied about Kitty. Ha ha ha. You didn't know I knew about you and Kitty. I knew it the next day. The very next day. If you don't believe me, I'll tell you where it happened and how it happened, and all about it. That was the great bond we had in common. You and Kitty, and I and this other boy."

"Then Kitty's a gentleman, because she never told me a word about you."

"I kissed every boy in our crowd except Pete, and I necked, heavy-necked two, as you well know, and stayed with one."

"The question is, did you stay with the other one that you heavy-necked with?"

"You'll never know, Jim, and please don't try to find out."

"I won't, but I won't be able to stop theorizing," I said.

We knew everything, everything there was to know. We were so far removed from the technical innocence of eighteen, sixteen, nineteen. I was a man of the world, and Bobbie was indeed a woman, who had borne a child and lived with a husband who had come the most recently to the knowledge we had acquired, but was already the most intricately involved in the complications of sex. We—Bobbie and I—could discuss him and still remain outside the problems of Pete McCrea. We could almost remain outside our own problems. We knew so much, and since what we knew seemed to be all there was to know, we were shockproof. We had come to our maturity and our knowledgeability during the long decade of cynicism that was usually dismissed as "a cynical disregard of the law of the land," but that was something else, something deeper. The law had been passed with a "noble" but nevertheless cynical disregard of men's right to drink. It was a law that had been imposed on some who took pleasure in drinking by some who did not. And when the law was an instant failure, it was not admitted to be a failure by those who had imposed it. They fought to retain the law in spite of its immediate failure and its proliferating corruption, and they fought as hard as they would have for a law that had been an immediate success. They gained no recruits to their own way; they had only deserters, who were not brave deserters but furtive ones; there was no honest mutiny but only grumbling and small disobediences. And we grew up listening to the grumbling, watching the small disobediences; laughing along when the grumbling was intentionally funny, imitating the small disobediences in other ways besides the customs of drinking. It was not only a cynical disregard for a law of the land; the law was eventually changed. Prohibition, the zealots' attempt to force total abstinence on a temperate nation, made liars of a hundred million men and cheats of their children; the West Point cadets who cheated in examinations, the basketball players who connived with gamblers, the thousands of uncaught cheats in the high schools and colleges. We had grown up and away from our earlier esteem of God and country and valour, and had matured at a moment when riches were vanishing for reasons that we could not understand. We were the losing, not the lost, generation. We could not blame Pete McCrea's troubles—and Bobbie's—on the Southern Baptists and the Northern Methodists. Since we knew everything, we knew that Pete's sudden release from twenty years of frustrations had turned him loose in a world filled with women. But Bobbie and I sat there in her mother-in-law's house, breaking several laws of possession, purchase, transportation and consumption of liquor, and with great calmness discussing the destruction of two lives—one of them hers—and the loss of her father's fortune, the depletion of her mother-in-law's, the allure of a chiropractor's divorcée, and our own promiscuity. We knew everything, but we were incapable of recognizing the meaning of our complacency.

I was wearing my dinner jacket, and someone was going to pick me up and take me to a dinner dance at the club. "Who's stopping for you?" said Bobbie.

"It depends. Either Joe or Frank. Depends on whether they go in Joe's car or Frank's. I'm to be ready when they blow their horn."

"Do me a favour, Jim. Make them come in. Pretend you don't hear the horn."

"If it's Joe, he's liable to drive off without me. You know Joe if he's had a few too many."

In a few minutes there was a blast of a two-tone horn, repeated. "That's Joe's car," said Bobbie. "You'd better go." She went to the hall with me and I kissed her cheek. The front door swung open and it was Joe Whipple.

"Hello, Bobbie," he said.

"Hello, Joe. Won't you all come in? Haven't you got time for one drink?" She was trying not to sound suppliant, but Joe was not deceived.

"Just you and Jim here?" he said.

"Yes. Pete went out a little while ago."

"I'll see what the others say," said Joe. He left to speak to the three in the sedan, and obviously he was not immediately persuasive, but they came in with him. They would not let Bobbie take their coats, but they were nice to her and with the first sips of our drinks we were all six almost back in the days when Bobbie Hammersmith's house was where so many of our parties started from. Then we heard the front door thumping shut and Pete McCrea looked in.

There were sounds of hello, but he stared at us over his horn-rims and said to Bobbie: "You didn't have to invite me, but you could have told me." He turned and again the front door thumped.

"Get dressed and come with us," said Joe Whipple.

"I can't do that," said Bobbie.

"She can't, Joe," said Phyllis Whipple. "That would only make more trouble."

"What trouble? She's going to have to sit here alone

till he comes home. She might as well be with us," said Joe.

"Anyway, I haven't got a dress that fits," said Bobbie. "But thanks for asking me."

"I won't have you sitting here——"

"Now don't make matters worse, Joe, for heaven's sake," said his wife.

"I could lend you a dress, Bobbie, but I think Phyllis is right," said Mary Lander. "Whatever *you* want to do."

"*Want* to do! That's not the question," said Bobbie. "Go on before I change my mind. Thanks, everybody. Frank, you haven't said a word."

"Nothing much for me to say," said Frank Lander. But as far as I was concerned he, and Bobbie herself, had said more than anyone else. I caught her looking at me quickly.

"Well, all right, then," said Joe. "I'm outnumbered. Or outpersuaded or something."

I was the last to say goodbye, and I whispered to Bobbie: "Frank, eh?"

"You're only guessing," she said. "Goodnight, Jim." Whatever they would be after we left, her eyes were brighter than they had been in years. She had very nearly gone to a party, and for a minute or two she had been part of it.

I sat in the back seat with Phyllis Whipple and Frank Lander. "If you'd had any sense you'd know there'd be a letdown," said Phyllis.

"Oh, drop it," said Joe.

"It might have been worth it, though, Phyllis," said

Mary Lander. "How long is it since she's seen anybody but that old battle-axe, Mrs. McCrea? God, I hate to think what it must be like, living in that house with Mrs. McCrea."

"I'm sure it would have been a *lot* easier if Bobbie'd come with us," said Phyllis. "That would have fixed things just right with Mrs. McCrea. She's just the type that wants Bobbie to go out and have a good time. Especially without Pete. You forget how the old lady used to call up all the mothers as soon as she heard there was a party planned. What Joe did was cruel because it was so downright stupid. Thoughtless. Like getting her all excited and then leaving her hung up."

"You've had too much to drink," said Joe.

"*I* have?"

"Yes, you don't say things like that in front of a bachelor," said Joe.

"Who's—oh, Jim? It is to laugh. Did I shock you, Jim?"

"Not a bit. I didn't know what you meant. Did you say something risqué?"

"My husband thinks I did."

"Went right over my head," I said. "I'm innocent about such things."

"So's your old man," said Joe.

"Do you think she should have come with us, Frank?" I said.

"Why ask me? No. I'm with Phyllis. What's the percentage for Bobbie? You saw that son of a bitch in the doorway, and you know damn well when he gets home from Muriel Nierhaus's, he's going to raise hell with Bobbie."

"Then Bobbie had nothing to lose," said Joe. "If Pete's going to raise hell with her, anyway, she might as well have come with us."

"How does he raise hell with her?" I said.

No one said anything.

"Do you know, Phyllis?" I said.

"What?" said Phyllis.

"Oh, come on. You heard me," I said. "Mary?"

"I'm sure I don't know."

"Oh, nuts," I said.

"Go ahead, tell him," said Frank Lander.

"Nobody ever knew for sure," said Phyllis, quietly.

"That's not true. Caroline English, for one. She knew for sure."

Phyllis spoke: "A few weeks before Bobbie had her baby she rang Caroline's doorbell in the middle of the night and asked Caroline if she could stay there. Naturally Caroline said yes, and she saw that Bobbie had nothing but a coat over her nightgown and had bruises all over her arms and shoulders. Julian was away, a lucky break because he'd have gone over and had a fight with Pete. As it was, Caroline made Bobbie have Dr. English come out and have a look at her, and nothing more was said. I mean, it was kept secret from everybody, especially Mr. Hammersmith. But the story got out somehow. Not widespread, but we all heard about it."

"We don't want it to get back to Mr. Hammersmith," said Mary Lander.

"He knows," said Frank Lander.

"You keep saying that, but I don't believe he does," said Mary.

"I don't either," said Joe Whipple. "Pete wouldn't be alive today if Phil Hammersmith knew."

"That's where I think you're wrong," said Phyllis. "Mr. Hammersmith might want to kill Pete, but killing him is another matter. And what earthly good would it do? The Hammersmiths have lost every penny, so I'm told, and at least with Pete still alive, Mrs. McCrea supports Bobbie. Barely. But they have food and a roof over their heads."

"Phil Hammersmith knows the whole damn story, you can bet anything on that. And it's why he's an old man all of a sudden. Have you seen him this trip, Jim?" said Frank Lander.

"I haven't seen him since the wedding."

"Oh, well——" said Mary.

"You won't——" said Joe.

"You won't recognize him," said Frank Lander. "He's bent over——"

"They say he's had a stroke," said Phyllis Whipple.

"And on top of everything else he got a lot of people sore at him by selling his bank stock to Ed Charney," said Joe. "Well, not a lot of people, but some that could have helped him. My old man, to name one. And I don't think that was so hot. Phil Hammersmith was a carpetbagger himself, and damn lucky to be in the bank. Then to sell his stock to a lousy stinking bootlegger . . . You should hear Harry Reilly on the subject."

"I don't want to hear Harry Reilly on any subject," said Frank Lander. "Cheap Irish Mick."

"I don't like him any better than you do, Frank, but call him something else," I said.

"I'm sorry, Jim. I didn't mean that," said Frank Lander.

"No. It just slipped out," I said.

"I apologize," said Frank Lander.

"Oh, all right."

"Don't be sensitive, Jim," said Mary.

"Stay out of it, Mary," said Frank Lander.

"*Everybody* calm down," said Joe. "Everybody knows that Harry Reilly is a cheap Irish Mick, and nobody knows it better than Jim, an Irish Mick but not a cheap one. So shut the hell up, everybody."

"Another country heard from," said Phyllis.

"Now *you*, for Christ's sake," said Joe. "Who has the quart?"

"I have my quart," said Frank Lander.

"I have mine," I said.

"I asked who has mine. Phyllis?"

"When we get to the club, time enough," said Phyllis.

"Hand it over," said Joe.

"Three quarts of whisky between five people. I'd like to know how we're going to get home tonight," said Mary Lander.

"Drunk as a monkey, if you really want to know," said Joe. "Tight as a nun's."

"Well, at least we're off the subject of Bobbie and Pete," said Phyllis.

"I'm not. I was coming back to it. Phyllis. The quart," said Joe.

"No," said Phyllis.

"Here," I said. "And remember where it came from." I handed him my bottle.

Joe took a swig in the corner of his mouth, swerving the car only slightly. "Thanks," he said, and returned the bottle. "Now, Mary, if you'll light me a cigarette like a dear little second cousin."

"Once removed," said Mary Lander.

"Once removed, and therefore related to Bobbie through her mother."

"No, *you* are but I'm not," said Mary Lander.

"Well, you're in it some way, through me. Now for the benefit of those who are not related to Bobbie or Mrs. Hammersmith, or Mary or me. Permit me to give you a little family history that will enlighten you on several points."

"Is this going to be about Mr. Hammersmith?" said Phyllis. "I don't think you'd better tell that."

"You're related only by marriage, so kindly keep your trap shut. If I want to tell it, I can."

"Everybody remember that I asked him not to," said Phyllis.

"Don't tell it, Joe, whatever it is," said Mary Lander.

"Yeah, what's the percentage?" said Frank Lander. "They have enough trouble without digging up past history."

"Oh, you're so noble, Lander," said Joe. "You fool nobody."

"If you're going to tell the story, go ahead, but stop insulting Frank," said Mary Lander.

"We'll be at the club before he gets started," said Phyllis.

"Then we'll sit there till I finish. Anyway, it doesn't take that long. So, to begin at the beginning. Phil Hammersmith. Phil Hammersmith came here before the war, just out of Lehigh."

"You're not even telling it right," said Phyllis.

"Phyllis is right. I'm screwing up my own story. Well, I'll begin again. Phil Hammersmith graduated from Lehigh, then a few years *later* he came to Gibbsville."

"That's better," said Phyllis.

"The local Lehigh contingent all knew him. He'd played lacrosse and he was a Sigma Nu around the time Mr. Chew was there. So he already had friends in Gibbsville."

"Now you're on the right track," said Phyllis.

"Thank you, love," said Joe.

"Where was he from originally?" I asked.

"Don't ask questions, Jim. It only throws me. He was from some place in New Jersey. So anyway he arrived in Gibbsville and got a job with the Coal & Iron Company. He was a civil engineer, and he had the job when he arrived. That is, he didn't come here looking for a job. He was hired before he got here."

"You've made that plain," said Phyllis.

"Well, it's important," said Joe.

"Yes, but you don't have to say the same thing over and over again," said Phyllis.

"Yes I do. Anyway, apparently the Coal & Iron people hired him on the strength of his record at Lehigh, plus asking a few questions of the local Lehigh contingent, that knew him, *plus* a very good recommendation he'd had from some firm in Bethlehem. Where he'd worked after getting out of college. But after he'd been here a while, and was getting along all right at the Coal & Iron, one day a construction engineer from New York arrived to talk business at the C. & I. Building. They took him down-cellar to the drafting-room and who should he see but Phil Hammersmith. But apparently Phil didn't see him. Well, the New York guy was a real wet smack, because he tattled on Phil.

"Old Mr. Duncan was general superintendent then and he sent for Phil. Was it true that Phil had once worked in South America, and if so, why hadn't he mentioned it when he applied for a job? Phil gave him the obvious answer. 'Because if I had, you wouldn't have hired me.' 'Not necessarily,' said Mr. Duncan. 'We might have accepted your explanation.' 'You say that now, but I tried telling the truth and I couldn't get a job.' 'Well, tell me the truth now,' said Mr. Duncan. 'All right,' said Phil. So he told Mr. Duncan what had happened.

"He was working in South America. Peru, I think. Or maybe Bolivia. In the jungle. And the one thing they didn't want the natives, the Indians, to get hold of was firearms. But one night he caught a native carrying an armful of rifles from the shanty, and when Phil yelled at him, the native ran, and Phil shot him. Killed him. The next day one of the other engineers was found with his throat cut. And the day after that the native chief came and called on the head man of the construction outfit. Either the Indians thought they'd killed the man that had killed their boy, or they didn't much care. But the chief told the white boss that the next time an Indian was killed, two white men would be killed. And not just killed. Tortured. Well, there were four or maybe five engineers, including Phil and the boss. The only white men in an area as big as Pennsylvania, and I guess they weighed their chances and being mathematicians, the odds didn't look so hot. So they quit. No hero stuff. They just quit. Except Phil. He was fired. The boss blamed Phil for everything and in his report to the New York office he put in a lot of stuff that just about fixed Phil for good. The boss, of course, was the same man that spotted Phil at the C. & I. drafting-room."

"You told it very well," said Phyllis.

"So any time you think of Phil Hammersmith killing Pete McCrea, it wouldn't be the first time," said Joe.

"And the war," I said. "He probably killed a few Germans."

"On the other hand, he never got over blaming himself for the other engineer's getting his throat cut," said Joe. "This is all the straight dope. Mr. Duncan to my old man."

We were used to engineers, their travels and adventures in far-off places, but engineers came and went and only a few became fixtures in our life. Phil Hammersmith's story was all new to Mary and Frank and me, and in the cold moonlight, as we sat in a heated automobile in a snow-covered parking area of a Pennsylvania country club, Joe Whipple had taken us to a dark South American jungle, given us a touch of fear, and in a few minutes covered Phil Hammersmith in mystery and then removed the mystery.

"Tell us more about Mr. Hammersmith," said Mary Lander.

Mary Lander. I had not had time to realize the inference that must accompany my guess that Frank Lander was the one boy in our crowd who had stayed with Bobbie. Mary Lander was the only girl who had not fought off Pete McCrea. She was the last girl I would have suspected of staying with Pete, and yet the one that surprised me the least. She had always been the girl our mothers liked us to take out, a kind of mothers' ideal for their sons, and possibly even for themselves. Mary Morgan Lander was the third generation of a family that had always been in the grocery business, the only store in the county that sold caviar and English biscuits and Sportsmen's Bracer chocolate, as well as the most expensive domestic items of fruit, vegetables, and tinned goods. Her brother Llewellyn Morgan still scooped out dried prunes and operated the rotary ham slicer, but no one seriously believed that all the Morgan money came from the store. Lew Morgan taught Sunday School in the Methodist Episcopal Church and played basketball at the Y.M.C.A., but he had been to Blair Academy and Princeton, and his father had owned one of the first Pierce-Arrows in Gibbsville. Mary had been unfairly judged a teaser, in previous years. She was not a teaser, but a girl who would kiss a boy and allow him to wander all over her body so long as he did not touch bare skin. Nothing surprised me about Mary. It was in character for her to have slapped Pete McCrea at a dinner party, and then to have let him stay with her and to have discussed with him a swap of husbands and wives. No casual dirty remark ever passed unnoticed by Mary; when someone made a slip we would all turn to see how Mary was taking it, and without fail she had heard it, understood it, and taken a pious attitude. But in our crowd she was the one person most conscious of sex and scatology. She was the only one of whom I would say she had a dirty mind, but I kept that observation to myself along with my theory that she hated Frank Lander. My theory, based on no information whatever, was that marriage and Frank Lander had not been enough for her and that Pete McCrea had become attractive to her because he was so awful.

"There's no more to tell," said Joe Whipple. We got out of the car and Mary took Joe's arm, and her evening was predictable: fathers and uncles and older brothers would cut in on her, and older women would comment as they always did that Mary Lander was *such* a sensible girl, *so* considerate of her elders, a *wonderful* wife to Frank. And we of her own age would dance with her because under cover of the dancing crowd Mary would wrap both legs around our right legs with a promise that had fooled us for years. Quiet little Mary Lander, climbing up a boy's leg but never forgetting to smile her Dr. Lyons smile at old Mrs. Ginyan and old Mr. Heff. And yet through some mental process that I did not take time to scrutinize, I was less annoyed with Mary than I had been since we were children. I was determined not to dance with her, and I did not, but my special knowledge about her and Pete McCrea reduced her power to allure. Bobbie had married Pete McCrea and she was still attractive in spite of it; but Mary's seductiveness vanished with the revelation that she had picked Pete as her lover, if only for once, twice, or how many times. I had never laughed at Mary before, but now she was the fool, not we, not I.

I got quite plastered at the dance, and so did a lot of other people. On the way home we sang a little— "Body and Soul" was the song, but Phyllis was the only one who could sing the middle part truly—and Frank Lander tried to tell about an incident in the smoking-room, where Julian English apparently had thrown a drink in Harry Reilly's face. It did not seem worth making a fuss about, and Frank never finished his story. Mary Lander attacked me: "You never danced with me, not once," she said.

"I didn't?"

"No, you didn't, and you know you didn't," she said. "And you always do."

"Well, this time I guess I didn't."

"Well, *why* didn't you?"

"Because he didn't want to," said Frank Lander. "You're making a fool of yourself. I should think you'd have more pride."

"Yeah, why don't you have more pride, Mary?" said Joe Whipple. "You'd think it was an honour to dance with this Malloy guy."

"It is," I said.

"That's it. You're getting so conceited," said Mary. "Well, I'm sure I didn't have to sit any out."

"Then why all the fuss?" said Frank Lander.

"Such popularity must be deserved," I said, quoting an advertising slogan.

"Whose? Mary's or yours?" said Phyllis.

"Well, I was thinking of Mary's, but now that you mention it . . ." I said.

"How many times did he dance with *you*, Phyllis?" said Joe.

"Three or four," said Phyllis.

"In that case, Frank, Jim has insulted your wife. I don't see any other way out of it. You have to at least slap his face. Shall I stop the car?"

"My little trouble-maker," said Phyllis.

"Come on, let's have a fight," said Joe. "Go ahead, Frank. Give him a punch in the nose."

"Yeah, like you did at the Dam, Frank," I said.

"Oh, God. I remember that awful night," said Phyllis. "What did you fight over?"

"Bobbie," I said.

"Bobbie was the cause of *more* fights," said Mary Lander.

"Well, we don't need her to fight over now. We have you," said Joe. "Your honour's been attacked and your husband wants to defend it. The same as I would if Malloy hadn't danced with *my* wife. It's a good thing you danced with Phyllis, Malloy, or you and I'd get out of this car and start slugging."

"Why did you fight over Bobbie? I don't remember that," said Mary.

"Because she came to the picnic with Jim and then went off necking with Frank," said Phyllis. "I remember the whole thing."

"Stop *talking* about fighting and let's *fight*," said Joe.

"All right, stop the car," I said.

"Now you're talking," said Joe.

"Don't be ridiculous," said Phyllis.

"Oh, shut up," said Joe. He pulled up on the side of the road. "I'll referee." He got out of the car, and so did Frank and I and Phyllis. "All right, put up your dukes." We did so, moved around a bit in the snow and slush. "Go on, mix it," said Joe, whereupon Frank rushed me and hit me on the left cheek. All blows were directed at the head, since all three of us were armoured in coonskin coats. "That was a good one, Frank. Now go get him, Jim." I swung my right hand and caught Frank's left eye, and at that moment we were all splashed by slush, taken completely by surprise as Phyllis, whom we had forgotten, drove the car away.

"That bitch!" said Joe. He ran to the car and got hold of a door handle but she increased her speed and he fell in the snow. "God damn that bitch, I should have known she was up to something. Now what? Let's try to bum a ride." The fight, such as it was, was over, and we tried to flag down cars on their way home from the dance. We recognized many of them, but not one would stop.

"Well, thanks to you, we've got a nice three-mile walk to Swedish Haven," said Frank Lander.

"Oh, she'll be back," said Joe.

"I'll bet you five bucks she's not," I said.

"Well, I won't bet, but I'll be damned if I'm going to walk three miles. I'm just going to wait till we can bum a ride."

"If you don't keep moving you'll freeze," said Frank.

"We're nearer the club than we are Swedish Haven. Let's go back there," I said.

"And have my old man see me?" said Joe.

"Your old man went home hours ago." I said.

"Well, somebody'll see me," said Joe.

"Listen, half the club's seen you already, and they wouldn't even stop," I said.

"Who has a cigarette?" said Joe.

"Don't give him one," said Frank.

"I have no intention of giving him one," I said. "Let's go back to the club. My feet are soaking wet."

"So are mine," said Frank. We were wearing pumps, and our feet had been wet since we got out of the car.

"That damn Phyllis, she knows I just got over a cold," said Joe.

"Maybe that's why she did it," I said. "It'd serve you right if you got pneumonia."

We began to walk in the middle of the road, in the direction of the clubhouse, which we could see, warm and comfortable on top of a distant plateau. "That old place never looked so good," said Joe. "Let's spend the night there."

"The rooms are all taken. The orchestra's staying there," I said.

We walked about a mile, our feet getting sorer at

every step, and the combination of exhaustion and the amount we had had to drink made even grumbling an effort. Then a Dodge touring car, becurtained, stopped about fifty yards from us and a spotlight was turned on each of our faces. A man in a short overcoat and fur-lined cap came towards us. He was a State Highway patrolman. "What happened to you fellows?" he said. "You have a wreck?"

"I married one," said Joe.

"Oh, a weisscrackah," said the patrolman, a Pennsylvania Dutchman. "Where's your car?"

"We got out to take a leak and my wife drove off with it," said Joe.

"You from the dance at the gulf club?"

"Yes," said Joe. "How about giving us a lift?"

"Let me see you' driwah's licence," said the cop.

Joe took out his billfold and handed over the licence. "So? From Lantenengo Street yet? All right, get in. Whereabouts you want to go to?"

"The country club," said Joe.

"The hell with that," said Frank. "Let's go on to Gibbsville."

"This ain't no taxi service," said the cop. "And I ain't taking you to no Gippsfille. I'm on my way to my sub-station. Swedish Haven. You can phone there for a taxi. Privileged characters, you think you are. A bunch of drunks, you ask me."

I had to go back to New York on the morning train and the events of the next few days, so far as they concerned Joe and Phyllis Whipple and Frank and Mary Lander, were obscured by the suicide, a day or two later, of Julian English, the man who had thrown a drink at Harry Reilly. The domestic crisis of the Whipples and the Landers and even the McCreas seemed very unimportant. And yet when I heard about English, who had not been getting along with his wife, I wondered about my own friends, people my own age but not so very much younger than Julian and Caroline English. English had danced with Phyllis and Mary that night, and now he was dead. I knew very little about the causes of the difficulties between him and Caroline, but they could have been no worse than the problems that existed in Bobbie's marriage and that threatened the marriage of Frank and Mary Lander. I was shocked and saddened by the English suicide; he was an attractive man whose shortcomings seemed out of proportion to the magnitude of killing himself. He had not been a friend of mine, only an acquaintance with whom I had had many drinks and played some golf; but friends of mine, my closest friends in the world, boys-now-men like myself, were at the beginning of the same kind of life and doing the same kind of thing that for Julian English ended in a sealed-up garage with a motor running. I hated what I thought those next few days and weeks. There is nothing young about killing oneself, no matter when it happens, and I hated this being deprived of the sweetness of youth. And that was what it was, that was what was happening to us. I, and I think the others, had looked upon our squabbles as unpleasant incidents but belonging to our youth. Now they were plainly recognizable as symptoms of life without youth, without youth's excuses or youth's recoverability. I wanted to love someone, and during the next year or two I confused the desperate need for love with love itself. I had put a hopeless love out of my life; but that is not part of this story, except to state it and thus to show that I knew what I was looking for.

2

When you have grown up with someone it is much easier to fill in gaps of five years, ten years, in which you do not see him, than to supply those early years in the life of a friend you meet in maturity. I do not know why this is so, unless it is a mere matter of insufficient time. With the friends of later life you may exchange boyhood stories that seem worth telling, but boyhood is not all stories. It is mostly not stories, but day-to-day, unepisodic living. And most of us are too polite to burden our later-life friends with unexciting anecdotes about people they will never meet. (Likewise we hope they will not burden us.) But it is easy to bring old friends up to date in your mental dossiers by the addition of a few vital facts. Have they stayed married? Have they had many more children? Have they made money or lost it? Usually the basic facts will do, and then you tell yourself that Joe Whipple is still Joe Whipple, plus two sons, a new house, a hundred thousand dollars, forty pounds, bifocals, fat in the neck, and a new concern for the state of the nation.

Such additions I made to my friends' dossiers as I heard about them from time to time; by letters from them, conversations with my mother, an occasional newspaper clipping. I received these facts with joy for the happy news, sorrow for the sad, and immediately went about my business, which was far removed from any business of theirs. I seldom went back to Gibbsville during the Thirties—mine and the century's—and when I did I stayed only long enough to stand at a grave, to toast a bride, to spend a few minutes beside a sickbed. In my brief encounters with my old friends I got no information about Bobbie and Pete McCrea, and only after I had returned to New York or California would I remember that I had intended to inquire about them.

There is, of course, some significance in the fact that no one volunteered information about Bobbie and Pete. It was that they had disappeared. They continued to live in Gibbsville, but in parts of the town that were out of the way for their old friends. There is no town so small that that cannot happen, and Gibbsville, a third-class city, was large enough to have all the grades of poverty and wealth and the many half grades in between, in which $10 a month in the husband's income could make a difference in the kind and location of the house in which he lived. No one had volunteered any information about Bobbie and Pete, and I had not remembered to inquire. In five years I had had no new facts about them, none whatever, and their disappearance from my ken might have continued but for a broken shoelace.

I was in Gibbsville for a funeral, and the year was 1938. I had broken a shoelace, it was evening and the stores were closed, and I was about to drive back to New York. The only place open that might have shoelaces was a poolroom that in my youth had had a two-chair bootblack stand. The poolroom was in a shabby section near the railroad stations and a couple of cheap hotels, four or five saloons, an automobile tyre agency, a barber shop, and a quick-lunch counter. I opened the poolroom door, saw that the bootblack's chairs were still there, and said to the man behind the cigar counter: "Have you got any shoelaces?"

"Sorry I can't help you, Jim," said the man. He was wearing an eyeshade, but as soon as he spoke I recognized Pete McCrea.

"Pete, for God's sake," I said. We shook hands.

"I thought you might be in town for the funeral," he said. "I should have gone, too, I guess, but I decided I wouldn't. It was nice of you to make the trip."

"Well, you know. He was a friend of my father's. Do you own this place?"

"I run it. I have a silent partner, Bill Charney. You remember Ed Charney? His younger brother. I don't know where to send you to get a shoelace."

"The hell with the shoelace. How's Bobbie?"

"Oh, Bobbie's fine. *You* know. A lot of changes, but this is better than nothing. Why don't you call her up? She'd love to hear from you. We're living out on Mill Street, but we have a phone. Call her up and say hello. The number is 3385-J. If you have time maybe you could go see her. I have to stay here till I close up at one o'clock, but she's home."

"What number on Mill Street? You call her up and tell her I'm coming? Is that all right?"

"Hell, yes."

Someone thumped the butt of a cue on the floor and called out: "Rack 'em up, Pete?"

"I have to be here. You go on out and I'll call her up," he said. "Keep your shirt on," he said to the pool player, then, to me: "It's 402 Mill Street, across from the open hearth, second house from the corner. I guess I won't see you again, but I'm glad we had a minute. You're looking very well." I could not force a comment on his appearance. His nose was red and larger, his eyes watery, the dewlaps sagging, and he was wearing a blue denim work shirt with a dirty leather bow tie.

"Think I could get in the Ivy Club if I went back to Princeton?" he said. "I didn't make it the first time around, but now I'm a big shot. So long, Jim. Nice to've seen you."

The open hearth had long since gone the way of all the mill equipment; the mill itself had been inactive for years, and as a residential area the mill section was only about a grade and a half above the poorest Negro slums. But in front of most of the houses in the McCreas' row there were cared-for plots; there always had been, even when the mill was running and the air was full of smoke and acid. It was an Irish and Polish neighbourhood, but knowledge of that fact did not keep me from locking all the doors of my car. The residents of the neighbourhood would not have touched my father's car, but this was not his car and I was not he.

The door of Number 402 opened as soon as I closed my car door. Bobbie waited for me to lock up and when I got to the porch, she said: "*Jim*. Jim, Jim, Jim. How nice. I'm so glad to see you." She quickly closed the door behind me and then kissed me. "Give me a real kiss and a real hug. I didn't dare while the door was open." I kissed her and held her for a moment and then she said: "Hey, I guess we'd better cut this out."

"Yes," I said. "It's nice, though."

"Haven't done that since we were—God!" She stood away and looked at me. "You could lose some weight, but you're not so bad. How about a bottle of beer? Or would you rather have some cheap whisky?"

"What are you drinking?"

"Cheap whisky, but I'm used to it," she said.

"Let's both have some cheap whisky," I said.

"Straight? With water? Or how?"

"Oh, a small slug of whisky and a large slug of water in it. I'm driving back to New York tonight."

She went to the kitchen and prepared the drinks. I recognized some of the furniture from the Hammersmith and McCrea houses. "Brought together by a shoestring," she said. "Here's to it. How do I look?"

"If you want my frank and candid opinion, good enough to go right upstairs and make up for the time we lost. Pete won't be home till one o'clock."

"If then," she said. "Don't think I wouldn't, but it's too soon after my baby. Didn't Pete tell you I finally produced a healthy son?"

"No."

"You'll hear him in a little while. We have a daughter, two years old, and now a son. Angus McCrea, Junior. Seven pounds two ounces at birth."

"Good for you," I said.

"Not so damn good for me, but it's over, and he's healthy."

"And what about your mother and father?" I said.

"Oh, poor Jim. You didn't know? Obviously you didn't, and you're going to be so sorry you asked. Daddy committed suicide two years ago. He shot himself. And Mother's in Swedish Haven." Swedish Haven was local lore for the insane asylum. "I'm sorry I had to tell you."

"God, why won't they lay off you?" I said.

"Who is they? Oh, you mean just—life?"

"Yes."

"I don't know, Jim," she said. "I've had about as much as I can stand, or so I keep telling myself. But I must be awfully tough, because there's always something else, and I go right on. Will you let me complain for just a minute, and then I'll stop? The only one of the old crowd I ever see is Phyllis. She comes out and never forgets to bring a bottle, so we get tight together. But some things we don't discuss, Phyllis and I. Pete is a closed subject."

"What's he up to?"

"Oh, he has his women. I don't even know who they are any more, and couldn't care less. Just as long as he doesn't catch a disease. I told him that, so he's been careful about it." She sat up straight. "I haven't been the soul of purity, either, but it's Pete's son. Both children are Pete's. But I haven't been withering on the vine."

"Why should you?"

"That's what *I* said. Why should I have nothing? Nothing? The children are mine, and I love them, but I need more than that, Jim. Children don't love you back. All they do is depend on you to feed them and

141

wash them and all the rest of it. But after they're in bed for the night—I never know whether Pete will be home at two o'clock or not at all. So I've had two tawdry romances, I guess you'd call them. Not you, but Mrs. McCrea would."

"Where is dear Mrs. McCrea?"

"She's living in Jenkintown, with an old maid sister. Thank heaven they can't afford carfare, so I'm spared that."

"Who are your gentlemen friends?"

"Well, the first was when we were living on the East Side. A gentleman by the name of Bill Charney. Yes, Ed's brother and Pete's partner. I was crazy about him. Not for one single minute in love with him, but I never even thought about love with him. He wanted to marry me, too, but I was a nasty little snob. I *couldn't* marry Bill Charney, Jim. I just couldn't. So he married a nice little Irish girl and they're living on Lantenengo Street in the house that used to belong to old Mr. Duncan. And I'm holding court on Mill Street, thirty dollars a month rent."

"Do you want some money?"

"Will you give me two hundred dollars?"

"More than that, if you want it."

"No, I'd just like to have two hundred dollars to hide, to keep in case of emergency."

"In case of emergency, you can always send me a telegram in care of my publisher." I gave her $200.

"Thank you. Now I have some money. For the last five or six years I haven't had any money of my own. You don't care how I spend this, do you?"

"As long as you spend it on yourself."

"I've gotten so stingy I probably won't spend any of it. But this is wonderful. Now I can read the ads and say to myself I could have some expensive lingerie. I think I will get a permanent, next month."

"Is that when you'll be back in circulation again?"

"Good guess. Yes, about a month," she said. "But not the same man. I didn't tell you about the second one. You don't know him. He came here after you left Gibbsville. His name is McCormick and he went to Princeton with Pete. They sat next to each other in a lot of classes, McC, McC, and he was sent here to do some kind of an advertising survey and ran into Pete. They'd never been exactly what you'd call pals, but they *knew* each other and Mac took one look and sized up the situation and—well, I thought, why not? He wasn't as exciting as Mr. Charney, but at one time I would have married him. *If* he'd asked me. He doesn't live here any more."

"But you've got the next one picked out?"

"No, but I know there will be a next one. Why lie to myself? And why lie to you? I don't think I ever have."

"Do you ever see Frank?"

"Frank? Frank Lander? What made you think of him?"

"Bobbie," I said.

"Oh, of course. That was a guess of yours, a long time ago," she said. "No, I never see Frank." She was smoking a cigarette, and sitting erect with her elbow on the arm of her chair, holding the cigarette high and with style. If her next words had been "Jeeves, have the

143

black Rolls brought round at four o'clock" she would not have been more naturally grand. But her next words were: "I haven't even thought about Frank. There was another boy, Johnny White, the one I was engaged to. *Engaged to*. That close to spending the rest of my life with him—or at least part of it. But because he wanted me to go away with him before we were married, I broke the engagement and married Pete."

"Is that all it was? That he wanted you to go away with him?"

"That's really all it was. I got huffy and said he couldn't really love me if he wanted to take that risk. Not that we hadn't been taking risks, but a pre-marital trip, that was something else again. My five men, Jim. Frank. Johnny. Bill and Mac. And Pete."

"Why didn't you and Frank ever get engaged?"

"I wonder. I *have* thought about *that*, so I was wrong when I said I never think of Frank. But Frank in the old days, not Frank now. What may have happened was that Frank was the only boy I'd gone all the way with, and then I got scared because I didn't want to give up the fun, popularity, good times. Jim, I have a confession to make. About you."

"Oh?"

"I told Frank I'd stayed with you. He wouldn't believe he was my first and he kept harping on it, so I really got rid of Frank by telling him you were the first."

"Why me?"

"Because the first time I ever stayed with Frank, or anybody, it was at a picnic at the Dam, and I'd gone to the picnic with you. So you were the logical one."

"Did you tell him that night?"

"No. Later. Days later. But you had a fight with him that night, and the fight made it all the more convincing."

"Well, thanks, little pal," I said.

"Oh, you don't care, do you?"

"No, not really."

"You had Kitty, after all," she said. "Do you ever see Kitty?"

"No. Kitty lives in Cedarhurst and they keep to themselves, Cedarhurst people."

"What was your wife like?"

"She was nice. Pretty. Wanted to be an actress. I still see her once in a while. I like her, and always will, but if ever there were two people that shouldn't have got married . . ."

"I can name two others," said Bobbie.

"You and Pete. But you've stuck to him."

"Don't be polite. I'm stuck with him. Can you imagine what Pete would be like if I left him?"

"Well, to be brutally frank, what's he like anyway? You don't have to go on paying for a dirty trick the rest of your life."

"It wasn't just a dirty trick. It would have been a dirty trick if I'd walked out on him the day we were getting married. But I went through with it, and that made it more than a dirty trick. I *should have* walked out on him, the day we got married. I even tried. And he'd have recovered—then. Don't forget, Pete McCrea was used to dirty tricks being played on him, and he might have got over it if I'd left him at the church. But once

145

I'd married him, he became a different person, took himself much more seriously, and so did everyone else. They began to dislike him, but that was better than being laughed at." She sipped her drink.

"Well, who did it? I did. Your little pal," she said. "How about some more cheap whisky?"

"No thanks, but you go ahead," I said.

"The first time I ever knew there *was* a Mill Street was the day we rented this house," she said, as she poured herself a drink. "I'd never been out this way before."

"You couldn't have lived here when the mill was operating. The noise and the smoke."

"I can live anywhere," she said. "So can anyone else. And don't be too surprised if you find us back on Lantenengo. Do you know the big thing nowadays? Slot machines and the numbers racket. Pete wants to get into The Numbers, but he hasn't decided how to go about it. Bill Charney is the kingpin in the county, although not the real head. It's run by a syndicate in Jersey City."

"Don't let him do it, Bobbie," I said. "Really don't."

"Why not? He's practically in it already. He has slot machines in the poolroom, and that's where people call up to find out what number won today. He might as well be in it."

"No."

"It's the only way Pete will ever have any money, and if he ever gets his hands on some money, maybe he'll divorce me. Then I could take the children and go away somewhere. California."

"That's a different story. If you're planning it that way. But stay out of The Numbers if you ever have any idea of remaining respectable. You can't just go in for a few years and then quit."

"Respectable? Do you think my son's going to be able to get into Princeton? His father is the proprietor of a poolroom, and they're going to know that when Angus gets older. Pete will never be anything else. He's found his niche. But if I took the children to California they might have a chance. And *I* might have a chance, before it's too late. It's our only hope, Jim. Phyllis agrees with me."

I realized that I would be arguing against a hope and a dream, and if she had that much left, and only that much, I had no right to argue. She very nearly followed my thinking. "It's what I live on, Jim," she said. "That—and this." She held up her glass. "And a little admiration. A little—admiration. Phyllis wants to give me a trip to New York. Would you take us to '21' and those places?"

"Sure."

"Could you get someone for Phyllis?"

"I think so. Sure. Joe wouldn't go on this trip?"

"And give up a chance to be with Mary Lander?"

"So now it's Joe and Mary?"

"Oh, that's old hat in Gibbsville. They don't even pretend otherwise."

"And Frank? What about him?"

"Frank is the forgotten man. If there were any justice he ought to pair off with Phyllis, but they don't like each other. Phyllis calls Frank a wishy-washy namby-pamby, and Frank calls Phyllis a drunken trouble-maker. We've all grown up, Jim. Oh, haven't we just? Joe doesn't like Phyllis to visit me because Mary says all we do is gossip. Although how she'd know *what* we do . . ."

"They were all at the funeral, and I thought what a dull, stuffy little group they've become," I said.

"But that's what they are," said Bobbie. "Very stuffy and very dull. What else is there for them to do? If I were still back there with them I'd be just as bad. Maybe worse. In a way, you know, Pete McCrea has turned out to be the most interesting man in our old crowd, present company excepted. Joe was a very handsome young man and so was Frank, and their families had lots of money and all the rest of it. But you saw Joe and Frank today. I haven't seen them lately, but Joe looks like a professional wrestler and I remember how hairy he was, all over his chest and back and his arms and legs. And Frank just the opposite, skin like a girl's and slender, but now we could almost call *him* Ichabod. He looks like a cranky schoolteacher, and his glasses make him look like an owl. Mary, of course, beautifully dressed I'm sure, and not looking a day older."

"Several days older, but damn good-looking," I said.

A baby cried and Bobbie made no move. "That's my daughter. Teething. Now she'll wake up my son and you're in for a lot of howling." The son began to cry, and Bobbie excused herself. She came back in a few minutes with the infant in her arms. "It's against my rules to pick them up, but I wanted to show him to you. Isn't he an ugly little creature? The answer is yes." She took him away and returned with the daughter. "She's begun to have a face."

"Yes, I can see that. Your face, for which she can be thankful."

"Yes, I wouldn't want a girl to look like Pete. It doesn't matter so much with a boy." She took the girl away and when she rejoined me she refilled her glass.

"Are you sorry you didn't have children?" she said.

"Not the way it turned out, I'm not," I said.

"These two haven't had much of a start in life, the poor little things. They haven't even been christened. Do you know why? There was nobody we could ask to be their godfathers." Her eyes filled with tears. "That was when I really saw what we'd come to."

"Bobbie, I've got a four-hour drive ahead of me, so I think I'd better get started."

"Four hours to New York? In that car?"

"I'm going to stop and have a sandwich halfway."

"I could give you a sandwich and make some coffee."

"I don't want it now, thanks."

We looked at each other. "I'd like to show how much I appreciate your coming out to see me," she said. "But it's probably just as well I can't. But I'll be all right in New York, Jim. That is, if I ever get there. I won't believe that, either, till I'm on the train."

If she came to New York I did not know about it, and during the war years Bobbie and her problems receded from my interest. I heard that Pete was working in a defence plant, from which I inferred that he had not made the grade in the numbers racket. Frank Lander was in the Navy, Joe Whipple in the War

Production Board, and by the time the war was over I discovered that so many other people and things had taken the place of Gibbsville in my thoughts that I had almost no active curiosity about the friends of my youth. I had even had a turnover in my New York friendships. I had married again, I was working hard, and most of my social life originated with my wife's friends. I was making, for me, quite a lot of money, and I was a middle-aged man whose physician had made some honest, unequivocal remarks about my life expectancy. It took a little time and one illness to make me realize that if I wanted to see my child grow to maturity, I had to retire from night life. It was not nearly so difficult as I had always anticipated it would be.

After I became reconciled to middle age and the quieter life I made another discovery: that the sweetness of my early youth was a persistent and enduring thing, so long as I kept it at the distance of years. Moments would come back to me, of love and excitement and music and laughter that filled my breast as they had thirty years earlier. It was not nostalgia, which only means homesickness, nor was it a wish to be living that excitement again. It was a splendid contentment with the knowledge that once I had felt those things so deeply and well that the throbbing urging of George Gershwin's "Do It Again" could evoke the original sensation and the pictures that went with it: a tea dance at the club and a girl in a long black satin dress and my furious jealousy of a fellow who wore a yellow foulard tie. I wanted none of it ever again, but all I had I wanted to keep. I could remember precisely the tone in which her brother had said to her: "Are you coming or aren't you?" and the sounds of his galoshes after she said: "I'm going home with Mr. Malloy." They were the things I knew before we knew everything, and, I suppose, before we began to learn. There was always a girl, and nearly always there was music; if the Gershwin tune belonged to that girl, a Romberg tune belonged to another and "When Hearts Are Young" became a personal anthem, enduringly sweet and safe from all harm, among the protected memories. In middle age I was proud to have lived according to my emotions at the right time, and content to live that way vicariously and at a distance. I had missed almost nothing, escaped very little, and at fifty I had begun to devote my energy and time to the last, simple but big task of putting it all down as well as I knew how.

In the midst of putting it all down, as novels and short stories and plays, I would sometimes think of Bobbie McCrea and the dinginess of her history. But as the reader will presently learn, the "they"—life— that had once made me cry out in anger, were not through with her yet. (Of course "they" are never through with anyone while he still lives, and we are not concerned here with the laws of compensation that seem to test us, giving us just enough strength to carry us in another trial.) I like to think that Bobbie got enough pleasure out of a pair of nylons, a permanent wave, a bottle of Phyllis Whipple's whisky, to recharge the brightness in her. As we again take up her story I promise the reader a happy ending, if only because I want it that way. It happens also to be the true ending. . . .

Pete McCrea did not lose his job at the end of the war. His Princeton degree helped there. He had gone into the plant, which specialized in aluminium extrusion, as a manual labourer, but his IBM card revealed that he had taken psychology courses in college, and he was transferred to Personnel. It seemed an odd choice, but it is not hard to imagine that Pete was better fitted by his experience as a poolroom proprietor than as a two-year student of psychology. At least he spoke both languages, he liked the work, and in 1945 he was not bumped by a returning veteran.

Fair Grounds, the town in which the plant was situated, was only three miles from Gibbsville. For nearly a hundred years it had been the trading centre for the Pennsylvania Dutch farmers in the area, and its attractions had been Becker's general store, the Fair Grounds Bank, the freight office of the Reading Railway, the Fair Grounds Hotel, and five Protestant churches. Clerks at Becker's and at the bank and the Reading, and bartenders at the hotel and the pastors of the churches, all had to speak Pennsylvania Dutch. English was desirable but not a requirement. The town was kept scrubbed, dusted, and painted, and until the erection of the aluminium plant, jobs and trades were kept in the same families. An engineman's son worked as waterboy until he was old enough to take the examinations for brakeman; a master mechanic would give his boy calipers for Christmas. There were men and women in Fair Grounds who visited Gibbsville only to serve on juries or to undergo surgery at the Gibbsville Hospital. There were some men and women who had never been to Gibbsville at all and regarded Gibbsville as some Gibbsville citizens regarded Paris, France. That was the pre-aluminium Fair Grounds.

To this town in 1941 went Pete and Bobbie McCrea. They rented a house no larger than the house on Mill Street but cleaner and in better repair. Their landlord and his wife went to live with his mother-in-law, and collected the $50 legally frozen monthly rent and $50 side payment for the use of the radio and the gas stove. But in spite of under-the-table and black-market prices Pete and Bobbie McCrea were financially better off than they had been since their marriage, and nylons at black-market prices were preferable to the no nylons she had had on Mill Street. The job, and the fact that he continued to hold it, restored some respectability to Pete, and they discussed rejoining the club. "Don't try it, I warn you," said Phyllis Whipple. "The club isn't run by your friends any more. Now it's been taken over by people that couldn't have got in ten years ago."

"Well, we'd have needed all our old friends to go to bat for us, and I guess some would think twice about it," said Pete. "So we'll do our drinking at the Tavern."

The Dan Patch Tavern, which was a new name for the renovated Fair Grounds Hotel bar, was busy all day and all night, and it was one of the places where Pete could take pleasure in his revived respectability. It was also one of the places where Bobbie could count on getting that little admiration that she needed to live on. On the day of Pearl Harbour she was only thirty-four years old and at the time of the Japanese surrender she was only thirty-eight. She was accorded admiration in abundance. Some afternoons just before the shift changed she would walk the three blocks to the Tavern and wait for Pete. The bartender on duty would say "Hi, Bobbie," and bring her currently favourite drink to her booth. Sometimes there would be four men sitting with her when Pete arrived from the plant; she was never alone for long. If one man tried to persuade her to leave, and became annoyingly insistent, the bartenders came to her rescue. The bartenders and the proprietor knew that in her way Bobbie was as profitable as the juke box. She was an attraction. She was a good-looking broad who was not a whore or a falling-down lush, and all her drinks were paid for. She was the Tavern's favourite customer, male or female, and if she had given the matter any thought she could have been declared in. All she wanted in return was a steady supply of Camels and protection from being mauled. The owner of the Tavern, Rudy Schau, was the only one who was aware that Bobbie and Pete had once lived on Lantenengo Street in Gibbsville, but far from being impressed by their background, he had a German opinion of aristocrats who had lost standing. He was actively suspicious of Bobbie in the beginning, but in time he came to accept her as a wife whose independence he could not condone and a good-looking woman whose morals he had not been able to condemn. And she was good for business. Beer business was good, but at Bobbie's table nobody drank beer, and the real profit was in the hard stuff.

In the Fair Grounds of the pre-aluminium days Bobbie would have had few women friends. No decent woman would have gone to a saloon every day—or any day. She most likely would have received warnings from the Ku Klux Klan, which was concerned with personal conduct in a town that had only a dozen Catholic families, no Negroes and no Jews. But when the aluminium plant (which was called simply The Aluminium or The Loomy) went into war production the population of Fair Grounds immediately doubled and the solid Protestant character of the town was changed in a month. Eight hundred new people came to town and they lived in apartments in a town where there were no apartments: in rooms in private houses, in garages and old stables, in rented rooms and haylofts out in the farming area. The newcomers wasted no time with complaints of double-rent, inadequate heating, holes in the roof, insufficient sanitation. The town was no longer scrubbed, dusted, or painted, and thousands of man-hours were lost while a new shift waited for the old to vacate parking space in the streets of the town. Bobbie and Pete were among the lucky early ones: they had a house. That fact of itself gave Bobbie some distinction. The house had two rooms and kitchen on the first floor, three rooms and bath on the second, and it had a cellar and an attic. In the identical houses on both sides there were a total of four families and six roomers. As a member of Personnel it was one of Pete's duties to find housing for workers, but Bobbie would have no roomers. "The money wouldn't do us much good, so let's live like human beings," she said.

"You mean there's nothing to buy with the money," said Pete. "But we could save it."

"If we had it, we'd spend it. You've never saved a cent in your life and neither have I. If you're thinking of the children's education, buy some more war bonds and have it taken out of your pay. But I'm not going to share my bathroom with a lot of dirty men. I'd have to do all the extra work, not you."

"You could make a lot of money doing their laundry. Fifty cents a shirt."

"Are you serious?"

"No."

"It's a good thing you're not, because I could tell you how else I could make a lot more money."

"Yes, a lot more," said Pete.

"Well, then, keep your ideas to yourself. I won't have boarders and I won't do laundry for fifty cents a shirt. That's final."

And so Bobbie had her house, she got the admiration she needed, and she achieved a moderate popularity among the women of her neighbourhood by little friendly acts that came spontaneously out of her friendly nature. There was a dinginess to the new phase: the house was not much, the men who admired her and the women who welcomed her help were the ill-advantaged, the cheap, the vulgar, and sometimes the evil. But the next step down from Mill Street would have been hopeless degradation, and the next step up, Fair Grounds, was at least up. She was envied for her dingy house, and when Pete called her the Queen of the Klondike she was not altogether displeased. There was envy in the epithet, and in the envy was the first sign of respect he had shown her in ten years. He had never suspected her of an affair with Mac McCormick, and if he had suspected her during her infatuation with Bill Charney he had been afraid to make an accusation; afraid to anticipate his own feelings in the event that Charney would give him a job in The Numbers. When Charney brought in a Pole from Detroit for the job Pete had wanted, Pete accepted $1,000 for his share of the poolroom and felt only grateful relief. Charney did not always buy out his partners, and Pete refused to wonder if the money and the easy dissolution of the partnership had been paid for by Bobbie. It was not a question he wanted to raise, and when the war in Europe created jobs at Fair Grounds he believed that his luck had begun to change.

Whatever the state of Pete's luck, the pace of his marriage had begun to change. The pace of his marriage —and not his alone—was set by the time he spent at home and what he did during that time. For ten years he had spent little more time at home than was necessary for sleeping and eating. He could not sit still in the same room with Bobbie, and even after the children were born he did not like to have her present during the times he would play with them. He would arrive in a hurry to have his supper, and in a short time he would get out of the house, to be with a girl, to go back to work at the poolroom. He was most conscious of time when he was near Bobbie; everywhere else he moved slowly, spoke deliberately, answered hesitantly. But after the move to Fair Grounds he spent more time in the house, with the children, with Bobbie. He would sit in the front room, doing paper work from the plant, while Bobbie sewed. At the Tavern he would say to Bobbie: "It's time we were getting home." He no longer darted in and out of the house and ate his meals rapidly and in silence.

He had a new girl, Martha—"Martie"—Klinger was a typist at the plant, a Fair Grounds woman whose husband was in the Coast Guard at Lewes, Delaware. She was Bobbie's age and likewise had two children. She retained a young prettiness in the now round face and her figure had not quite reached the stage of plumpness. Sometimes when she moved an arm the flesh of her breast seemed to go all the way up to her neckline, and she had been one of the inspirations for a plant memo to women employees, suggesting that tight sweaters and tight slacks were out of place in wartime industry. Pete brought her to the Tavern one day after work, and she never took her eyes off Bobbie. She looked up and down, up and down, with her mouth half open as though she were listening to Bobbie through her lips. She showed no animosity of a defensive nature and was not openly possessive of Pete, but Bobbie knew on sight that she was Pete's new girl. After several sessions at the Tavern Bobbie could tell which of the men had already slept with Martie and which of them were likely to again. It was impossible to be jealous of Martie, but it was just as impossible not to feel superior to her. Pete, the somewhat changed Pete, kept up the absurd pretence that Martie was just a girl from the plant whom he happened to bring along for a drink, and there was no unpleasantness until one evening Martie said: "Jesus, I gotta go or I won't get any supper."

"Come on back to our house and have supper with us," said Pete. "That's okay by you, isn't it, Bobbie?"

"No, it isn't," said Bobbie.

"Rudy'll give us a steak and we can cook it at home," said Pete.

"I said no," said Bobbie, and offered no explanation.

"I'll see you all tomorrow," said Martie. "Goodnight, people."

"Why wouldn't you let her come home with us? I could have got a steak from Rudy. And Martie's a hell of a good cook."

"When we can afford a cook I may hire her," said Bobbie.

"Oh, that's what it is. The old snob department."

"That's exactly what it is."

"We're not in any position——"

"*You're* not."

"*We're* not. If I can't have my friends to my house," he said, but did not know how to finish.

"It's funny that she's the first one you ever asked. Don't forget what I told you about having boarders, and fifty cents a shirt. You keep your damn Marties out of my house. If you don't, I'll get a job and you'll be just another boarder yourself."

"Oh, why are you making such a stink about Martie?"

"Come *off* it, Pete, for heaven's *sake*."

The next statement, he knew, would have to be a stupidly transparent lie or an admission, so he made no statement. If there had to be a showdown he preferred to avert it until the woman in question was someone more entertaining than Martie Klinger. And he liked the status quo.

They both liked the status quo. They had hated each other, their house, the dinginess of their existence on Mill Street. When the fire whistle blew it was within the hearing of Mill Street and of Lantenengo Street; rain from the same shower fell on Mill Street and on Lantenengo Street; Mill Street and Lantenengo Street read the same Gibbsville newspaper at the same time every evening. And the items of their proximity only made the nearness worse, the remoteness of Mill Street from Lantenengo more vexatious. But Fair Grounds was a new town, where they had gone knowing literally nobody. They had spending money, a desirable house, the respectability of a white-collar job, and the restored confidence in a superiority to their neighbours that they had not allowed themselves to feel on Mill Street. In the Dan Patch Tavern they would let things slip out that would have been meaningless on Mill Street, where their neighbours' daily concern was a loaf of bread and a bottle of milk. "Pete, did you know Jimmy Stewart, the movie actor?" "No, he was several classes behind me, but he was in my club." "Bobbie, what's it like on one of them yachts?" "I've only been on one, but it was fun while it lasted." They could talk now about past pleasures and luxuries without being contradicted by their surroundings, and their new friends at the Tavern had no knowledge of the decade of dinginess that lay between that past and this present. If their new friends also guessed that Pete McCrea was carrying on with Martie Klinger, that very fact made Bobbie more credibly and genuinely the woman who had once cruised in a yacht. They would have approved Bobbie's reason for not wanting Martie Klinger as a guest at supper, as they would have fiercely resented Pete's reference to Bobbie as the Queen of the Klondike. Unintentionally they were creating a symbol of order that they wanted in their lives as much as Bobbie needed admiration, and if the symbol and the admiration were slightly ersatz, what, in war years, was not?

There was no one among the Tavern friends whom Bobbie desired to make love with. "I'd give a week's pay to get in bed with you, Bobbie," said one of them.

"Fifty-two weeks' pay, did you say?" said Bobbie.

"No dame is worth fifty-two weeks' pay," said the man, a foreman named Dick Hartenstein.

"Oh, I don't know. In fifty-two weeks you make what?"

"A little over nine thousand. Nine gees, about."

"A lot of women can get that, Dick. I've heard of women getting a diamond necklace for just one night, and they cost a lot more than nine thousand dollars."

"Well, I tell you, Bobby, if I ever hit the crap game for nine gees I'd seriously consider it, but not a year's pay that I worked for."

"You're not romantic enough for me. Sorry."

"Supposing I did hit the crap game and put nine gees on the table in front of you? Would you and me go to bed?"

"No."

"No, I guess not. If I asked you a question would you give me a truthful answer? No. You wouldn't."

"Why should I?"

"Yeah, why should you? I was gonna ask you, what does it take to get you in bed with a guy?"

"I'm a married woman."

"I skipped all that part, Bobbie. You'd go, if it was the right guy."

"You could get to be an awful nuisance, Dick. You're not far from it right this minute."

"I apologize."

"In fact, why don't you take your drink and stand at the bar?"

"What are you sore at? You get propositioned all the time."

"Yes, but you're too persistent, and you're a bore. The others don't keep asking questions when I tell them no. Go on, now, or I'll tell Rudy to keep you out of here."

"You know what you are?"

"Rudy! Will you come here, please?" she called. "All right, Dick. What am I? Say it in front of Rudy."

Rudy Schau made his way around from the bar. "What can I do for you, Bobbie?"

"I think Dick is getting ready to call me a nasty name."

"He won't," said Rudy Schau. He had the build of a man who had handled beer kegs all his life and he was now ready to squeeze the wind out of Hartenstein. "Apolochise to Bobbie and get the hell outa my place. And don't forget you got a forty-dollar tab here. You won't get a drink nowheres else in tahn."

"I'll pay my God damn tab," said Hartenstein.

"That you owe me. Bobbie you owe an apolochy."

"I apologize," said Hartenstein. He was immediately clipped behind the ear, and sunk to the floor.

"I never like that son of a bitch," said Rudy Schau. He looked down at the unconscious Hartenstein and very deliberately kicked him in the ribs.

"Oh, *don't*, Rudy," said Bobbie. "*Please* don't."

Others in the bar, which was now half filled, stood waiting for Rudy's next kick, and some of them looked at each other and then at Rudy, and they were ready to rush him. Bobbie stood up quickly. "Don't, Rudy," she said.

"All right. I learned him. Joe, throw the son of a bitch out," said Rudy. Then suddenly he wheeled and grabbed a man by the belt and lifted him off the floor, holding him tight against his body with one hand and making a hammer of his other hand. "You, you son of a bitch, you was gonna go after me, you was, yeah? Well, go ahead. Let's see you, you son of a bitch. You son of a bitch, I break you in pieces." He let go and the man retreated out of range of Rudy's fist. "Pay your bill and don't come back. Don't ever show your face in my place again. And any other son of a bitch was gonna gang me. You gonna gang Rudy, hey? I kill any two of you." Two of the men picked Hartenstein off the floor before the bartender got to him. "Them two, they paid up, Joe?"

"In the clear, Rudy," said the bartender.

"You two. Don't come back," said Rudy.

"Don't worry. We won't," they said.

Rudy stood at Bobbie's table. "Okay if I sit down with you, Bobbie?"

"Of course," said Bobbie.

"Joe, a beer, please, hey? Bobbie, you ready?"

"Not yet, thanks," she said.

Rudy mopped his forehead with a handkerchief. "You don't have to take it from these bums," said Rudy. "Any time any them get fresh, you tell me. You're what keeps this place decent, Bobbie. I know. As soon as you go home it's a pigpen. I get sick of hearing them, some of the women as bad as the men. Draft-dotchers. Essengial industry! Draft-dotchers. A bunch of 4-F draft-dotchers. I like to hear what your Daddy would say about them."

"Did you know him, my father?"

"Know him? I was in his platoon. Second platoon, C Company. I went over with him and come back with him. Phil Hammersmith."

"I never knew that."

Rudy chuckled. "Sure. Some of these 4-F draft-dotchers from outa town, they think I'm a Nazi because I never learn to speak good English, but my Daddy didn't speak no English at all and he was born out in the Walley. My old woman says put my dischartch papers up over the back-bar. I say what for? So's to make the good impression on a bunch of draft-dotchers? Corporal Rudolph W. Schau. Your Daddy was a good man and a good soldier."

"Why didn't you ever tell me you knew him?"

"Oh, I don't know, Bobbie. I wasn't gonna tell you now, but I did. It don't pay to be a talker in my business. A listener, not a talker."

"You didn't approve of me, did you?"

164

"I'm a saloon-keeper. A person comes to my——"

"You didn't approve of me. Don't dodge the issue."

"Well, your Daddy wouldn't of liked you coming to a saloon that often. But times change, and you're better off here than the other joints."

"I hope you don't *mind* my coming here."

"Listen, you come here as much as you want."

"Try and stop me," she said, smiling.

Pete joined them. "What happened to Dick Hartenstein?" he said.

"The same as will happen to anybody gets fresh with your wife," said Rudy, and got up and left them.

"There could be a hell of a stink about this. Rudy could lose his licence if the Company wanted to press the point."

"Well, you just see that he doesn't," said Bobbie.

"Maybe it isn't such a good idea, your coming here so often."

"Maybe. On the other hand, maybe it's a wonderful idea. I happen to think it's a wonderful idea, so I'm going to keep on coming. If *you* want to go to one of the other places, that's all right. But I like Rudy's. I like it better than ever, now."

No action was taken against Rudy Schau, and Bobbie visited the Tavern as frequently as ever. Hartenstein was an unpopular foreman and the women said he got what had been coming to him for a long time. Bobbie's friends were pleased that their new symbol had such a forthright defender. It was even said that Bobbie had saved Hartenstein from a worse beating, a rumour that added to the respect she was given by the men and the women.

The McCrea children were not being brought up according to Lantenengo Street standards. On the three or four afternoons a week that Bobbie went to the Tavern she would take her son and daughter to a neighbour's yard. On the other afternoons the neighbours' children would play in her yard. During bad weather and the worst of the winter the McCreas' house was in more frequent service as a nursery, since some of the neighbours were living in one- or two-room apartments. But none of the children, the McCreas' or the neighbours', had individual supervision. Children who had learned to walk were separated from those who were still crawling, on the proven theory that the crawling children were still defenceless against the whimsical cruelties of the older ones. Otherwise there was no distinction, and all the children were toughened early in life, as most of their parents had been. "I guess it's all right," Pete once said to Bobbie. "But I hate to think what they'll be like when they get older. Little gangsters."

"Well, that was never your trouble, God knows," said Bobbie. "And I'm no shining example of having a nannie take care of me. Do you remember my nannie?"

"Vaguely."

" 'Let's go and see the horsies,' she'd say. And we'd go to Mr. Duncan's stable and I'd come home covered with scratches from the stable cat. And I guess Patrick was covered with scratches from my nannie. Affectionate scratches, of course. Do you remember Mr. Duncan's Patrick?"

"Sure."

"He must have been quite a man. Phyllis used to go there with her nannie, too. But the cat liked Phyllis."

"I'm not suggesting that we have a nannie."

"No. You're suggesting that I stay away from the Tavern."

"In the afternoon."

"The afternoon is the only time the mothers will watch each other's children, except in rare cases. Our kids are all right. I'm with them all day most of the time, and we're home every evening, seven nights a week."

"What else is there to do?"

"Well, for instance once a month we could go to a movie."

"Where? Gibbsville?"

"Yes. Two gallons of gas at the most."

"Are you getting the itch to move back to Gibbsville?"

"Not at all. Are you?"

"Hell, no."

"We could get some high school kid to watch the children. I'd just like to have a change once in a while."

"All right. The next time there's something good at the Globe."

Their first trip to the Globe was their last. They saw no one they knew in the theatre or in the bar of the John Gibb Hotel, and when they came home the high school kid was naked in bed with a man Pete recognized from the plant. "Get out of here," said Pete.

"Is she your kid, McCrea?"

"No, she's not my kid. But did you ever hear of statutory rape?"

"Rape? This kid? I had to wait downstairs, for God's sake. She took on three other guys tonight. Ten bucks a crack."

The girl put on her clothes in sullen silence. She never spoke except to say to the man: "Do you have a room some place?"

"Well," said Pete, when they had gone. "Where did you get her from? The Junior League?"

"If you'd stared at her any more you'd have had to pay ten dollars too."

"For sixteen she had quite a shape."

"She won't have it much longer."

"You got an eyeful, too, don't pretend you didn't."

"Well, at least she won't get pregnant that way. And she *will* get *rich*," said Bobbie.

Pete laughed. "It was really quite funny. Where *did* you get her?"

"If you want her name and telephone number, I have it downstairs. I got her through one of the neighbours. She certainly got the word around quickly enough, where she'd be. There's the doorbell. Another customer?"

Pete went downstairs and informed the stranger at the door that he had the wrong address.

"Another customer, and I think he had two guys with him in the car. Seventy dollars she was going to make tonight. I guess I'm supposed to report this at the plant. We have a sort of a V-D file of known prostitutes. We sic the law on them before they infect the whole outfit, and I'll bet this little character——"

"Good heavens, yes. I must burn everything. Bed linen. Towels. Why that little bitch. Now I'm getting sore." She collected the linen and took it downstairs and to the trash burner in the yard. When she returned Pete was in bed, staring at the ceiling. "I'm going to sleep in the other room," she said.

"What's the matter?"

"I didn't like that tonight. I don't want to sleep with you."

"Oh, all right then, go to hell," said Pete.

She made up one of the beds in the adjoining room. He came and sat on the edge of her bed in the dark. "Go away, Pete," she said.

"Why?"

"Oh, all right, I'll *tell* you why. Tonight made me think of the time you wanted to exchange with Mary and Frank. That's all I've been able to think of."

"That's all passed, Bobbie. I'm not like that any more."

"You would have got in bed with that girl. I saw you."

"Then I'll tell you something. You would have got in bed with that man. I saw you, too. You were excited."

"How could I help being excited, to suddenly come upon something like that. But I was disgusted, too. And still am. Please go away and let me try to get some sleep."

She did not sleep until first light, and when the alarm

clock sounded she prepared his and the children's break-fasts. She was tired and nervous throughout the day. She could not go to the Tavern because it was her turn to watch neighbours' children, and Pete telephoned and said bluntly that he would not be home for supper, offering no excuse. He got home after eleven that night, slightly drunk and with lipstick on his neck.

"Who was it? Martie?" said Bobbie.

"What difference does it make who it was? I've been trying to give up other women, but you're no help."

"I have no patience with that kind of an excuse. It's easy enough to blame me. Remember, Pete, I can pick up a man just as easily as you can make a date with Martie."

"I know you can, and you probably will."

It was the last year of the war, and she had remained faithful to Pete throughout the life of their son Angus. A week later she resumed her affair with Bill Charney. "You never forgot me," he said. "I never forgot you, either, Bobbie. I heard about you and Pete living in Fair Grounds. You know a couple times I took my car and dro' past your house to see which one it was. I didn't know, maybe you'd be sitting out on the front porch and if you saw me, you know. Maybe we just say hello and pass the time of day. But I didn't think no such thing, to tell you the God's honest truth. I got no-thing against my wife, only she makes me weary. The house and the kids, she got me going to Mass every Sunday, all like that. But I ain't built that way, Bobbie. I'm the next thing to a hood, and you got that side of you, too. I'll make you any price you say, the other jerks you slept with, they never saw that side of you. You know, you hear a lot about love, Bobbie, but I guess I came closer to it with you than any other woman I ever knew. I never forgot you any more than you ever forgot me. It's what they call a mutual attraction. Like you know one person has it for another person."

"I know."

"I don't see how we stood it as long as we did. Be honest, now, didn't you often wish it was me instead of some other guy?"

"Yes."

"All right, I'll be honest with you. Many's the time in bed with my wife I used to say to myself, 'Peggy, you oughta take lessons from Bobbie McCrea.' But who can give lessons, huh? If you don't have the mutual attraction, you're nothin'. How do you think I look?" He slapped his belly. "You know I weigh the same as I used to weigh? You look good. You put on a little. What? Maybe six pounds?"

"Seven or eight."

"But you got it distributed. In another year Peggy's gonna weigh a hundred and fifty pounds, and I told her, I said either she took some of that off or I'd get another girl. Her height, you know. She can't get away with that much weight. I eat everything, but I do a lot of walking and standing. I guess I use up a lot of excess energy. Feel them muscles. Punch me in the belly. I got no fat on me anywhere, Bobbie. For my age I'm a perfect physical specimen. I could get any amount of insurance if I got out of The Numbers. But nobody's gonna knock me off so why do I want insurance? I may even give up The Numbers one of these days. I got a couple of things lined up, strictly, strictly legitimate, and when my kids are ready to go away to school, I may just give up The Numbers. For a price, naturally."

"That brings up a point."

"You need money? How much do you want? It's yours. I *mean* like ten, fifteen gees."

"No, no money. But everybody knows you now. Where can we meet?"

"What's the matter with here? I told you, I own this hotel."

"But I can't just come and go. People know me, too. I have an idea, though."

"What?"

"Buy a motel."

"Buy a motel. You know, that thought crossed me a year ago, but you know what I found out? They don't make money. You'd think they would, but those that come out ahead, you be surprised how little they make."

"There's one near Swedish Haven. It's only about a mile from my house."

"We want a big bed, not them twin beds. I tell you what I could do. I could rent one of the units by the month and move my own furniture in. How would that suit you?"

"I'd like it better if you owned the place."

"Blackmail? Is that what you're thinking about? Who'd blackmail me, Bobbie? Or my girl? I'm still a hood in the eyes of some people."

There was no set arrangement for their meetings. Bill Charney postponed the purchase of the motel until she understood he had no intention of buying it or of making any other arrangement that implied permanence. At first she resented his procrastination, but she discovered that she preferred his way; he would telephone her, she would telephone him whenever desire became urgent, and sometimes they would be together within an hour of the telephone call. They spaced out their meetings so that each one produced novelty and excitement, and a year passed and another and Bobbie passed the afternoon of her fortieth birthday with him.

It was characteristic of their relationship that she did not tell him it was her birthday. He always spoke of his wife and children and his business enterprises, but he did not notice that she never spoke of her home life. He was a completely egocentric man, equally admiring of his star sapphire ring on his strong short-fingered hand and of her slender waist, which in his egocentricity became his possession. Inevitably, because of the nature of his businesses, he had a reputation for being close-mouthed, but alone with Bobbie he talked freely. "You know, Bobbie, I laid a friend of yours?"

"Was it fun?"

"Aren't you gonna ask me who?"

"You'll tell me."

"At least I guess she's a friend of yours. Mary Lander."

"She used to be a friend of mine. I haven't seen her in years."

173

"Yeah. While her husband was in the service. Frank."

"You're so busy, with all your women."

"There's seven days in the week, honey, and it don't take up too much of your time. This didn't last very long, anyway. Five, maybe six times I slept with her. I took her to New York twice, that is I met her there. The other times in her house. You know, she's a neighbour of mine."

"And very neighbourly."

"Yeah, that's how it started. She come to my house to collect for something, some war drive, and Peggy said I took care of all them things so when I got home I made out a cheque and took it over to the Landers' and inside of fifteen minutes—less than that—we were necking all over the parlour. Hell, I knew the minute she opened the door——"

"One of those mutual attractions?"

"Yeah, sure. I gave her the cheque and she said, 'I don't know how to thank you,' and I said if she had a couple minutes I'd show her how. 'Oh, Mr. Charney,' but she didn't tell me to get out, so I knew I was in."

"What ever broke up this romance?"

"Her. She had some guy in Washington, D.C., she was thinking of marrying, and when I finally got it out of her who the guy was, I powdered out. Joe Whipple. I gotta do business with Joe. We got a home-loan proposition that we're ready to go with any day, and this was three years ago when Joe and I were just talking about it, what they call the talking stage."

"So you're the one that broke it off, not Mary."

"If a guy's looking at you across a desk and thinking

you're laying his girl, you stand to get a screwing from that guy. Not that I don't trust Joe, because I do."

"Do you trust Mary?"

"I wondered about that, if she'd blab to Joe. A dame like Mary Lander, is she gonna tell the guy she's thinking of marrying that she's been laying a hood like me? No. By the way, she's queer. She told me she'd go for a girl."

"I'm surprised she hasn't already."

"Maybe she has. I couldn't find out. I always try to find out."

"You never asked me."

"I knew you wouldn't. But a dame like Mary, as soon as she opened the door I knew I was in, but then the next thing is you find out what else she'll go for. In her case, the works, as long as it isn't gonna get around. I guess I always figured her right. I have to figure all angles, men *and* women. That's where my brother Ed was stupid. I used to say to him, find out what kind of a broad a guy goes for before you declare him in. Ed used to say all he had to do was play a game of cards with a guy. But according to my theory, everybody goes into a card game prepared. Both eyes open. But not a guy going after a broad. You find out more from broads, like take for instance Mary. Now I know Frank is married to a dame that is screwing his best friend, laid a hood like me, and will go for a girl. You think I'd ever depend on Frank Lander? No. And Joe Whipple. Married to a lush, and sleeping with his best friend's wife, Mary."

"Then you wouldn't depend on Joe, either?"

"Yes, I would. Women don't bother him. He don't care if his wife is a lush, he'll get his nooky from his best friend's wife, he *isn't* going to marry her because that was three-four years ago, and he's tough about everybody. His wife, his dame, his best friend, *and* the United States government. Because I tell you something, if we ever get going on the home-loan proposition, don't think Joe didn't use his job in Washington every chance he got. The partnership is gonna be me and Joe Whipple, because he's just as tough as I am. And one fine day he'll fall over dead from not taking care of himself, and I'll be the main guy. You know the only thing I don't like about you, Bobbie, is the booze. If you'd lay off the sauce for a year I'd get rid of Peggy, and you and I could get married. But booze is women's weakness like women are men's weakness."

"Men are women's weakness."

"No, you're wrong. Men don't make women talk, men don't make women lose their looks, and women can give up men for a hell of a long time, but a female lush is the worst kind of a lush."

"Am I a lush?"

"You have a couple drinks every day, don't you?"

"Yes."

"Then you're on the way. Maybe you only take three-four drinks a day now, but five years from now three or four drinks will get you stewed, so you'll be stewed every day. That's a lush. Peggy eats like a God damn pig, but if she ever started drinking, I'd kick her out. Fortunately her old man died with the D.T.'s, so she's afraid of it."

"Would you mind getting me a nice double Scotch with a little water?"

"Why should I mind?" He grinned from back molar to back molar. "When you got a little load on, you forget home and mother." He got her the drink, she took it in her right hand and slowly poured it down his furry chest. He jumped when the icy drink touched him.

"Thank you so much," she said. "Been a very pleasant afternoon, but the party's over."

"You sore at me?"

"Yes, I am. I don't like being called a lush, and I certainly don't like you to think I'd make a good substitute for Peggy."

"You *are* sore."

"Yes."

The children did not know it was her birthday, but when Pete came home he handed her two parcels. "For me?" she said.

"Not very much imagination, but I didn't have a chance to go to Gibbsville," he said.

One package contained half a dozen nylons, the other a bottle of Chanel Number 5. "Thank you. Just what I wanted. I really did."

He suddenly began to cry, and rushed out of the room.

"Why is Daddy crying?" said their daughter.

"Because it's my birthday and he did a very sweet thing."

"Why should he cry?" said their son. He was nine years old, the daughter eleven.

"Because he's sentimental," said the daughter.

177

"And it's a very nice thing to be," said Bobbie.

"Aren't you going to go to him?"

"Not quite yet. In a minute. Angus, will you go down to the drug store and get a quart of ice cream? Here's a dollar, and you and your sister may keep the change, divided."

"What flavour?" said the boy.

"Vanilla and strawberry, or whatever else they have."

Pete returned. "Kids gone to bed?"

"I sent them for some ice cream."

"Did they see me bawling?"

"Yes, and I think it did them good. Marjorie understood it. Angus was a little mystified. But it was good for both of them."

"Marjorie understood it? Did you?"

"She said it was because you were sentimental."

He shook his head. "I don't know if you'd call it sentimental. I just couldn't help thinking you were forty years old. Forty. You forty. Bobbie Hammersmith. And all we've been through, and what I've done to you. I know why you married me, Bobbie, but why did you stick it out?"

"Because I married you."

"Yes. Because you married Ichabod. You know, I wasn't in love with you when we were first married. You thought I was, but I wasn't. It was wonderful, being in bed with you and watching you walking around without any clothes on. Taking a bath. But it was too much for me and that's what started me making passes at everybody. And underneath it all I knew damn well why you married me and I hated you. You were making a fool of me and I kept waiting for you to say this farce was over. If you had, I'd have killed you."

"And I guess rightly."

"And all the later stuff. Running a poolroom and living on Mill Street. I blamed all of that on you. But things are better now since we moved here. Aren't they?"

"Yes, much better, as far as the way we live——"

"That's all I meant. If we didn't have Lantenengo Street and Princeton and those things to look back on, this wouldn't be a bad life for two ordinary people."

"It's not bad," she said.

"It's still pretty bad, but that's because we once had it better. Here's what I want to say. Any time you want to walk out on me, I won't make any fuss. You can have the children, and I won't fight about it. That's my birthday present to you, before it's too late. And I have no plans for myself. I'm not trying to get out of this marriage, but you're forty now and you're entitled to whatever is left."

"Thank you, Pete. I have nobody that wants to marry me."

"Well, maybe not. But you may have, sometime. I love you now, Bobbie, and I never used to. I guess you can't love anybody else while you have no self-respect. When the war was over I was sure I'd get the bounce at the plant, but they like me there, they've kept me on, and that one promotion. We'll never be back on Lantenengo Street, but I think I can count on a job here maybe the rest of my life. In a couple of years we can move to a nicer house."

"I'd rather buy this and fix it up a little. It's a better-built house than the ones they're putting up over on Fair Grounds Heights."

"Well, I'm glad you like it too," he said. "The other thing, that we hardly ever talk about. In fact never talk about. Only fight about sometimes. I'll try, Bobbie. I've been trying."

"I know you have."

"Well—how about you trying, too?"

"I did."

"But not lately. I'm not going to ask you who or when or any of that, but why is it you're faithful to me while I'm chasing after other women, and then when I'm faithful to you, you have somebody else? You're forty now and I'm forty-four. Let's see how long we can go without cheating?"

"You don't mean put a time limit on it, or put up a trophy, like an endurance contest? That's the way it sounds. We both have bad habits, Pete."

"Yes, and I'm the worst. But break it off, Bobbie, whoever it is. Will you please? If it's somebody you're not going to marry, and that's what you said, I've—well, it's a long time since I've cheated, and I like it much better this way. Will you stop seeing this other guy?"

"All right. As a matter of fact I *have* stopped, but don't ask me how long ago."

"I won't ask you anything. And if you fall in love with somebody and want to marry him——"

"And he wants to marry me."

"And he wants to marry you, I'll bow out." He

leaned down and kissed her cheek. "I know you better than you think I do, Bobbie."

"That's an irritating statement to make to any woman."

"I guess it is, but not the way I meant it."

Now that is as far as I need go in the story of Pete and Bobbie McCrea. I promised a happy ending, which I shall come to in a moment. We have left Pete and Bobbie in 1947, on Bobbie's fortieth birthday. During the next thirteen years I saw them twice. On one occasion my wife and I spent the night with them in their house in Fair Grounds, which was painted, scrubbed, and dusted like the Fair Grounds houses of old. My wife went to bed early, and Pete and Bobbie and I talked until past midnight, and then Pete retired and Bobbie and I continued our conversation until three in the morning. Twice she emptied our ash trays of cigarette butts, and we drank a drip-flask of coffee. It seemed to me that she was so thorough in her description of their life because she felt that the dinginess would vanish if she once succeeded in exposing it. But as we were leaving in the morning I was not so sure that it had vanished. My wife said to me: "Did she get it all out of her system?"

"Get what out of her system?"

"I don't know, but I don't think she did, entirely."

"That would be asking too much," I said. "But I guess she's happy."

"Content, but not happy," said my wife. "But the children are what interested me. The girl is going to be attractive in a few more years, but that boy! You didn't talk to him, but do you know about him? He's four-teen, and he's already passed his senior mathematics. He's *finished* the work that the high school seniors are supposed to be taking. The principal is trying to arrange correspondence courses for him. He's the brightest student they ever had in Fair Grounds High School, ever, and all the scientific men at the aluminium plant know about him. And he's a good-looking boy, too."

"Bobbie didn't tell me any of this."

"And I'll bet I know why. He's their future. With you she wanted to get rid of the past. She adores this boy, adores him. That part's almost terrifying."

"Not to me," I said. "It's the best thing that could have happened to her, and to Pete. The only thing that's terrifying is that they could have ruined it. And believe me, they could have."

In 1960, then, I saw Pete and Bobbie again. They invited me, of all their old friends, to go with them to the Princeton commencement. Angus McCrea, Junior, led his class, was awarded the mathematics prize, the physics prize, the Eubank Prize for scholarship, and some other honours that I am sure are listed in the programme. I could not read the programme because I was crying most of the time. Pete would lean forward in his chair, listen-ing to the things that were being said about his son, but in an attitude that would have been more suitable to a man who was listening to a pronouncement of sentence. Bobbie sat erect and smiling, but every once in a while I could hear her whisper, "Oh, God. Oh, God."

There, I guess, is our happy ending.

WE'RE FRIENDS AGAIN

I KNOW of no quiet quite like that of a men's club at about half past nine on a summer Sunday evening. The stillness is a denial of the meaning and purpose of a club, and as you go from empty room to empty room and hear nothing but the ticking of clocks and your own heel taps on the rugless floor, you think of the membership present and past; the charming, dull, distinguished, vulgar, jolly, bibulous men who have selected this place and its company as a refuge from all other places and all other company. For that is what a club is, and to be alone in it is wrong. And at half past nine on a summer Sunday evening you are quite likely to be alone. The old men who live there have retired for the night, sure that if they die before morning they will be discovered by a chambermaid, and that if they survive this night they will have another day in which their loneliness will be broken by the lunch crowd, the cocktail crowd, and the presence of a few men in the dining-room in the evening. But on a summer Sunday evening the old men are better off in their rooms, with their personal possessions, their framed photographs and trophies of accomplishment and favourite books. The lounge, the library, the billiard and card rooms have a deathly emptiness on summer Sunday evenings, and the old men need no additional reminder of emptiness or death.

It is always dark in my club at half past nine in the evening, and darker than ever on Sunday in summer, when only the fewest possible lights are left burning. If you go to the bar the bartender slowly folds his newspaper, which he has been reading by the light from the back-bar, takes off his glasses, says "Good evening," and unconsciously looks up at the clock to see how much longer he must stay. Downstairs another club servant is sitting at the telephone switchboard. There is the spitting buzz of an incoming call and he says, "'Devening, St. James Club? . . . No sir, he isn't . . . No sir, no message for you . . . Mr. Crankshaw went to bed about an hour ago. Orders not to disturb him, sir . . . You're welcome. Goodnight." The switchboard buzzes, the loudest, the only noise in the club, until the man pulls out the plug and the weight pulls the cord back into place, and then it is quiet again.

I had been a member of the St. James for about ten years, but I could not recall ever having been there on a Sunday until this night a year or so ago. I was summoned on the golf course by an urgent message to call the New York operator, which I did immediately. "Jim, I'm sorry to louse up your golf, but can you get a train in to New York? I don't advise driving. The traffic is terrible."

"There's a train that will get me to Penn Station about eight-thirty," I said. "But what's this all about?"

The man I was speaking to was Charles Ellis, one of my best friends.

"Charley? What's it all *about*?" I repeated.

"Nancy died this afternoon. She had a stroke after lunch."

"Oh, no. Charley, I can't tell you——"

"I know, and thanks. Are you still a member at the St. James?"

"Yes, why?"

"Will you meet me there? I'll tell you why when I see you."

"Of course. What time will you get there?"

"As soon after eight-thirty as I can."

For a little while the stillness of the club was a relief from the noise and unpleasantness of the train, which was filled with men and women and children who had presumably been enjoying themselves under the Long Island sun but were now beginning to suffer from it, and if not from the damage to their skin, from the debilitating effects of too much picnic food and canned beer. At Jamaica there was an angry scramble as we changed trains, and all the way from Jamaica to Penn Station five men fought over some fishing tackle on the car platform while three young men with thick thatches and blue jeans tormented two pansies in imitation Italian silk suits.

The bartender gave me some cold cuts and bread and cheese and made me some instant coffee. "How late do you work, Fred?" I said.

"Sundays I'm off at ten," he said, looking at the clock for the fifth or sixth time. "Don't seem worth the while, does it?"

"I'm expecting a friend, he's not a member."

"Then if I was you I'd make sure Roland knows about

it. He's just as liable to fall asleep. You know, asleep at the switchboard? You heard the old saying, asleep at the switch. That fellow can go to sleep with his eyes open."

"I've already spoken to him," I said. I wandered about in the lounge and the library, not to be out of earshot when Charley Ellis arrived. As all the clocks in the club struck ten Fred came to me, dressed for the street, and said: "Can I get you anything before I go?"

"Can you let me have a bottle of Scotch?"

"I can do that, and a bowl of ice. You want soda, Mr. Malloy?"

"Just the Scotch and the ice, thanks."

"About the only place you can drink it is in your room, if you want water with it. I have to close up the bar."

"It's all right if we sit here, isn't it?"

"Jesus, if you *want* to," said Fred.

At that moment Charles Ellis arrived, escorted by Roland.

"Oh, it's Mr. Ellis," said Fred. "Remember me? Fred, from the Racquet Club?"

"Yes, hello, Fred. Is this where you are now?"

"Six and a half years," said Fred.

"Thanks very much, Fred," I said. "Goodnight."

"I'll bring you the bottle," said Fred.

"I don't want a drink, if that's what you mean," said Charles Ellis. "Unless *you've* fallen off the wagon."

"Then never mind, thanks, Fred. Goodnight."

Fred left, and I switched on some lights in the lounge.

"You saddled with that bore?" said Charley.

"I don't see much of him," I said.

"I'm sorry I'm so late. I got here as soon as I could. I called this number but it didn't answer."

"That's all right. I guess Roland had the buzzer turned off."

"Hell of an imposition, taking you away from golf and so forth. How is Kay?"

"Very distressed, naturally. She said to give you her love."

"I almost asked her to come in with you."

"She almost came," I said. "But she has her grand-children coming tomorrow."

He was silent, obviously wondering where to begin.

"Take your time," I said.

He looked up at me and smiled. "Thanks." He reached over and patted my knee. "Thanks for every-thing, Jim."

"Well, what the hell?"

"First, why did I want to see you here? Because I didn't want to ask you to come to the apartment, and I didn't want to go to the Racquet Club."

"I figured something like that."

"How did it happen, and all that? Nancy and I were spending the week-end at her uncle's. We went out to dinner last night, and when we came home she said she had a headache, so I gave her some aspirin. This morn-ing she still had the headache and I asked her if she wanted me to send for a doctor, but she didn't. She said she hadn't slept very well, and I probably should have called the doctor, but I didn't. Then there were four guests for lunch and I didn't have a chance to speak to her. In fact the last thing I said to her was before lunch, I told her that if she didn't feel better after lunch, she should make her excuses and lie down. And that's what she did. She excused herself, shook her head to me not to follow her, and about twenty minutes later the maid came and told us she was dead. Found her lying on the bathroom floor. I can't believe it. I can't be devoid of feeling, but I just can't believe it."

"Did the doctor give you anything?"

"You mean sedative? Tranquillizers? No, I haven't needed anything. I guess I must be in some sort of shock."

"Where are the children?"

"Well, of course Mike is in Germany, still in the Army. And I finally located Janey about an hour ago, at a house in Surrey where she's spending the week-end. She's been abroad all summer. She's flying home to-morrow and Mike has applied for leave. The Army or the Red Cross or somebody will fly him home in time for the funeral." He paused.

"Wednesday morning at eleven o'clock. Church of the Epiphany, on York Avenue. I decided Wednesday so that Mike could be here, in case there's any hitch." He looked about him. "You couldn't ask for a gloomier place than this, could you?"

"No, it's certainly appropriate."

"Well, what do I do now, Jim? You've been through it."

"Yes, I've been through it. The answer is, you're going to be so damn busy with details the next few weeks that you won't have too much time to know what hit you. You're going to find out how really nice people can be. Maybe you haven't thought about that lately, but you're going to find out. You're also going to find out that some people are shits. Real shits. I'll give you the two worst. The old friend that won't make any effort at all except maybe to send you a telegram, if that. You'll be shocked by that, so you ought to be prepared for it. I mean very close friends, guys and women you grew up with that just won't come near you. Then there's the second type, just as bad. He'll write you a letter in a week or two, and it'll be all about himself. How sad *he* is, how well he knew Nancy, how much he appreciated her, and rather strongly implying that *you* didn't know her true worth as well as he did. You'll read one of those letters and reread it, and if you do what I did, you'll throw it in the wastebasket. But the next time you see the son of a bitch, he'll say, 'Hey, Ellis, I wrote you a letter. Didn't you ever get it?' So be prepared for those two. But against them, the nice people. The *kind* people, Charley, sometimes where you'd least expect it. A guy that I thought was about as cold a fish as there is in the world, he turned out to have more real heart than almost anybody. In my book he can never do another wrong thing. The third group I haven't mentioned. The lushes. But they're obvious and you can either put up with them or brush them off. The only advice I can give you—keep busy. Don't take any more time off from your work than you absolutely have to."

"And when will it really hit me?"

"I don't know when, but I know how. Suddenly,

and for no apparent reason. When your guard is down. You'll be in the subway, or walking along the street, not any favourite street full of memories, but any anonymous street. Or in a cab. And the whole God damn thing will come down on you and you'll be weeping before you know it. That's where nobody can help you, because it's unpredictable and you'll be alone. It'll only happen when you're relaxed and defenceless. But you're not relaxed, really. It's just that you're weak, *been* weakened without realizing what it's taken out of you. Emotional exhaustion, I guess it is. Then there are two other things, but I won't talk about them now. They may not happen to you, and I've told you enough."

"Thanks, Jim."

"Charley, you know what let's do? Let's go for a walk. We won't run into anybody."

"Yes. Nothing against your club, but I think I've had it here."

So the two of us went for a not too brisk walk, down Fifth Avenue, up Fifth Avenue, and to the door of Charley's apartment house. The doorman saluted him and said: "Sorry fur yur trouble, Mr. Ellis. A foine lovely woman, none foiner."

I happened, and only happened, to be looking at Charley as the doorman spoke. He nodded at the doorman but did not speak. I took his arm and led him to the elevator. "Mr. Ellis's apartment," I said, and frowned the elevator man into silence. He understood.

We got off at Charley's floor, the only apartment on that floor, and he went to the living-room and sat down and wept without covering his face. I stayed in the foyer. Five minutes passed and then he said: "Okay, Jim. I'm okay now. What can I give you? Ginger ale? Coke? Glass of milk?"

"A ginger ale."

"It hit me sooner than we expected," he said. "Do you know what it was? Or what I think it was? It was the doorman saying nice things, and he didn't really know her at all. He's only been here a few weeks. He doesn't know either of us very well. Why don't you stay here tonight, instead of going back to that God damn dreary place?"

"I will if you'll go to bed. And don't worry, you'll sleep."

"Will I?"

"Yes, you'll sleep tonight. Twenty blocks to a mile, we walked damn near four miles, I make it. Take a lukewarm tub and hit the sack. I'll read for a while and I'll be in Mike's room. Goodnight, Charley."

"Goodnight, Jim. Thanks again."

One afternoon in 1937 I was having breakfast in my apartment in East Fifty-fifth Street. I had worked the night before until dawn, as was my custom, and I was smoking my third cigarette and starting on my second quart of coffee when the house phone rang. Charley Ellis was in the vestibule. I let him in and he shook his head at me in my pyjamas, unshaven, and with the coffee and newspapers beside my chair. "La Vie de Boheme," he said.

"That's right," I said. "Come on out, Mimi, and stop that damn coughing."

Charley looked at me with genuine alarm. "You haven't got a dame here, have you? I'm sorry if——"

"No dame."

"I don't want to interrupt anything."

"I wouldn't have let you in," I said. "But I've just been reading about you, so maybe I would have. Curiosity. Who is Nancy Preswell?"

"Oh, you saw that, did you? Well, she's the wife of a guy named Jack Preswell."

"All right, who is *Jack* Preswell?" I said. "Besides being the husband of a girl named Nancy Preswell."

"Well, you've met him. With me. Do you remember a guy that we went to the ball game with a couple of years ago?"

"I do indeed. I remember everything about him but his name. A very handsome guy, a little on the short side. Boyish-looking. And now I know who she is because I've seen them together, but I never could remember his name. Not that it mattered. He didn't remember me at all, but she's quite a beauty. Not *quite* a beauty. She *is* a beauty. And you're the home-wrecker."

"According to Maury Paul I am, if you believe what he writes."

"He's often right, you know," I said. "He had me in his column one time with a woman I'd never met, but I met her a year or so later and he turned out to be a very good prophet. So it's only your word against his."

"I didn't come here to be insulted," he said, taking a chair.

"Well, what did you come here for? I haven't seen or

heard from you in God knows how long." It always took a little while for Charley Ellis to get started on personal matters, and if I didn't talk a lot or kid him, he would sometimes go away without saying what he had intended to say. "Now I understand *why*, of course, but I gather Mrs. Preswell hasn't even gone to Reno yet."

"If you'll lay off this heavy-handed joshing, I guess you'd call it, I'd like to talk seriously for a minute."

"All right. Have a cup of coffee, or do you want a drink? If you want a drink, you know where it is."

"I don't want anything but your respectful attention and maybe some sound advice. What I really want is someone to talk to, to talk things out with."

Charley Ellis was about thirty-three years old then, and not a young thirty-three. He had stayed single because he had been in love with his first cousin, a lovely girl who was the wife of Junior Williamson, Ethridge B. Williamson, Junior; he had wanted to write, and instead had gone to work for his father's firm, Willetts & Ellis. His father knew about the second frustration, but I was now more convinced than ever that I was the only person to whom Charley had confided both.

"You may be right, you know," he said. "I probably am the home-wrecker. At least a good case could be made out against me. Nancy and Jack never have got along very well, and made no secret of the fact. But I guess I'm the first one that shall we say took advantage of the situation. They had a couple of trial separations but they always went back together until I happened to come into the picture during the last one."

"But you're not blaming yourself or anything like that, I hope."

"Not one bit. That's a form of boasting, or so it always seemed to me."

"And to me, too. That's why I'm glad you're not doing the *mea culpa* act."

"Oh, hell no. I didn't create the situation," he said.

"Do you know who did?"

"Yes, I do," said Charley. "Franklin D. Roosevelt, your great pal."

"Yeah. The inventor of bubonic plague and the common cold, and now the louser-up of the Preswell marriage. You've been spending too much time at Willetts & Ellis. You ought to come up for air."

"You were bound to say something like that, but it happens to be a fact. Preswell was one of the bright young boys that went to Washington five years ago, and that didn't sit too well with Nancy or her family. Then two years ago Preswell himself saw the light and got out, but he'd made a lot of enemies while he was defending Roosevelt, and he came back to New York hating everybody. He said to me one time, 'They call me a traitor to my class, like the Glamour Boy himself, but my class has been a traitor to me.' He used to go around telling everybody that they ought to be grateful to him, that he and Roosevelt were holding the line for the American system. But then when he quit, he was just as violent against Roosevelt as anybody, but nobody would listen. He'd been so God damn arrogant when he was *with* Roosevelt, said a lot of personal things, so nobody cared whose side he was on. And of course he began to take it out on Nancy."

"What does this gentleman do for a living?"

"He *was* with Carson, Cass & Devereux, but they don't want him back. That's just the point. Nobody wants him."

"Was he a good lawyer?"

"Well, *Harvard Law Review*, assistant editor, I think. I don't really know how good a lawyer he was. With a firm like Carson, Cass, you don't get any of the big stuff till you've been there quite a while. He has nothing to worry about financially. His father left him very well fixed and Nancy has money of her own. Her father was, or *is*, Alexander McMinnies, Delaware Zinc."

"Oh, that old crook."

"Why do you say that? You don't know whether he's a crook or a philanthropist."

"He could be both, but even if he is your girl's father, Charley, you know damn well what he is. I'll bet the boys at Carson, Cass have sat up many a night trying to keep him out of prison."

"And succeeded, in spite of Roosevelt and Homer S. Cummings."

"Those things take time," I said.

"Get your facts right. Mr. McMinnies won in the Supreme Court. Unless you were looking forward to the day when Franklin D. decides to abolish the courts and all the rest of that stuff. Which is coming, I have very little doubt."

"You don't really think that, but you have proved

beyond a doubt that Roosevelt loused up Preswell's marriage. Aren't you grateful?"

"You're a tricky bastard."

"It's so easy with you guys. You have a monomania about Roosevelt."

"Monophobia."

"No, wise guy. Monophobia means fear of being alone. So much for you and your four years at the Porcellian."

"I could correct you on that four years, but I hate to spoil your good time."

"All right, we're even," I said. "What's on your mind, Charley?"

"Yes, we can't even have a casual conversation without getting into politics," he said. "Can we forget about politics?"

"Sure, I like to rib you, but what's on your mind? Nancy Preswell, obviously."

He was smoking a cigarette, and rubbing the ashes from the glowing end into the ash tray as they formed, turning the cigarette in his fingers. And not looking at *me*. "Jim, I read a short story of yours a few months ago. Nancy read it, too. She liked it, and she said she'd like to meet you. It was that story about two people at a skiing place."

"Oh, yes. 'Telemark.' "

"That's the one," he said. "They agree to get married even though they weren't in love. Was that based on your own experience—if you don't mind my asking?"

"No. I was in love when I got married, we both

were. But it didn't last. No, that story was invention on my part. Well, not all invention. What is? When I was in Florida two years ago I saw this couple always together and always talking so earnestly, so seriously, and I began to wonder what they were talking about. So I thought about them, forgot them, and remembered them again and changed the locale to a skiing place, and that was the story."

"Nancy liked the story, but she didn't agree with you. You seemed to imply that they *should* have gotten married."

"Yes, I believe that, and they did."

"That's what Nancy didn't agree with. She said they were both willing to face the fact that they weren't in love, but where they were dishonest was in thinking they could make a go of it without being in love."

"I didn't imply that they'd make a go of it," I said. "But it seemed to me they had a chance. Which is as much as any two people have."

"I didn't get that, and neither did Nancy. We both thought you were practically saying that this was as good a start as two people could have."

"So far, so good, but that's *all* I implied."

"Do you think they *really* had a chance? Nancy says no. That marriage hasn't any chance without love, and not too much of a chance with it."

"Well, what do you think? How do you feel about it?"

"I wasn't ready for that question."

"I know damn well you weren't, Charley, and that's what's eating you. It may also be what's eating Nancy.

Does she know you were in love with Polly Williamson?"

"Never. You're the only one that knows that. But here I am, thirty-three, Jim. Why can't I get rid of something that never *was* anything?"

"Go to Polly and tell her that you've always been in love with her, and can't be in love with anyone else."

"I'm afraid to," he said, and smiled. "Maybe I'm afraid she'll say she feels the same way, and divorce Junior."

"Well, that's not true. She doesn't feel the same way, or you'd have found out before this. But if you admit to yourself that you're afraid, then I think you don't really love Polly as much as you think you do, or like to think you do. I was in love with Polly for one afternoon, and I told her so. I meant it, every word of it. But every now and then I see her with Williamson and I thank God she had some sense. A girl with less sense might conceivably have divorced Williamson and married me, and how long would that have lasted? Polly is Williamson's wife, prick though he may be. And if she wants Williamson, she certainly doesn't want me, and probably not you. Has Polly ever stepped out on her own?"

"I think she did, with a guy from Boston. An older guy. I don't think you'd even know his name. A widower, about forty-five. Not a playboy type at all. Very serious-minded. Just right for Polly. You know, Polly has her limitations when it comes to a sense of humour, the lighter side. She was born here, but her father and mother both came from Boston and she's always been more of a Boston type than New York.

200

Flowers and music and the children. But she does her own work in the garden, and she often goes to concerts by herself. What I'm saying is, no *chi-chi*. She's a good athlete, but there again it isn't what you might call public sport. The contest is always between her and the game itself, and the things she's best at are games like golf or trap-shooting. Skiing. Figure-skating. Polly damn near doesn't need anyone else to enjoy herself. And God knows she never needed me." He paused. "Did you ever hear her play the piano?"

"No."

"She's good. You know, Chopin. Rachmaninoff. Tschaikovsky."

"Charley, I just discovered something about you," I said.

"What?"

"*You're* a Bostonian."

"Maybe."

"The admiring way you talk about Polly, and of course you're a first cousin. Isn't it practically a tradition in Boston that you fall in love with your first cousin?"

"It's been known to happen, but I assure you, it had nothing to do with my falling in love with Polly."

"Do you mind if I take issue with you on that point? I have a theory that it had a *lot* to do with your falling in love with Polly, and that your present love affair, with Nancy, is your New York side."

He laughed. "Oh, God. How facile, and how stupid . . . I take back stupid, but you're wrong."

"Why am I wrong? You haven't given the theory

any thought. And I have, while listening to you. You'd better give it some thought, and decide whether you want to be a New Yorker or a Bostonian."

"Or you might be wrong and I won't have to make the choice."

"Yes, but don't reject my theory out of hand. You're a loner. You wanted to be a writer. You're conventional, as witness working in the family firm against your will, but doing very well I understand. And you were talking about yourself as much as you were about Polly."

"Not at all. I was a great team-sport guy. Football in school, and rowing in college."

"Rowing. The obvious joke. Did you ever meet that Saltonstall fellow that rowed Number 5?"

"I know the joke, and it was never very funny to us. A Yale joke. Or more likely Princeton." He seemed to ignore me for a moment. He sat staring at his outstretched foot, his elbow on the arm of his chair, his cheek resting on the two first fingers of his left hand while the other two fingers were curled under the palm. "And yet, you may have a point," he said, judicially. "You just may have a point. Dr. Jekyll and Mr. Hyde. Larry Lowell and Jimmy Walker. Waldo Emerson and Walter Winchell. This conversation may be the turning point of my whole life, and I'll owe it all to you, you analytical son of a bitch."

"That's the thanks I get. Watery compliments."

He rose. "Gotta go." he said.

"How come you're uptown at this hour?"

"I took the afternoon off," he said. "I have a perfectly

legitimate reason for being uptown, but I know your nasty mind.   Will you be in town next week? How about dinner Tuesday?"

"Tuesday, no. Wednesday, yes."

"All right, Wednesday. Shall we pick you up here? I'd like Nancy to see the squalor you live in."

"Others have found it to have a certain Old World charm," I said. "All right, Mimi. You can come out now."

"Listen, don't have any Mimi here Wednesday, will you, please?"

"That's why I said Wednesday instead of Tuesday."

"Degrading. And not even very instructive," he said.

"Not if you don't want to learn."

My apartment was actually a comfortable, fairly expensively furnished two rooms and bath, which was cleaned daily by a coloured woman who worked full-time elsewhere in the building. But Charley Ellis's first remark when he arrived with Nancy Preswell was: "Why, look, he's had the place all spruced up. Is all this new?"

"All goes back to Sloane's in the morning," I said. "How do you do, Mrs. Preswell?"

"Wait a minute. You haven't been introduced," said Charley. "You could have put me in a hell of a spot. What if this hadn't been Mrs. Preswell?" He was in high good humour, determined to make this a pleasant evening.

"I often wish I weren't," she said, without bitterness, but as her first words to me they were an indication that she knew Charley confided in me. "By the way, how do you do?"

"I've often seen you. Well, pretty often," I said.

"And always pretty," said Charley.

I looked at him and then at her: "You've done wonders with this guy. I hardly recognize the old clod." My remark pleased her, and she smiled affectionately at Charley. "Gallantry, yet," I said.

"It was always there," said Charley. "It just took the right person to bring it out."

"I like your apartment, Mr. Malloy. Is this where you do all your writing?"

"Most of it. Practically all of it."

"Oh, you type your stories?" she said, looking at my typewriter. "But don't you write them in longhand first?"

"No. I don't even write letters in longhand."

"Love letters?"

"I type them," I said.

"And mimeographs them," said Charley. "Shall we have a free drink here, saving me two and a quarter?"

"The market closed firm, but have you ever noticed that Charley hates to part with a buck?"

"No, that's not fair," said Nancy Preswell.

"Or true. What's the name of that friend of yours, that writes the Broadway stories?"

"Mark Hellinger?"

"Hellinger. Right. I thought he was going to have a stroke that night when I paid a bill at '21'."

"I very nearly had one myself."

"No, now that isn't fair," said Nancy Preswell.

"I'm softening him up for later," I said.

We had some drinks and conversation, during which Nancy slowly walked around, looking at my book-shelves and pictures. "I gather you don't like anything very modern," she said.

"Not in this room. Some abstract paintings in the bathroom."

"May I see your bedroom?"

"Believe me, that's the best offer he's had today," said Charley.

"A four-poster," she said.

"Early Wanamaker," I said. "*Circa* 1930."

"All you need is a rag rug and a cat curled up on it. I like it. That's not your father, is it?"

"My grandfather. Practically everything in this room is a copy of stuff I remember from when I was a kid. I depended entirely on their taste."

"But you bought it all yourself, so it's your taste, too," said Nancy Preswell. "Very interesting, and very revealing, considering what some of the critics say about your writings."

"What does it reveal to you?" I said.

"That basically you're very conventional."

"I could have told you that," I said.

"Yes, but I probably wouldn't have believed you if I hadn't seen your apartment."

"I think I ought to tell you, though. I went through an all-modernistic phase when I lived in the Village."

"Why are you for Roosevelt?" she said.

"No! Not tonight, please," said Charley.

"You shouldn't be, you know," she persisted.

"Shall we not argue about it? I'm for him, and you're not, and that's where we'd be if we argued till tomorrow morning," I said.

"Except that I think I could convince you. You don't know my husband, do you? I know you've met him, but you've never talked with him about Roosevelt."

"When was *he* most convincing?" I said. "When he was with him, or against him?"

"He was never in the least convincing when he was for him. And he's not very convincing now. But as a writer you should be able to disregard a lot of things he says and go beneath the surface. Then you'd see what a man like Roosevelt can do to an idealist. And my husband *was* an idealist."

"Don't look at me. I'm not saying a word," said Charley.

"I do look at you, for corroboration. Jack *was* an idealist. You may not have liked him, but you have to admit that."

"Yes, he was," said Charley.

"And so were you. But Jack did something about it. You played it safe."

"Jim is wondering why I'm not taking this big. The reason is we've had it out before," said Charley.

"Many times," said Nancy Preswell. "And probably will again."

"But not tonight, shall we?" said Charley Ellis.

"I hate Mr. Roosevelt," she said. "And I can't stand it when a writer that I think is good is *for* him. I'm one of those people that think he ought to be assassinated,

206

and I just hope somebody else does it, not my poor, drunken, disillusioned husband."

"Is he liable to, your husband?" I said.

"I don't suppose there's any real danger of it. But it's what he thinks of day and night. I don't want you to think I love my husband. I haven't for years. But Jack Preswell was an idealist, and Roosevelt turned him into a fanatic."

"He might have been a fanatical idealist."

"*He was!* Four years ago, that's what he was. But there's nothing left now but the fanaticism. Don't you see that, Mr. Malloy? Mr. Roosevelt took away his ideals."

"How are you on ideals, Mrs. Preswell?"

"If that's supposed to be a crusher, it isn't . . . I have a few, but they're not in any danger from—that awful man. Now I've said enough, and you probably don't want to have dinner with us."

"Yes, I would. You're a very attractive girl."

"As long as I don't say what I think? That's insulting, and now I'm not sure *I* want to have dinner with *you.*"

There was a silence, broken by Charley: "Well, what shall we do? Toss a coin? Heads we dine together, tails we separate."

"I'll agree to an armistice if Mr. Malloy will."

"All right," I said. "Let's go. Maybe if we have a change of scenery . . ."

"I promise I'll be just as stupid as you want me to be," said Nancy Preswell.

There was not another word about politics all evening, and at eleven o'clock we took a taxi to a theatre where I was to meet an actress friend of mine, Julianna Moore, the female heavy in an English mystery play. Julie was about thirty, a girl who had been prematurely starred after one early success, and had never again found the right play. Her father was a history professor at Yale, and Julie was a well-educated girl whom I had first known in our Greenwich Village days. We had been lovers then, briefly, but now she was a friend of my ex-wife's and the mistress of a scenic designer.

Nancy Preswell began with compliments to Julie, ticking off six plays in which Julie had appeared.

"You must go to the theatre all the time, to have seen some of those sad little turkeys," said Julie.

"I go a lot," said Nancy.

"Did you ever do any acting?"

"*Did* I? 'Shall I speak ill of him that is my husband?/ Ah, poor my lord, what tongue shall smooth thy name . . .'"

"'When I, thy three-hours wife, have mangled it?' Where and when did you do Juliet?" said Julie.

"At Foxcroft."

"I'll bet you were a very pretty Juliet," said Julie.

"Thank you. If I was, that says it all. I was cured."

"Well, I was the kind of ham that never was cured, if you don't mind a very small joke . . . I always thought it would have been fun to go to Foxcroft. All that riding and drilling."

"Where *did* you go?"

"A Sacred Heart school in Noroton, Connecticut, then two years at Vassar."

"Where did you go to school, Charley," I said.

"I don't know. Where did you?" he said.

"Oh, a Sacred Heart school in Noroton, Connecticut. Then two years at Foxcroft," I said.

"Too tarribly fonny, jost too tarribly fonny," said Julie.

"That's her Mickey Rooney imitation. Now do Lionel Barrymore," I said.

"Too tarribly fonny, jost too tarribly fonny," said Julie.

"Isn't she good?" I said. "Now do Katharine Hepburn."

"Who?" said Julie.

"She's run out of imitations," I said.

We went to "21", the 18 Club, LaRue, and El Morocco. We all had had a lot to drink, and Julie, who played two performances that day, had soon caught up with the rest of us by drinking double Scotches. "Now the big question is, the all-important question—*is*," said Julie.

"What is the big question, Julie dear?" said Nancy.

"Ah, you like me, don't you? I like you, too," said Julie. "I like Charley, too. And I used to like Jim, didn't I, Jim?"

"Used to, but not any more."

"Correct. Jim is a rat. Aren't you, Jim?"

"Of course he's a rat," said Nancy. "He's a Franklin D. Roosevelt rat."

"I'm a Franklin D. Roosevelt rat. You be careful what you say," said Julie.

"The hell with that. What was the big question?" said Charley.

"*My* big question?" said Julie.

"Yes," said Charley.

"I didn't know I had one. Oh, yes. The big *question*. *Is*. Do we go to Harlem and I can't go on tomorrow night and I give my understudy a break. *Or*. *Or*. Do I go home to my trundle bed—and you stay out of it, Jim. You're a rat. I mean stay out of my trundle. Nevermore, quoth the raven. Well, what did my understudy ever do for me? So I guess we better go home. Right?"

"Yeah. I haven't got an understudy," said Charley. He signalled for the bill.

"Jim, why are you such a rat? If you weren't such a rat. But that's what you are, a rat," said Julie.

"Pretend I'm not a rat."

"How can I pretend a thing like that? I'm the most promising thirty-year-old ingénue there is, but I can't pretend you're not a rat. Because that's what you are. Your ex-wife is my best friend, so what else are you but a rat? Isn't that logical, Jim? Do you remember Bank Street? That was before you were a rat."

"No, I was a rat then, Julie."

"No. No, you weren't. If you were a rat then, you wouldn't be one now. That's logical."

"But he's not a bad rat," said Nancy.

"Oh, there you're wrong. If he was a good little rat I'd take him home with me. But I don't want a rat in my house."

"Then you come to my house," I said.

"All right," said Julie. "That solves everything. I don't know *why* I didn't think of that before. Remember Bank Street, Jim?"

"Sure."

She stood up. "*Good*night, Nancy. *Good*night, Charley." On her feet she became dignified, the star. She held her mink so that it showed her to best advantage and to the captains who said, "Goodnight, Miss Moore," she nodded and smiled. In the taxi she was ready to be kissed. "Ah, Jim, what a Christ-awful life, isn't it? You won't tell Ken, will you?"

"No. I won't tell anybody."

"Just don't tell Ken. I don't want him to think I care that much. He's giving me a bad time. Kiss me, Jim. Tell me I'm nicer than Nancy."

"You're much nicer than Nancy. Or anybody else."

She smiled. "You're a rat, Jim, but you're a nice old rat. It's all right if I call you a rat, isn't it? Who the hell is she to say you aren't a bad rat? She's not in our game, is she?"

"No."

"We don't have to let her in our game. But *he* does, the poor son of a bitch."

When she saw my bedroom she said: "Good Lord, Jim, I feel pregnant already. That's where Grandpa and Grandma begat. Isn't it? I hope *we* don't beget."

I was still asleep when she left, and on my desk there was a note from her:

Dear Rat:

You didn't use to snore on Bank Street. Am going home to finish my sleep. It is eight-fifteen and you seem good for many more hours. I had a lovely time and have the hangover to prove it. Want to be home in case K. calls as he said he would. In any case we are better off than Nancy and Charles. Are they headed for trouble!!!

Love,

J.

P.S.: The well-appointed bachelor's apartment has a supply of extra toothbrushes. My mouth tastes like the inside of the motorman's glove. Ugh!!!

J.

The motorman's glove. Passé collegiate slang of the previous decade, when the word whereupon was stuck into every sentence and uzza-mattera-fact and wet-smack and swell caught on and held on. I read Julie's note a couple of times, and "the motorman's glove" brought to mind two lines from *Don Juan* that had seemed strangely out of character for Byron:

Let us have wine and women, mirth and laughter,
Sermons and soda-water the day after.

The mirth and laughter, the wine and women were not out of character, but there was something very vulgar about Byron's taking soda-water for a hangover as I took Eno's fruit salts. An aristocrat, more than a century dead, and a man I disliked as cordially as if he were still alive. But he had said it all, more than a hundred years ago. I made a note to buy a copy of *Don Juan* and send it, with that passage marked, to Julie. At that moment, though, I was trying to figure out what she meant by Nancy and Charley, headed for trouble. There was trouble already, and more to come.

I waited until four o'clock and then telephoned Julie. "It's the rat," I said. "How are you feeling?"

"I'll live. I'll be able to go on tonight. Actually, I'm feeling much better than I have any right to, considering the amount I drank. I went home and took a bath and fiddled around till Ken called——"

"He called, did he?"

"Yes. There isn't going to be anything in the columns about you and me, is there?"

"My guess is a qualified no. If we went out again tonight there would be, but——"

"But we're not going out again tonight," she said. "I don't have to tell you that last night was a lapse."

"You don't have to, but you did," I said.

"Now don't get huffy," she said. "It wouldn't have happened with anyone else, and it wouldn't have happened with you if it hadn't been for the old days on Bank Street."

"I know that, Julie, and I'm not even calling you for another date. I want to know what you meant by—I have your note here—Nancy and Charley headed for trouble. Was something said? Did something happen that I missed?"

"Oh, God, I have to think. It seems to me I wrote that ages ago. And it was only this morning. Is it important? I could call you back?"

"Not important."

"*I* know. I know what it was. Is Nancy's husband a man named Jack Preswell?"

"Yes."

"Well, he was at Morocco last night. Standing at the

213

bar all alone and just staring at us. Staring, staring, staring. I used to know him when I was a prom-trotter, back in the palaeolithic age."

"How did you happen to see him and we didn't?"

"Because I was facing that way and you weren't," she said. "Maybe I should have said something. Maybe I did."

"No, you didn't."

"I don't think I did. No, I guess I didn't, because now I remember thinking that I wasn't positively sure it was he. But when you and I left I caught a glimpse of him, and it was. If anybody was tighter than we were, he was. His eyes were just barely open, and he was holding himself up by the elbows. I'll bet he didn't last another ten minutes."

"Well, just about," I said.

"What do you mean?"

"Have you seen the early editions of the afternoon papers?"

"No. I don't get the afternoon papers here."

"Preswell was hit by a taxi at 54th and Lexington. Fractured his skull and died before the ambulance got there. According to the cops he just missed being hit by a northbound cab, and then walked in front of a southbound. Four or five witnesses said the hack driver was not at fault, which is another way of saying Preswell was blind drink."

"Well, I guess I could almost swear to that, but I'm glad I don't have to. I won't, will I?"

"Not a chance. He wasn't with us, and none of us ever spoke to him. The *Times* and the *Trib* will print the bare facts and people can draw their own conclusions. The *News* and the *Mirror* will play it up tonight, but it's only a one-day story. However, there is one tabloid angle. If the *Mirror* or the *News* finds out that Nancy was in Morocco with Charley—well, they could do something with that."

"And would you and I get in the papers?"

"Well, if I were the city editor of the *News* or the *Mirror*, and a prominent actress and an obscure author——"

"Oh, Lord. And I told Ken I went straight home from the theatre. Jim, you know a lot of those press people . . ."

"Julie, if they find out, your picture's going to be in the tabloids. I couldn't prevent that."

"And they *are* going to find out, aren't they?"

"The only straight answer is yes. You spoke to a lot of people as we were leaving. Waiter captains. People at the tables. If you can think of a story to tell Ken, I'll back you up. But maybe the best thing is to tell him the truth, up to a certain point."

"He'll supply the rest, after that certain point. He knows about Bank Street."

"That was eight years ago. Can't you have an evening out with an old friend?"

"Would you believe that line?"

"No," I said. "But I have a very suspicious nature."

"You're a blind man trusting a boy scout compared to Ken. He didn't believe me when I told him I went straight home from the theatre. But in the absence of proof—now he's got his proof."

"Well, then have a date with me tonight. Make the son of a bitch good and jealous."

"I'm almost tempted. When will we know about the *News* and the *Mirror*?"

"Oh, around nine o'clock tonight."

"You'll see them when they come out, before I can. If they mention me, will you stop for me at the theatre? That isn't much of an offer, Jim, but for old time's sake?"

"And if you're not mentioned, you have a date with Ken?"

"Yes," she said.

"All right. You understand, of course, this is something I wouldn't do for just anybody, take second best."

"I understand exactly why you're doing it, and so do you," she said.

"I detect the sound of *double entendre*."

"Well, that's how I meant it. You're being nice, but you also know that nice little rats get a piece of candy. And don't make the obvious remark about piece of what. Seriously, Jim, I can count on you, can't I?"

"I would say that you are one of the few that can always count on me, Julie. For whatever that's worth."

"Right now, a great deal."

"Well, I wish you luck, even though I'll be the loser in the deal."

"You didn't lose anything last night. And I may have lost a husband. He was talking that way today."

"Do you want to marry him?"

"Yes, I do. Very much. Too much. So much that all he ever sees is my phony indifference. Too smart for

216

my own good, I am. Jim, ought I to call Nancy Preswell, or write her a note?"

"A note would be better, I think."

"Yes, I do, too."

"I've been calling Charley all afternoon, and nobody knows where he is. But he'll be around when he wants to see me."

"It's a hateful thing for me to say, but in a way he's stuck, isn't he?"

"He wants to be."

"He's still stuck," said Julie.

At about eleven-twenty I was standing with the backstage doorman, who was saying goodnight to the actors and actresses as they left the theatre. "Miss Moore's always one of the last to leave," he said. "We us'ally break about five to eleven, but tonight she's later than us'al. I told her you was here. I told her myself."

"That's all right," I said.

"She dresses with Miss Van, one flight up. I'll just go tell her you're here."

"No. No thanks. Don't hurry her," I said.

"She's us'ally one of the last out, but I don't know what's keeping her tonight."

"Making herself look pretty," I said.

"She's a good little actress. You know, they had to change the curtain calls so she could take a bow by herself."

There were footsteps on the winding iron stairway, the cautious, high-heeled footsteps of all actresses descending all backstage stairways, but these were made

217

by Julie. She did not make any sign of recognition of me but took my arm. "Goodnight, Mike," she said.

"Goodnight, Miss Moore. See you tomorrow. Have a good time," said the doorman.

"Let's go where we won't see anybody. Have you got the papers? I don't mind being seen with you, Jim, but I don't want to be seen crying. As soon as Mike said 'Mr. Malloy,' I knew. Tomorrow the press agent will thank me for the publicity break. Irony."

I took her to a small bar in the New Yorker Hotel, and she read the *News* and the *Mirror*. The *Mirror* had quite a vicious little story by a man named Walter Herbert, describing the gay foursome and the solitary man at the bar of El Morocco, and leaving the unmistakable inference that Jack Preswell had stumbled out into the night and thrown himself in front of a taxi. The *News*, in a story that had two by-lines, flatly said that Preswell had gone to the night club in an attempt to effect a reconciliation with his wife, who was constantly in the company of Charles Ellis, multi-millionaire stockbroker and former Harvard oarsman, and onetime close friend of the dead man. The *Mirror* ran a one-column cut of Julie, an old photograph from the White Studios; the *News* had a more recent picture of her in the décolleté costume she wore in the play. There was a wedding picture of Preswell and Nancy in the *News*, which also came up with a manly picture of Charley Ellis in shorts, shirt, and socks, holding an oar. There was no picture of me, and in both papers the textual mention of Julie and me was almost identical: Julie was the beautiful young actress, I was the sensational young novelist.

"Were we as gay as they say we were? I guess we were," said Julie.

"The implication is, that's what happens to society people when they mix with people like you and me."

"Exactly. They only got what they deserved. By the way, what did they get, besides a little notoriety? I'm beginning to feel sorry for Preswell. I lose a possible husband, but it must hurt to be hit by a taxi, even if you do die right away."

"You're taking it very well," I said.

"I thought Ken might show up, if only to demand an explanation. He loves to demand explanations. Have you talked to Ellis?"

"No. I'd like to know if there's anything in that *News* story, about Preswell and the reconciliation. I doubt it, and nobody will sue, but either the *News* has a very good rewrite man or they may have something. If it's something dreamed up by the rewrite man he ought to get a bonus, because he's taken a not very good story and dramatized the whole scene at Morocco."

"Thank goodness for one thing. They left my father and mother out of it," she said. "Poor Daddy. He groans. He comes to see me in all my plays, and then takes me to one side and asks if it's absolutely necessary to wear such low-cut dresses, or do I always *have* to be unfaithful to my husband? He told Thornton Wilder I'd have been just right for the girl in *Our Town*. Can you imagine how I'd have had to hunch over to play a fourteen-year-old?"

We were silent for a moment and then suddenly she said: "Oh, the hell with it. Let's go to '21'?"

"I'll take you to '21', but no night clubs."

"I want to go to El Morocco and the Stork Club."

"No, you can't do it."

"I'm not in mourning."

"I used to be a press agent, Julie. If you want to thumb your nose at Ken, okay. But if you go to El Morocco tonight, you're asking for the worst kind of publicity. Capitalizing on those stories in the *News* and *Mirror*. You're better than that."

"Oh, the hell I am."

"Well, you used to be."

"The hell with what I used to be. I was a star, too, but now I'm just a sexy walk-on. And a quick lay, for somebody that calls me up after eight years. Why *did* you take me out last night?"

"Because you're a lady, and so is Nancy."

"Oh, it was Nancy you were trying to impress? I wish I'd known *that*."

"I have no desire to impress Nancy. I merely thought you'd get along with her and she with you."

"Why? Because she did Juliet at Foxcroft?"

"Oh, balls, Julie."

"Would you say that to Nancy?"

"If she annoyed me as much as you do, yes, I would. If you'll shut up for a minute, I'll tell you something. I don't like Nancy. I think she's a bitch. But I like Charley."

"Why do you like Charley? He's not your type. As soon as you make a little money you want to join the

Racquet Club and all the rest of that crap. That apartment, for God's sake! And those guns. You're not Ernest Hemingway. Would you know how to fire a gun?"

"If I had one right now I'd show you."

"When did you get to be such pals with Charley Ellis?"

"I was hoping you'd get around to that. I knew him before I knew you, before I ever wrote anything. As to the armament, the shotguns belonged to my old man, including one that he gave me when I was fourteen. I do admit I bought the rifle four years ago. As to the apartment—well, you liked it last night. If you want to feel guilty about it, go ahead. But you said yourself it was a damned sight more comfortable than that studio couch on Bank Street. What do you want to do? Do you want to go to '21' and have something to eat, or shall I take you home?" I looked at my watch.

"It isn't too late to get another girl, is it?"

"That's exactly what I was thinking."

"Some girl from one of the night clubs?"

"Yes."

"I thought they only went out with musicians and gangsters."

"That's what you thought, and you go on thinking it. Do you want to go to '21'?"

"How late can you get one of those girls?"

"Two-thirty, if I'm lucky."

"You mean if you call up now and make the date?"

"Yes."

"You're a big liar, Jim. They have a two o'clock

221

show that lasts an hour, so you can call this girl any time between now and two o'clock, and you won't meet her till after three. I know the whole routine. A boy in our play is married to one of them."

"The girl I had in mind isn't a show girl and she isn't in the line. She does a specialty."

She put her chin in her hand and her elbow on the table, in mock close attention. "*Tell* me about her specialty, Jim. Is it something I should learn? Or does one have to be double-jointed?"

"You want to go to '21'?"

"I'm dying to go to '21'," she said.

"Well, why didn't you say so?"

"Because you're such a grump, and I had to get a lot of things out of my system."

We used each other for a couple of weeks in a synthetic romance that served well in place of the real thing; and we were conscientious about maintaining the rules and customs of the genuine. We saw only each other and formed habits: the same taxi driver from the theatre, the same tables in restaurants, exchanges of small presents and courtesies; and we spoke of the wonder of our second chance at love. It was easy to love Julie. After the first few days and nights she seemed to have put aside her disappointment as easily as I was overcoming my chronic loneliness. We slept at my apartment nearly every night, and when she stayed at hers we would talk on the telephone until there was nothing more to say. We worried about each other: I, when the closing notice was put up at her theatre, and she when a story of mine was rejected. A couple of weeks became a couple of months and our romance was duly noted in the gossip columns: we were sizzling, we were hunting a preacher. "Would you ever go back to the Church?" she said, when it was printed that we were going to marry.

"I doubt it. Would you?"

"If Daddy wanted me to get married in the Church, I would."

"We've never talked about this."

"You mean about marriage?"

"*Or* the Church. Do you want to talk about marriage?"

"Yes, I have a few things I want to say. I love you, Jim, and you love me. But we ought to wait a long time before we do anything about getting married. If I'm married in the Church I'm going to stick to it."

"You wouldn't have with Ken."

"No, but he never was a Catholic. If I married you, in the Church, I'd want a nuptial Mass and you'd have to go to confession and the works. With a Protestant—Ken—I couldn't have had a nuptial Mass and I'd have been half-hearted about the whole thing. But marrying you would be like going back to the Church automatically. I consider you a Catholic."

"Do you consider yourself a Catholic?"

"Yes. I never go to Mass, and I haven't made my Easter duty since I was nineteen, but it's got me. I'm a Catholic."

"It's gone from me, Julie. The priests have ruined it for me."

"They've almost ruined it for me, but not quite. I

don't listen to the priests. I can't tell that in confession, but that's why I stay away. Well, one of the reasons. I don't believe that going to bed with you is a sin."

"The priests do."

"Let them. They'll never be told unless I marry a Catholic and go to confession. That's why I say we ought to wait a long time. I'm thinking of myself. If I marry a Catholic, I'll be a Catholic. If I don't I'll be whatever I am. A non-practising member of the faithful. I'll never be anything else."

"Well, neither will I. But I'm a heretic on too many counts, and the priests aren't going to accept me on my terms. It wouldn't be the Church if they did. It would be a new organization called the Malloyists."

"I'll be a Malloyist until we get married."

"There's one thing, Julie. If you get pregnant, what?"

"If I get pregnant, I'll ask you to marry me. I've had two abortions, but the father wasn't a Catholic. It was Ken. I paid for the abortions myself and never told him I was pregnant. I didn't want to have a baby. I wanted to be a star. But if I ever get pregnant by you, I'll tell you, and I hope you'll marry me."

"I will."

"However, I've been very, very careful except for that first night."

I have never been sure what that conversation did to us. I have often thought that we were all right so long as we felt a future together without getting down to plans, without putting conditional restrictions on ourselves, without specifying matters of time or event. It is also quite possible that the affection and passion that we identified as love was affection and passion and tenderness, but whatever sweetness we could add to the relationship, we could not add love, which is never superimposed. In any event, Julie stayed away one night and did not answer her telephone, and the next day I was having my coffee and she let herself in.

"Hello," I said.

"I'm sorry, Jim."

"I suppose you came to get your things," I said. I took a sip of coffee and lit a cigarette.

"Not only to get my things."

"You know, the awful thing is, you look so God damn—oh, nuts." She was wearing a blue linen dress that was as plain as a Chinese sheath, but there was more underneath that dress than Chinese girls have, and I was never to have it again. Someone else had been having it only hours ago.

"All right," I said. "Get your things."

"Aren't you going to let me say thank-you for what we had?"

"Yes, and I thank you, Julie. But I can't be nice about last night and all this morning." I took another sip of coffee and another drag on my cigarette, and she put her hand to her face and walked swiftly out of the room. I waited a while, then got up and went to the bedroom. She was lying face down on my unmade bed and she was crying.

"You'll wrinkle your dress," I said.

"The hell with my dress," she said, and slowly turned and sat up. "Jim." She held out her arms.

"Oh, no," I said.

"I couldn't help it. He came to the theatre."

"Oh, hell, I don't want to hear about that."

"I promised him I wouldn't see you again, but I had to come here."

"No you didn't, Julie. I could have sent you your things. It would have been much better if you'd just sent me a telegram."

"Put your arms around me."

"Oh, now that isn't like you. What the hell do you think I am? I've had about two hours' sleep. I'm on the ragged edge, but you don't have to do that to me."

She stood up and slipped her dress over her head, and took off her underclothes. "Can I make up for last night?" she said. "I'll never see you again. Will you put your arms around me now?"

"I wish I could say no, but I wanted you the minute I saw you."

"I know. That's why you wouldn't look at me, isn't it?"

"Yes."

She was smiling, and she could well afford to, with the pride she had in her breasts. "How do you want to remember me? I'll be whatever you want."

"What is this, a performance?"

"Of course. A farewell performance. Command, too. You don't want me as a virgin, do you?"

"No."

"No, that would take too much imagination on *your* part. But I could be one if that's what you want. But you don't. You'd much rather remember me as a slut, wouldn't you?"

"Not a slut, Julie. But not a virgin. Virgin's aren't very expert."

"You'd rather remember me as an expert. A whore. Then you'll be able to forget me and you won't have to forgive me. All right."

She knew things I had never told her and there was no love in the love-making, but when she was dressed again and had her bag packed she stood in the bed-room doorway. "Jim?"

"What?"

"I'm not like that," she said. "Don't remember me that way, please?"

"I hope I don't remember you at all."

"I love him. I'm going to marry him."

"You do that, Julie."

"Haven't you got one nice thing to say before I go?"

I thought of some cruel things and I must have smiled at the thought of them, because she began to smile too. But I shook my head and she shrugged her shoulders and turned and left. The hall door closed and I looked at it, and then I saw that the key was being pushed under it. Twenty-three crowded years later I still remember the angle of that key as it lay on the dark-green carpet. My passion was spent, but I was not calm of mind; by accident the key was pointed towards me, and I thought of the swords at a court-martial. I was being re-sentenced to the old frenetic loneliness that none of us would admit to, but that governed our habits and our lives.

In that state of mind I made a block rejection of a thousand men and women whom I did not want to see, and reduced my friendships to the five or ten, the three or five, and finally the only person I felt like talking to. And that was how I got back in the lives of Charley Ellis and Nancy McMinnies Preswell Ellis.

They had been married about a month, and I was not sure they would be back from their wedding trip, but I got Charley at his office and he said he had started work again that week. He would stop in and have a drink on his way home.

"Gosh, the last time I was in this apartment——" he said, and it was not necessary to go on.

"You ended up getting married, and I damn near did myself."

"To Julia Murphy?"

"Close. Julianna Moore. In fact, your coming here rounds out a circle, for me. She ditched me today."

"Are you low on account of it?"

"Yes, so tell me about you and Nancy. I saw the announcement of your wedding, in the papers."

"That's all there was. We didn't send out any others."

"You lose a lot of loot that way," I said.

"I know, but there were other considerations. We wanted people to forget us in a hurry, so Nancy's mother sent short announcements to the *Tribune* and the *Sun*. You can imagine we'd had our fill of the newspapers when Preswell was killed."

"I don't have to imagine. It was the start of my romance, the one that just ended." I told him what had happened, a recital which I managed to keep down to about fifteen minutes. I lied a little at the end: "So this morning she called me up and said she'd gone back to her friend Mr. Kenneth Kenworthy."

"Well, you might say our last meeting here did end in two marriages," said Charley.

"If he marries her. He's been married three times and if she marries him she's going to have to support herself. He has big alimony to pay. I hope they do get married. Selfishly. I don't want any more synthetic romances. They're just as wearing as the real thing, and as Sam Hoffenstein says, what do you get yet?"

"Everything, if it turns out all right. You remember Nancy and her theory that nobody should get married without love, the real thing? That story of yours we talked about—'Telemark'?"

"Yes."

"Well, to be blunt about it, I really forced Nancy to marry me. All that notoriety—I put it to her that if she didn't marry me, *I'd* look like a shitheel. So on that basis——"

"Oh, come on."

"It's true. That's why she took the chance. But what was true then isn't true now. I want you to be the twenty-fifth to know. We're having a child."

"She never had any by Preswell?"

"No, and she wanted one, but his chemistry was all wrong. We expect ours in March or April."

"Congratulations."

"Thank you. Needless to say, I'm an altogether different person."

"You mean you have morning sickness?"

"I mean just the opposite. I'm practically on the wagon, for one thing, and for the first time in my life I'm thinking about someone besides myself. Get married, Malloy, and have a baby right away."

"I *like* to think about myself," I said.

"That's bullshit, and it's a pose. All this crazy life you lead, I think you're about the lonesomest son of a bitch I know."

I bowed my head and wept. "You shouldn't have said that," I said. "I wish you'd go."

"I'm sorry, Jim. I'll go. But why don't you drop in after dinner if you feel like it?"

"Thanks," I said, and he left.

He had taken me completely unawares. His new happiness and my new misery and all that the day had taken out of me made me susceptible of even the slightest touch of pity or kindness. I stopped bawling after two minutes, and then I began again, but during the second attack I succumbed to brain fag and fell asleep. I slept about three hours and was awakened by the telephone.

"This is Nancy Ellis. I hope you're coming up, we're expecting you. I'll bet you haven't had your dinner. Tell me the truth?"

"As a matter of fact, I was asleep."

"Well, how about some lamb chops? Do you like them black on the outside and pink on the inside? And have you any pet aversions in the vegetable line?"

"Brussels sprouts. But do you mean to say you haven't had your dinner?"

"We've had ours, but I can cook. Half an hour?"

It was a pleasant suburban evening in a triplex apartment in East Seventy-first Street, with one of the most beautiful women in New York cooking my supper and serving it; and it was apparent from their avoidance of all intimate topics that they had decided how they would treat me. At ten-thirty Nancy went to bed, at eleven Charley went in to see how she was, and at eleven-thirty I said goodnight. I went home and slept for ten hours. Had it not been for Nancy and Charley Ellis I would have gone on a ten-day drunk. But during those ten days I met a fine girl, and in December of that year we were married and we stayed married for sixteen years, until she died. As the Irish would say, she died on me, and it was the only unkind thing she ever did to anyone.

The way things tie up, one with another, is likely to go unnoticed unless a lawyer or a writer calls our attention to it. And sometimes both the writer and the lawyer have some difficulty in holding things together. But if they are men of purpose they can manage, and fortunately for writers they are not governed by rules of evidence or the whims of the court. The whim of the reader is all that need concern a writer, and even that should not concern him unduly; Byron, Scott, Milton, and Shakespeare, who have been quoted in this chronicle, are past caring what use I make of their words, and at the appointed time I shall join them and the other millions of writers who have said their little say and then become forever silent—and in the public domain. I shall join them with all due respect, but at the first sign of a patronizing manner I shall say: "My dear sir, when you were drinking it up at the Mermaid Tavern, did you ever have the potman bring a telephone to your table?"

I belonged to the era of the telephone at the tavern table, and the thirty-foot extension cord that enabled the tycoon to talk and walk, and to buy and sell and connive and seduce at long distances. It is an era already gone, and I may live to see the new one, in which extra-sensory perception combines with transistors, enabling the tycoon to dispense with the old-fashioned cord and *think* his way into new power and new beds. I may see the new era, but I won't belong to it. The writer of those days to come will be able to tune in on the voice of Lincoln at Gettysburg and hear the clanking of pewter mugs at the Mermaid, but he will never know the feeling of accomplishment that comes with the successful changing of a typewriter ribbon. A writer belongs to his time, and mine is past. In the days or years that remain to me, I shall entertain myself in contemplation of my time and be fascinated by the way things tie up, one with another.

I was in Boston for the tryout of a play I had written, and Charley Ellis's father had sent me a guest card to his club. "The old man said to tell you to keep your ears open and be sure and bring back any risqué stories you hear."

"At the Somerset Club?"

"The best. Where those old boys get them, I don't know, but that's where they tell them."

I used the introduction only once, when I went for a walk to get away from my play and everyone concerned with it. I stood at the window and looked out at the Beacon Street traffic, read a newspaper, and wandered to a small room to write a note to Mr. Ellis. There was only one other man in the room, and he looked up and half nodded as I came in, then resumed his letter-writing. A few minutes later there was a small angry spatter and I saw that a book of matches had exploded in the man's hand. "*Son* of a *bitch!*" he said.

His left hand was burned and he stared at it with loathing.

"Put some butter on it," I said.

"What?"

"I said, put some butter on it."

"I've heard of tea, but never butter."

"You can put butter on right away, but you have to wait for the water to boil before you have tea."

"What's it supposed to do?"

"Never mind that now. Just put it on. I've used it. It works."

He got up and disappeared. He came back in about ten minutes. "You know, it feels much better. I'd never heard of butter, but the man in the kitchen had."

"It's probably an old Irish remedy," I said.

"Are you Irish?"

"Yes. With the name Malloy I couldn't be anything else."

"Howdia do. My name is Hackley. Thanks very much. I wonder what it does, butter?"

"It does something for the skin. I guess it's the same principle as any of the greasy things."

"Of course. And it's cooling. It's such a stupid accident. I thought I closed the cover, but I guess I didn't." He hesitated. "Are you stopping here?"

"No, staying at the Ritz, but I have a guest card from Mr. Ellis in New York."

"Oh, of course. Where did you know *him*?"

"His son is a friend of mine."

"You're a friend of Charley's? I see. He's had another child, I believe. A daughter, this time."

"Yes. They wanted a daughter. I'm one of the god-fathers of the boy."

"Oh, then you know him very well."

"Very," I said.

"I see. At Harvard?"

"No, after college. Around New York."

"Oh, yes. Yes," he said. Then: "Oh, *I* know who you are. You're the playwright. Why, I saw your play night before last."

"That wasn't a very good night to see it," I said.

"Oh, I didn't think it was so bad. Was I right in thinking that one fellow had trouble remembering his lines? The bartender?"

"Indeed you were,"

"But aside from that, I enjoyed the play. Had a few good chuckles. That what-was-she, a chorus girl? They do talk that way, don't they? It's just that, uh, when you hear them saying those things in front of an audience. Especially a Boston audience. You know how we are. Or do you? We look about to see how the others are taking it. Tell me, Mr. Malloy, which do you prefer? Writing books, or writing for the stage?"

"At the moment, books."

"Well, of course with an actor who doesn't remember lines. A friend of mine in New York knows you. She sent me two of your books. I think one was your first and the other was your second."

"Oh? Who was that?"

"Polly Williamson is her name."

So here he was, the serious-minded widower who had been Polly Williamson's only lover. "That was damn nice of Polly. She's a swell girl."

"You *like* Polly. So do I. Never see her, but she's a darn nice girl and I hear from her now and again. Very musical, and I like music. Occasionally she'll send me a book she thinks I ought to read. I don't always like what she likes, and she knows I won't, but she does it to stimulate me, you know."

I had an almost ungovernable temptation to say something coarse. Worse than coarse. Intimate and anatomical and in the realm of stimulation, about Polly in bed. Naturally he misread my hesitation. "However," he said. "I enjoyed your first book very much. The second, not quite as much. So you're James J. Malloy?"

"No, I'm not James J. Malloy. I'm James Malloy, but my middle initial isn't J."

"I beg your pardon. I've always thought it was James J."

"People do. Every Irishman has to be James J. or John J."

"No. There was John L. Sullivan," said Hackley.

"Oh, but he came from Boston."

"Indeed he did. But then there was James J. Wadsworth. I know he wasn't Irish."

"No, but he was sort of a friend of Al Smith's."

"*Was he really?* I didn't know that. Was—he—really? Could you by any chance be thinking of his father, James *W*. Wadsworth?"

"I am. Of course I am. The senator, James *W*. Wadsworth."

"Perfectly natural mistake," said Hackley. "Well, I have to be on my way, but it's been nice to've had this chat with you. And thank you for the first-aid, I'll remember butter next time I set myself on fire."

On the evening of the next day I was standing in the lobby of the theatre, chatting with the press agent of the show and vainly hoping to overhear some comment that would tell me in ten magic words how to make the play a success. It was the second intermission. A hand lightly touched my elbow and I turned and saw Polly Williamson. "Do you remember me?" she said.

"Of course I remember you. I told you once I'd never forget you." Then I saw, standing with but behind her, Mr. Hackley, and I was sorry I was quite so demonstrative. "Hello, Mr. Hackley. How's the hand?"

He held it up. "Still have it, thanks to you."

"Just so you can applaud long and loud."

"The bartender fellow is better tonight, don't you think?"

"Much better," I said. "I'm glad you can sit through it a second time."

"He has no choice," said Polly Williamson.

"I hadn't, either," said Hackley. "I'll have you know this lady came all the way from New York just to see your play."

"You did, Polly?"

"Well, yes. But I don't know that I ought to tell you why."

"Why did you?" I said.

"Well, I read excerpts from some of the reviews, and I was afraid it wouldn't reach New York."

"We've tightened it up a little since opening night. I think the plan is now to take it to Philadelphia. But it was awfully nice of you to come."

"I wouldn't have missed it. I'm one of your greatest fans, and I like to tell people I knew you when."

"Well, I like to tell people I know you."

"I suppose you're terribly busy after the show," said Hackley.

"Not so busy that I couldn't have a drink with Polly and you, if that's what you had in mind."

They waited for me in the Ritz Bar. Two tweedy women were sitting with them, but they got up and left before I reached the table. "I didn't mean to drive your friends away," I said.

"They're afraid of you. Frightened to death," said Hackley.

"They're pretty frightening themselves," I said, angrily.

"They are, but before you say any more I must warn you, one of them is *my* cousin *and* Charley Ellis's cousin," said Polly Williamson.

"They thought your play was frightful," said Hackley.

"Which should assure its success," said Polly. "Maisie, my cousin, goes to every play that comes to Boston and she hasn't liked anything since I don't know when."

"*The Jest*, with Lionel and Jack Barrymore, I think was the last thing she really liked. And not so much the play as Jack Barrymore."

"I don't think she'd *really* like John Barrymore," I said.

"Oh, but you're wrong. She met him, and she does," said Hackley. It seemed to me during the hour or more that we sat there that he exerted a power over Polly that was effortless on his part and unresisted by her. He never allowed himself to stay out of the conversation, and Polly never finished a conversational paragraph that he chose to interrupt. I was now sure that their affair was still active, in Boston. She had occasion to remark that he never went to New York, which led me to believe that the affair was conducted entirely on his home ground, on his terms, and at as well as for his pleasure. I learned that he lived somewhere in the neighbourhood—two or three minutes' walk from the hotel; and that she always stayed with an aunt who lived on the other side of the Public Garden. Since they had not the slighest reason to suspect that I knew any more about them than they had told me, they unconsciously showed the whole pattern of their affair. It was a complete reversal of the usual procedure, in which the Boston man goes to New York to be naughty. Polly went to Boston under the most respectable auspices and with the most innocent excuses—and as though she were returning home to sin. (I did not pass that judgment on her.) Williamson was an ebullient, arrogant boor; Hackley was a Bostonian, who shared her love of music, painting, and flowers; and whatever they did in bed, it was almost certainly totally different from whatever she did with Williamson, which was not hard to guess at. I do know that in the dimly lighted bar of the hotel she seemed more genuinely at home and at ease than in her own house or at the New York parties where I would see her, with the odd difference that in Boston she was willingly under the domination of a somewhat epicene aesthete, while in New York she quietly but, over the years, noticeably resisted Williamson's habit of taking control of people's lives. After fifteen years of marriage to Williamson she was regarded in New York as a separate and individual woman, who owed less and less to her position as the wife of a spectacular millionaire. But none of that was discernible to me in her relations with Hackley. She did what he wanted to do, and in so doing she completed the picture of her that Charley Ellis had given me. In that picture, her man was missing. But now I saw that Hackley, not the absent Williamson, was her man.

It was hardly a new idea, that the lover was more husband than the husband; but I had never seen a case in which geography, or a city's way of life, had been so influential. Polly not only returned to Hackley; she returned to Boston and the way of life that suited her best and that Hackley represented. There was even

something appropriately austere about her going back
to New York and Williamson. Since divorce was un-
desirable, with Williamson, the multi-millionaire, she
was making-do. The whole thing delighted me. It is
always a pleasure to discover that someone you like and
have underestimated on the side of simplicity turns out
to be intricate and therefore worthy of your original
interest. (Intricacy in someone you never liked is, of
course, just another reason for disliking him.)

"I have to go upstairs now and start working on the
third act," I said.

"Oh, I hope we didn't keep you," said Hackley.

"You did, and I'm very glad you did. The director
and the manager have had an hour to disagree with each
other. Now I'll go in and no matter what I say, one of
them will be on my side and the other will be left out
in the cold. That's why I prefer writing books, Mr.
Hackley . . . Polly, it's been very nice to've seen you
again. Spread the good word when you go back. Tell
everybody it's a great play."

"Not great, but it's good," said Polly. "When will
you be back in New York?"

"Leaving tomorrow afternoon."

"So am I. Maybe I'll see you on the train."

There was a situation in my play that plainly needed
something to justify a long continuing affair, something
other than an arbitrary statement of love. In the elevator
it came to me: it was Polly's compromise. In continuing
her affair with Hackley, Polly—and the woman in my
play—would be able to make a bad marriage appear
to be a good one. The character in the play was a movie

240

actress, and if Polly saw the play again she never would recognize herself. The director, the manager, and I agreed that we would leave the play as-is in Boston, and open with the new material in Philadelphia. Only three members of the cast were affected by the new material, and they were quick studies. One of them was Julianna Moore.

I had said to my wife: "Would you object if I had Julie read for the part?"

"No. You know what I'd object to," she said.

"Well, it won't happen. There won't be any flare-up. Kenworthy is doing the sets, and they seem to be making a go of it."

There was no flare-up. Julie worked hard and well and got good notices in Boston, and I got used to having her around. I suppose that if she had come to my room in the middle of the night, my good intentions would have vanished. But we had discussed that. "If people that have slept together can never again work together," she said, "then the theatre might as well fold up. They'd never be able to cast a play on Broadway. And as to Hollywood . . ."

"Well, if you get too attractive, I'll send for my wife," I said.

"You won't have to. Ken will be there most of the time," she said. "Anyway, Jim, give me credit for some intelligence. I know you thought this all out and talked it over with your wife. Well, *I* talked it over with Ken, too. He hates you, but he respects you."

"Then we're in business," I said, and that was really all there was to it. I made most of my comments to the actors through the director, and Julie was not the kind of woman or actress who would use acquaintance with the author to gain that little edge.

Polly Williamson was at the Back Bay station and we got a table for two in the diner. "Do you think Mr. Willkie has a chance?" she said.

"I think he did have, but not now. Roosevelt was so sure he was a shoo-in that he wasn't going to campaign, and that was when Willkie had his chance. But luckily I was able to persuade the President to make some speeches."

"You did?"

"Not really," I said. "But I did have a talk with Tim Cochran in August, and I told him that Roosevelt was losing the election. I was very emphatic. And then one of the polls came out and showed I was right."

"Are you a New Dealer? I suppose you are."

"All the way."

"Did you ever know Jack Preswell? I know you know Nancy, Nancy Ellis, but did you know her first husband?"

"I once went to a baseball game with him, that's all."

"That's a tragic story. You know how he was killed and all that, I'm sure, but the real tragedy happened several years before. Jack was a brilliant student in Law School and something of an idealist. He had a job with Carson, Cass & Devereux, but he quit it to get into the New Deal. I probably shouldn't be saying this . . ."

"You can say anything to me."

"Well, I *want* to. Nancy is married to my cousin and

I know you and he are very good friends, but all is far from well there, you know."

"No, I didn't know. I haven't seen them lately."

"Nancy and her father hounded Jack Preswell. They were very contemptuous of his ideals, and when he went to Washington Nancy wouldn't go with him. She said it would be a repudiation of everything she believed in and her father believed in and everything Jack's *family* believed in. As a woman I think Nancy was just looking for an excuse. Nancy is *so* beautiful and has been told so *so* many times that she'd much rather be admired for her brains. Consequently she can be very intolerant of other people's ideas, and she made Jack's life a hell. Not that Jack was any rose. I didn't agree with him, but he had a perfect right to count on Nancy's support, and he never got it. Not even when he got out of the New Deal. She should have stuck by him, at least publicly."

"Yes, as it turned out, Preswell became as anti–New Deal as she was, or Old Man McMinnies. I knew a little about this, Polly."

"Well, did I tell it fairly? I don't think you could have known much of it, because she was at her worst in front of his friends. She's a very destructive girl, and now she's up to the same old tricks with Charley. You don't know *that*, do you?"

"No."

"She's gotten Charley into America First. You knew that?"

"No, I didn't."

"Yes. And even my husband, as conservative as he

is, and his father, they've stayed out of it. What's the use of isolationism now, when we're practically in it already? I agree with you, I think Roosevelt's going to win, although I just can't vote for him. But he'll get in and then it's only a question of another *Lusitania*, and we'll be in it too. So I don't see the practical value of America First. We ought to be getting stronger and stronger and the main reason I won't vote for Mr. Roosevelt is that he's such a hypocrite. He won't come out and honestly say that we're headed towards war."

"A little thing about neutrality and the head of the United States government."

"Oh, come. Do you think Hitler and Mussolini are hoping for a last-minute change of heart? Roosevelt should be uniting the country instead of playing politics. This nonsense about helping the democracies is sheer hypocrisy. There is no France, there's only England."

"You're very fiery, Polly."

"Yes. We have two English children staying with us. Their father was drowned coming back from Dunkerque. Nancy has Charley convinced that their presence in our house is a violation of neutrality. She said it wouldn't be fashionable to have two German children. When have I ever given a darn about fashion? That really burned me up."

I became crafty. "How do they feel about this in Boston? What does Mr. Hackley think?"

"Ham? The disappointment of his life was being turned down by the American Field Service. He'd have been wonderful, too. Speaks French, German, and

Italian, and has motored through all of Europe. He'd make a wonderful spy."

"They'd soon catch on to him."

"Why?"

"If he burnt his hand, he'd say 'Son of a bitch', and they'd know right away he was an American."

"Oh, yes." She smiled. "He told me about that. He's nice, don't you think?"

She was so nearly convincingly matter-of-fact. "Yes. He and I'd never be friends, but of his type I like him. Solid Boston."

"I don't know," she said. "Charley's almost that, and you and he have been friends quite a long time. Poor Charley. I don't know what I hope. Oh, I do. I want him to be happy with Nancy. I just hate to see what I used to like in him being poisoned and ruined by that girl."

"And you think it is?"

"The Charley Ellis I used to know would have two English children staying with him, and he'd probably be in the Field Service, if not actually in the British army."

"Well, my wife and I haven't taken any English children, and I'm not in the Field Service, so I can't speak. However, I'm in agreement with you in theory about the war. And in sentiment."

"Look up Charley after your play opens. Talk to him."

"Do you think I'd get anywhere in opposition to Nancy?"

"Well, you can have a try at it," she said.

I did have a try at it, after my play opened to re-strained enthusiasm and several severe critical notices. Charley and I had lunch one Saturday and very nearly his opening remark was: "I hear you caught up with Polly and her bosom companion?"

I was shocked by the unmistakable intent of the phrase. "Yes, in Boston," I said.

"Where else? He never leaves there. She nips up there every few weeks and comes home full of sweetness and light, fooling absolutely no one. Except herself. Thank God I didn't go to Oxford."

"Why?"

"Well, you saw Hackley. He went to Oxford—after Harvard, of course."

"You sound as if you had a beef against Harvard, too."

"There are plenty of things I don't like about it, beginning with der Fuehrer, the one in the White House," he said. "Polly fill you up with sweetness and light, and tell you how distressed she was over Nancy and me?"

"No, we had my play to talk about," I said.

"Well, she's been sounding off. She's imported a couple of English kids and gives money to all the British causes. She'd have done better to have a kid by Hackley, but maybe they don't *do* that."

"What the hell's the matter with you, Charley? If I or anyone else had said these things about Polly a few years ago, you'd have been at their throat."

"That was before she began saying things about Nancy, things that were absolutely untrue, and for no reason except that Nancy has never gone in for all that phony Thoreau stuff. Nature-lover stuff. You know, I think Polly has had us all fooled from 'way back. You fell for it, and so did I, but I wouldn't be surprised if she'd been screwing Hackley all her life. One of those children that Junior thinks is his, *could* very well be Hackley's. The boy."

"Well, I wouldn't know anything about that. I've never seen their children. But what turned you against Polly? Not the possibility of her having had a child by Hackley."

"I've already told you. She's one of those outdoor-girl types that simply can't tolerate a pretty woman. And she's subtle, I'll give her that. She puts on this act of long-suffering faithful wife, while Junior goes on the make, and of course meanwhile Polly is getting hers in Boston."

"But you say not getting away with it."

"She got away with it for a long time, but people aren't that stupid. Even Junior Williamson isn't that stupid. He told Nancy that he's known about it for years, but as long as she didn't interfere with his life, he might as well stay married to her. Considering the nice stories Polly spread about Preswell and Nancy, I think Nancy showed considerable restraint in not making any cracks about Hackley and Polly's son. Nancy has her faults, but she wouldn't hurt an innocent kid."

The revised portraits of Junior Williamson, tolerating his wife's infidelity for years, and of Nancy Ellis, withholding gossip to protect a blameless child, were hard to get accustomed to. I did not try very hard. I was so astonished to see what a chump Nancy had made of my old friend, and so aggrieved by its effect on him, that I cut short our meeting and went home. Three or four months later the war news was briefly interrupted to make room for the announcement that Mrs. Ethridge Williamson, Jr., had established residence in Reno, Nevada. "A good day's work, Nancy," I said aloud. Much less surprising, a few months later, was the news item that Mrs. Smithfield Williamson, former wife of Ethridge Williamson, Jr., millionaire sportsman and financier, had married Hamilton Hackley, prominent Boston art and music patron, in Beverly, Massachusetts. The inevitable third marriage did not take place until the summer of 1942, when Lieutenant Commander Williamson, U.S.N.R., married Ensign Cecilia G. Reifsnyder, of the Women Accepted for Volunteer Emergency Service, in Washington, D.C. It seemed appropriate that the best man was Lieutenant Charles Ellis, U.S.N.R. The bride's only attendant was her sister, Miss Belinda Reifsnyder, of Catasauqua, Pennsylvania. I gave that six months, and it lasted twice that long.

My war record adds up to a big, fat nothing, but for a time I was a member of an Inverness-and-poniard organization, our elaborate nickname for cloak-and-dagger. In Washington I moved about from "Q" Building to the Brewery to South Agriculture and houses that were only street addresses. One day in 1943 I was on my way out of "Q" after an infuriatingly frustrating meeting with an advertising-man-turned-spy, a name-dropper who often got his names a little bit wrong. In the corridor a man fell in step with me and addressed me by my code nickname, which was Doc. "Do I know you?" I said.

"The name is Ham," said Hackley.

"We can't be too careful," I said.

"Well, we can't, as a matter of fact, but you can relax. I called you Doc, didn't I?" He smiled and I noticed that he needed dental work on the lower incisors. He had grown a rather thick moustache, and he had let his hair go untrimmed. "Come have dinner with Polly and me."

"I can think of nothing I'd rather do," I said.

"Irritating bastard, isn't he?" he said, tossing his head backward to indicate the office I had just left.

"The worst. The cheap, pompous worst," I said.

"One wonders, one wonders," said Hackley.

We got a taxi and went to a house in Georgetown. "Not ours," said Hackley. "A short-term loan from some friends."

Polly was a trifle thick through the middle and she had the beginnings of a double chin, but her eyes were clear and smiling and she was fitting into the description of happy matron.

"You're not at all surprised to see me," I said.

"No. I knew you were in the organization. Charley told me you'd turn up one of these days."

"Charley Who?"

"Heavens, have you forgotten all your old friends? Charley Ellis. Your friend and my cousin."

"I thought he was at CINCPAC."

"He's back and forth," she said. She put her hand on

249

her husband's arm. "I wish this man got back as often. Would you like to see Charley? He's not far from here."

"Yes, but not just now. Later. I gather you're living in Boston?"

"Yes. My son is at Noble's and my daughter is still home with me. How is your lovely wife? I hear nothing but the most wonderful things about her. Aren't we lucky? Really, aren't we?"

"We are that," I said. Hackley had not said a word. He smoked incessantly, his hand was continually raising or lowering his cigarette in a slow movement that reminded me of the royal wave. I remembered the first time I had seen him and Polly together, when he would tack on his own thought to everything she said. "Are you still with us?" I said.

"Oh, very much so," he said.

"Can you tell Jim what you've been doing?"

"Well, now that's very indiscreet, Polly. Naturally he infers that I've told you, and he could report me for that. And should," said Hackley. "However, I think he can be trusted. He and I dislike the same man, and that's a great bond."

"And we like the same woman," I said.

"Thank you," said Polly.

"I've been in occupied territory," said Hackley. "Hence the hirsute adornment, the neglected teeth. I can't get my teeth fixed because I'm going back, and the Gestapo would take one look at the inside of my mouth and ask me where I'd happened to run across an American dentist. Hard question to answer. So I've been sitting here literally sucking on a hollow tooth. Yes, I'm still with you."

"I wish I were with *you*—not very much, but a little."

"You almost were, but you failed the first requirement. I had to have someone that speaks nearly perfect French, and you took Spanish."

"I'm highly complimented that you thought of me at all. I wish I did speak French."

"Yes, the other stuff you could have learned, as I had to. But without the French it was no go. French French. Not New Orleans or New Hampshire."

"Do you go in by parachute—excuse me, I shouldn't ask that."

"You wouldn't have got an answer," said Hackley. He rose. "I wonder if you two would excuse me for about an hour? I'd like to have a bath and five minutes' shut-eye."

As soon as he left us Polly ceased to be the happy matron. "He's exhausted. I wish they wouldn't send him back. He's over fifty, you know. I wish they'd take me, but do you know why they won't? The most complicated reasoning. The French would think I was a German agent, planted in France to spy on the Resistance. And the Germans would know I was English or American, because I don't speak German. But imagine the French thinking I was a German. My colouring, of course, and I *am* getting a bit dumpy."

"Where are your English children?"

"One died of leukemia, and their mother asked to have the other sent back, which was done. John

R   251

Winant helped there. The child *is* better off with her mother, and the mother is too, I'm sure."

"Ham wants to go back, of course," I said.

"I wonder if he really does. Every time he goes back, his chances—and the Germans are desperate since we invaded Italy. It's young men's work, but a man of Ham's age attracts less attention. Young men are getting scarcer in France. Oh, I'm worried and I can't pretend I'm not. I can to Ham, but that's because I have to. But you saw how exhausted he is, and he's had——"

"Don't tell me. You were going to tell me how long he's been home. Don't. I don't want to have that kind of information."

"Oh, I understand. There's so little I want to talk about that I'm permitted to. Well, Charley Ellis is a safe subject. Shall I ask him to come over after dinner?"

"First, brief me on Charley and Nancy. I haven't seen him for at least a year."

"Nancy is living in New York, or you could be very sure I'd never see Charley. I didn't want to ever again. It was Nancy that stirred up the trouble between Junior and me, and I'm very grateful to her now but I wasn't then. Junior'd had lady friends, one after another, for years and years, and if he'd been a different sort of man it would have been humiliating. But as Charley pointed out to me, oh, twenty years ago, there are only about half a dozen Junior Williamsons in this country, and they make their own rules. So, in order to survive, I made mine, too. I really led a double life, the one as Mrs. Ethridge Williamson, Junior, and the other, obviously, as Ham's mistress. You knew that, didn't you?"

"Well, yes."

"I didn't take anything away from Junior that he wanted. Or withhold anything. And several times over the years I did stop seeing Ham, when Junior would be going through one of his periods of domesticity. I was always taken in by that, and Junior can be an attractive man. To women. He has no men friends, do you realize that? He always has some toady, or somebody that he has to see a lot of because of business or one of his pet projects. But he has no real men friends. Women of all ages, shapes, and sizes and, I wouldn't be surprised, colours. He married that Wave, and the next thing I heard was she caught him in bed with her sister. Why not? One meant as much to him as the other, and I'm told they were both pretty. That would be enough for Junior. A stroke of luck, actually. He's paying off the one he married. A million, I hear. And she's not going to say anything about her sister. What will those girls do with a million dollars? And think how much more they would have asked for if they'd ever been to the house on Long Island. But I understand he never took her there. That's what he considers home, you know. Christmas trees, and all the servants' children singing carols, and the parents lining up for their Christmas cheques. But the Wave was never invited. Oh, well, he's now an aide to an admiral, which should make life interesting."

"Having your commanding officer toady to you?"

"That, yes. But being able to pretend that you're

just an ordinary commander, or maybe he's a captain now, but taking orders and so on. An admiral that would have him for an aide is the kind that's feathering his nest for the future, so I don't imagine Junior has any really unpleasant chores."

"Neither has the admiral. He's chair-borne at Pearl."

"Yes, Charley implied as much. I've talked too much about Junior, and you want to know about Charley and Nancy. Well, Nancy stirred up the trouble. I never would have denied that I was seeing Ham, if Junior'd asked me, but that isn't what he asked me. He asked me if Ham were the father of our son, and I felt so sick at my stomach that I went right upstairs and packed a bag and took the next train to Boston, not saying a single word. When I got to my aunt's house, Junior was already there. He'd flown in his own plane. He said, 'I asked you a question, and I want an answer. *Entitled* to an answer.' So I said, 'The answer to the question is no, and I never want to say another word to you.' Nor have I. If he was entitled to ask the question, which I don't concede, he was entitled to my answer. He got it, and all communication between us since then has been through the lawyers."

"What about Nancy, though?"

"Oh, bold as brass, she told people that she thought my son's father was Ham. Which shows how well she doesn't know old Mr. Williamson. The boy looks exactly like his grandfather, even walks like him. But she also didn't know that Mr. Williamson is devoted to the boy, wouldn't speak to Junior for over a year, and worst of all, from Mr. Williamson's point of view, I have my son twelve months of the year and at school in Boston, so his grandfather has to come to Boston to see him. I refuse to take him to Long Island. And Mr. Williamson says I'm perfectly right, after Junior's nasty doubts. Doubts? Accusations."

"But you and Charley made it up," I said.

"Yes and no. Oh, we're friends again, but it'll never be what it used to be. Shall I tell you about it? You may be able to write it in a story sometime."

"Tell me about it."

"Charley was getting ready to ship out, his first trip to the Pacific, and he wrote me a letter. I won't show it to you. It's too long and too—private. But the gist of it was that if anything happened to him, he didn't want me to remember him unkindly. Then he proceeded to tell me some things that he'd said about me, that I hadn't heard, and believe me, Jim, if I'd ever heard them I'd have remembered him *very* unkindly. He put it all down, though, and then said, 'I do not believe there is a word of truth in any of these things.' Then he went on to say that our friendship had meant so much to him and so forth."

"It does, too, Polly," I said.

"Oh, James Malloy, you're dissembling. You know what he really said, don't you?"

"You're dissembling, too. I know what he used to feel."

"*I* never did. I always thought he was being extra kind to an awkward younger cousin," she said. "And he never liked Junior. Well, since you've guessed, or always knew, you strange Irishman, I'll tell you the rest.

255

I wrote to him and told him our friendship was just where it had always been, and that I admired him for being so candid. That I was hurt by the things he had said, but that his first loyalty was to Nancy. That I never wanted to see Nancy again, and that therefore I probably would never see him. But since we lived such different lives, in different cities, I probably wouldn't see him anyway, in war or peace."

"But you did see him."

"Yes. We're friends again. I've seen him here in Washington. We have tea together now and then. To some extent it's a repetition of my trips to Boston to see Ham. Needless to say, with one great difference. I never have been attracted to Charley that way. But I'm his double life, and the piquancy, such as it is, comes from the fact that Nancy doesn't know we see each other. Two middle-aged cousins, more and more like the people that come to my aunt's house in Louisburg Square."

"Do you remember the time we came down from Boston?"

"Had dinner on the train. Of course."

"You said then, and I quote, that all was far from well between Nancy and Charley."

She nodded. "It straightened itself out. It wasn't any third party or anything of that kind. It was Nancy reshaping Charley to her own ways, and Charley putting up a fight. But she has succeeded. She won. Except for one thing that she could never understand."

"Which is?"

"That Charley and I like to have tea together. If she

256

found out, and tried to stop it, that's the one way she'd lose Charley. So she mustn't find out. You see, Jim, I don't want Charley, as a lover or as a husband. I have my husband and he was my lover, too. As far as I'm concerned, Charley is first, last, and always a cousin. A dear one, that I hope to be having tea with when we're in our seventies. But that's all. And that's really what Charley wants, too, but God pity Nancy if she tries to deprive him of that."

For a little while neither of us spoke, and then she said something that showed her astuteness. "I'll give you his number, but let's not see him tonight. He doesn't like to be discussed, and if he came over tonight he'd know he had been."

"You're right," I said. "Polly, why did you divorce Williamson?"

"You're not satisfied with the reason I gave you?"

"It would be a good enough reason for some women, but not for you."

She looked at me and said nothing, but she was disturbed. She fingered her circle of pearls, picked up her drink and put it down without taking a sip.

"Never mind," I said. "I withdraw the question."

"No. No, don't. You gave me confidence one day when I needed it. The second time I ever saw you. I'll tell you."

"Not if it's an ordeal," I said.

"It's finding the words," she said. "The day Junior asked me point-blank if he was the father of my son, I had just learned that I was pregnant again. By him, of course. One of his periods of domesticity. So I had an abortion, something I'd sworn I'd never do, and I've never been pregnant since. I had to have a hysterectomy, and Ham and I did want a child. You see, I couldn't answer your question without telling you the rest of it."

After the war my wife and I saw the Ellises punctiliously twice every winter; they would take us to dinner and the theatre, we would take them. Dinner was always in a restaurant, where conversation makes itself, and in the theatre it was not necessary. Charley and I, on our own, lunched together every Saturday at his club or mine, with intervals of four months during the warm weather and time out for vacations in Florida or the Caribbean. Every five years on Charley's birthday they had a dance in the ballroom of one of the hotels, and I usually had a party to mark the occasion of a new book or play. We had other friends, and so had the Ellises, and the two couples had these semi-annual evenings together only because not to do so would have been to call pointed attention to the fact that the only friendship was that of Charley and me. Our wives, for example, after an early exchange of lunches never had lunch together again; and if circumstances put me alone with Nancy, I had nothing to say. In the years of our acquaintance she had swung from America First to Adlai Stevenson, while I was swinging the other way. She used the word valid to describe everything but an Easter bonnet, another favourite word of hers was denigrate, and still another was challenge. When my wife died Nancy wrote me a note in which she "questioned the validity of it all" and told me to "face the challenge". When I married again she said I had made the only valid decision by "facing up to the challenge of a new life". I had ceased to be one of the authors she admired, and in my old place she had put Kafka, Kierkegaard, Rilke, and Camus. I sent her a copy of Kilmer to make her velar collection complete, but she did not think it was comical or cute.

Charley and I had arrived at a political rapprochement: he conceded that some of the New Deal had turned out well, I admitted that Roosevelt had been something less than a god. Consequently our conversations at lunch were literally what the doctor ordered for men of our age. To match my Pennsylvania reminiscences he provided anecdotes about the rich, but to him they were not the rich. They were his friends and enemies, neighbours and relatives, and it was a good thing to hear about them as such. Charley Ellis had observed well and he remembered, and partly because he was polite, partly because he had abandoned the thought of writing as a career, he gave me the kind of information I liked to hear.

We seldom mentioned Nancy and even less frequently, Polly. If he continued to have tea with her, he did not say so. But one day in the late Forties we were having lunch at his club and he bowed to a carefully dressed man who limped on a cane and wore a patch over his left eye. He was about sixty years old. "One of your boys," said Charley.

"You mean Irish?"

"Oh, no. I meant O.S.S."

"He must have been good. The Médaille Militaire. That's one they don't hand out for travelling on the French Line."

"A friend of Ham Hackley's. He told me how Hackley died."

All I knew was that Hackley had never come back from France after my evening with him in Washington. "How did he?" I said.

"The Germans caught him with a wad of plastic and a fuse wire in his pocket. He knew what he was in for, so he took one of those pills."

"An 'L' pill," I said.

"Whatever it is that takes about a half a minute. You didn't know that about Ham?"

"I honestly didn't."

"That guy, the one I just spoke to, was in the same operation. He blew up whatever they were supposed to blow up, but he stayed too close and lost his eye and smashed up his leg. You wouldn't think there was that much guts there, would you? He knew he couldn't get very far, but he set off the damn plastic and hit the dirt." Charley laughed. "Do you know what he told us? He said, 'I huddled up and put my hands over my crotch, so I lost an eye. But I saved everything else.' We got him talking at a club dinner this winter."

"I wish I'd been here."

"Not this club. This was at the annual dinner of my club at Harvard. He was a classmate of Ham's. I don't usually go back, but I did this year."

"Did you see Polly?"

"Yes, I went and had tea with her. Very pleasant.

Her boy gets out of Harvard this year. Daughter's married."

"We got an announcement. What does Polly do with her time?"

"Oh, why, I don't know. She always has plenty of things to do in Boston. A girl like Polly, with all her interests, she'd keep herself very busy. I must say she's putting on a little weight."

"What would she be now?"

"How old? Polly is forty-one, I think."

"Still young. Young enough to marry again."

"I doubt if she will," said Charley. "I doubt it very much. Boston isn't like New York, you know. In New York a woman hates to go to a party without a man, but in Boston a woman like Polly goes to a party by herself and goes home by herself and thinks nothing of it."

"Nevertheless she ought to have a husband. She's got a good thirty years ahead of her. She ought to marry if only for companionship."

"Companionship? Companionship is as hard to find as love. More so. Love can sneak up on you, but when you're looking for companionship you shop around."

"Maybe that's what Polly's doing, having a look at the field."

"Maybe. There's one hell of a lot of money that goes with her, and she's not going to marry a fortune-hunter. Oh, I guess Polly can take care of herself."

"Just out of curiosity, how *much* money is there?"

"How much money? Well, when Polly's father died, old Mr. Smithfield, he left five million to Harvard, and another million to a couple of New York hospitals, and a hundred thousand here and a hundred thousand there. I happen to know that he believed in tithes. All his life he gave a tenth of his income to charity. So if he followed that principle in his will, he was worth around seventy million gross. I don't know the taxes on that much money, but after taxes it all went to Polly. In addition, Ham Hackley left her all his money, which was nothing like Cousin Simon Smithfield's, but a tidy sum nonetheless. I also know that when Polly divorced Junior Williamson, old Mr. Williamson changed his will to make sure that the grandchildren would each get one-third, the same as Junior. That was quite a blow to Junior. So all in all, Polly's in a very enviable position, financially."

"Good God," I said. "It embarrasses me."

"Why you?"

"Don't you remember that day I told her I loved her?"

"Oh, yes. Well, she took that as a compliment, not as a business proposition. She's never forgotten it, either."

"Well, I hope Polly holds on to her good sense. When I was a movie press agent I made a great discovery that would have been very valuable to a fortune-hunter. And in fact a few of them had discovered it for themselves. Big stars, beautiful and rich, would come to New York and half the time they had no one to take them out. They depended on guys in the publicity department. I never would have had to work for a living."

"How long could you have stood that?"

"Oh, a year, probably. Long enough to get tired of a

Rolls and charge accounts at the bespoke tailors. Then I suppose I'd have read a book and wished I'd written it. I knew a fellow that married a movie star and did all that, and he wasn't just a gigolo. He'd taught English at Yale. He took this doll for God knows how much, then she gave him the bounce and now he's living in Mexico. He's had a succession of fifteen-year-old wives. Once every two or three years he comes to New York for a week. He subsists entirely on steak and whisky. One meal a day, a steak, and all the whisky he can drink. He's had a stroke and he knows he's going to die. I could have been that. In fact, I don't like to think how close I came."

"I don't see you as Gauguin."

"Listen, Gauguin wasn't unhappy. He was doing what he wanted to do. I don't see myself as Gauguin either. What I don't like to think of is how close I came to being my friend that married the movie actress. That I could have been."

"No, you were never really close. You were no closer than I was to marrying Polly. You thought about it, just as I did about marrying Polly. But I wasn't meant to marry Polly, and you weren't meant to steal money from a movie actress and go on the beach in Mexico."

"Go on the beach? Why did you say that?"

"It slipped. I knew the fellow you're talking about. Henry Root?"

"Yes."

"Before he taught at Yale he had the great distinction of teaching me at Groton. You know why he

stopped teaching at Yale? Bad cheques. Not just
bouncing cheques. Forgeries. There was one for a
thousand dollars signed Ethridge B. Williamson, Junior.
That did it. He had Junior's signature to copy from, but
that wasn't the way Junior signed his cheques. He
always signed E. B. Williamson J R, so his cheques
wouldn't be confused with his father's, which had
Ethridge written out. Henry was a charming, facile
bum, and a crook. You may have been a bum, but you
were never a crook. Were you?"

"No, I guess I wasn't. I never cheated in an exam, and
the only money I ever stole was from my mother's
pocketbook. And got caught, every time. My mother
always knew how much was in her purse."

"Now let me ask you something else. Do you think
Henry Root would ever have been a friend of Polly's?
As good a friend, say, as you are?"

"Well—I'd say no."

"And you'd be right. When she was Polly Smithfield
he'd always give her a rush at the dances, and it was an
understood thing that Junior and I would always cut
in. I don't think we have to worry about Polly and
fortune-hunters, or you about how close you came to
being Henry Root. I don't even worry about how close
that damn story of yours came to keeping Nancy from
marrying me."

"Oh, that story. 'Christiana.' No. 'Telemark.' That
was it, 'Telemark.' "

"You don't even remember your own titles, but that
was the one."

"I may not remember the title, but the point of the

story was that two people could take a chance on marriage without love."

"Yes, and Nancy was so convinced that you were wrong that she had it on her mind. You damn near ruined my life, Malloy."

"No I didn't."

"No, you didn't. My life was decided for me by Preswell, when he walked in front of that taxi."

I knew this man so well, and with his permission, but I had never heard him make such an outright declaration of love for his wife, and on my way home I realized that until then I had not known him at all. It was not a discovery to cause me dismay. What did he know about me? What really, can any of us know about any of us, and why must we make such a thing of loneliness when it is the final condition of us all? And where would love be without it?